## "Now you've ruined my entire life."

"Why?" she continued unsteadily. "Why me?"

"I think you know the answer to that," Alexis answered smoothly. His straying fingers threaded the tumbled softness of her hair.

"Stop it!" Rachel managed to protest as he probed her nape and aroused an unwanted film of goose bumps.

"Stop what, Rachel? Stop tormenting you?" he questioned. "Or stop this unnecessary delay—" and bending his head, he replaced his fingers with his lips.

Rachel pushed desperately against his unyielding chest, but the hard strength beneath her protesting fingers was disturbingly appealing.

"Stop fighting it," Alexis murmured. "Stop fighting *me*...you want this too!"

"No!" Rachel m the word seco claimed hers.

D1115349

# Books by Anne Mather

STORMSPELL
WILD CONCERTO

## HARLEQUIN PRESENTS

## HARLEQUIN ROMANCES

These books may be available at your local bookseller.

For a free catalog listing all titles currently available, send your name and address to:

Harlequin Reader Service
P.O. Box 52040, Phoenix, AZ 85072-2040
Canadian address: Stratford, Ontario N5A 6W2

# ANNE MATHER

## sirocco

**Harlequin Books**

TORONTO • NEW YORK • LONDON
AMSTERDAM • PARIS • SYDNEY • HAMBURG
STOCKHOLM • ATHENS • TOKYO • MILAN

Harlequin Presents first edition April 1984
ISBN 0-373-10683-1

Original hardcover edition published in 1983
by Mills & Boon Limited

# CHAPTER ONE

THE man was slumped over the steering wheel of the car, evidently unconscious, and possibly in need of medical attention. The car itself was expensive—one of those powerful continental sports cars, with long silver wings—and from the look of it, it had not been involved in a traffic accident. On the contrary, it was parked sedately at the kerb, like any one of a dozen others parked in Kimbel Square—except that none of the others had an apparently senseless male reclining on the steering wheel.

Rachel stopped and sighed and glanced around her. But as was generally the case in such circumstances, she appeared to be the only pedestrian about at this particular moment, and she reflected rather wryly that if she had not decided to abandon Roger's party for personal reasons, she would not have found herself in this uncertain position. There were, inevitably, few people walking in the quiet London square at half-past eleven at night, and had her car been parked outside the building where Roger had his apartment, she would not have been one of them. As it was, she was faced with the uncomfortable awareness that if she ignored the man, he could conceivably lie there until morning before anyone else noticed him.

If only she had accepted Roger's offer to walk her to her car, she thought impatiently. Roger would have known what to do. But after the row they had just had, she had not felt capable of speaking civilly to him, and instead, she had flounced off without even saying goodbye. Of course, she could always go back there and get assistance, but the idea of approaching Roger again after the things they had said to one another did not bear thinking about right now, and her only alternative seemed to be the police station.

But where was the nearest police station? she

wondered, drawing her lower lip between her teeth.
Like pedestrians, police stations were few and far
between in this fashionable district of London, and
there was always the possibility that when she returned
with help the car might have gone.

Sighing again, she cast another look about her. If she
could only ascertain what was wrong with him, she
thought, stepping nearer to the car. It was difficult to
draw any real conclusions with a pane of laminated
glass between them, and with a resigned shrug of her
shoulders she touched the handle of the door. It was
unlocked, and feeling distinctly like a criminal, Rachel
swung it open.

The man did not stir, but in the illumination cast by the
courtesy light, she was able to examine him more closely.
He was, she surmised, in his late twenties or early thirties,
with straight wheat-coloured hair that looked silver at
present, and unusually dark skin. She guessed that either
he was not English or he spent much of his life out of
doors to account for his dark colouring, but as he was
lying face-down on the steering wheel, it wasn't easy to
make an accurate assessment. The watch on his wrist was
made by Cartier, and his jacket, like the car and the gold
bracelet on his other wrist, bore the imprint of wealth and
influence. Other than that, she had no clues to his identity,
and once again her eyes swept the Square searching for
assistance.

But there was still no one else within calling distance,
and bending down she put a tentative hand on his
sleeve. As she drew nearer, she could smell the
unmistakable tang of leather and good tobacco that
drifted from inside the car—that, and something else,
something Rachel was slow to identify, but which
became evident when she shook his sleeve. A bottle
rolled from his lap on to the floor of the car, and
although she automatically bent to retrieve it, she
guessed before she lifted it what it was.

*Gin!* she murmured to herself, staring at the bottle,
which was almost empty. That the man might be blind
drunk had seemed such an uncharitable conclusion, but
now she gripped the bottle impatiently, strongly

tempted to bring it down upon the unconscious man's head. He must be crazy, she thought scornfully, shaking her head. If a policeman strolled across Kimbel Square and observed him, he could face a criminal conviction. Being drunk in charge of a car was not consequent upon one actually driving the vehicle, and these days such offences were given the maximum penalty.

With a helpless shrug, she bent and pushed the empty bottle behind the front seat. It was nothing to do with her if he chose to invite prosecution, she told herself. But as she straightened, the man stirred and groaned, and her initial intention to close the door again was hindered when he slumped sideways towards her.

'Oh, *lord*!'

His weight almost threw her off her feet, and she had to grasp the roof of the car to save herself and him. Luckily, she was quite a strong girl and she was able to use her knees to propel him back into his seat, but the rocking motion had aroused him and when she attempted to draw away, his hand fastened tenaciously about her wrist.

'*Bon sang!*' he swore, in a muffled voice, confirming her opinion that he might not be English. '*Qu'est-ce que vous êtes en train de faire?*'

Trying rather unsuccessfully to pull her wrist away, Rachel realised belatedly that her efforts could be misconstrued. It was possible that he might think she had been trying to rob him, and she was glad she had interpreted the situation before trying to unfasten his tie or loosen his collar.

'I was trying to stop you from falling out of the car,' she declared now, albeit a little unsteadily as he lifted his head and looked at her. 'I'm sorry—I thought you were ill. It serves me right for being so inquisitive.'

'Ill?' he echoed, speaking good English now, though with a slight accent overlaying his drawling tone. 'How was I ill?' His eyes grew sardonic. 'Do you often open the doors of strangers' cars?'

'Of course not.' Rachel shifted rather uncomfortably beneath his appraising gaze. 'You were slumped over the wheel. I was—concerned.'

'The good Samaritan!'

'If you like.' Rachel took a deep breath. 'Now, will you let me go? It's late, and one of us has to work tomorrow.'

The man hesitated a moment and then, with a faint grimace, he let her hand free, flexing his shoulders against the back of his seat as if his unconventional repose had left him feeling rather stiff. Rachel didn't wait to find out. With an unwelcome sense of anticlimax, she started towards her car, only to halt uncertainly when the man's voice arrested her.

'Wait!'

He had extricated himself from behind the wheel now, and was standing on the pavement, supporting himself with the roof of the sports car. He was taller than average, Rachel saw, and leaner than she had thought, judging from the width of his shoulders. He was attractive, too, his lean dark features contrasting effectively with his pale hair, and Rachel guessed she wasn't the first woman to think so. Hooded eyes, which could be any shade from grey to blue to hazel, acknowledged her hesitation, and the thin lips below the narrow cheekbones twisted mockingly.

'What is your name?' he asked, arching one dark brow. 'I should know the name of my saviour. Without your intervention, I might have slept much longer, and to be found in that position could have been embarrassing.'

'Slept?' Rachel's mouth compressed. 'You weren't asleep! You were out—cold! You're lucky it was me and not a policeman who brought you back to consciousness.'

'You think that?' He left the car to walk towards her, moving easily, if slightly unsteadily. 'You think I was—drunk, hmm? Isn't that what you mean by—out cold?'

Rachel glanced behind her. Her car was still some yards away along the pavement, and she instinctively measured the distance should she have to make a run for it.

Drawing the suede holdall hanging from her shoulder in front of her, Rachel wrapped her arms about it as she replied: 'I found the bottle. On your knee?' she prompted, with a mock sweet smile. 'I'm sorry, but I don't buy that story about feeling sleepy and putting your head down.'

The man pushed his hands into his trouser pockets as he halted in front of her. 'You didn't tell me your name,' he reminded her tolerantly. 'Let me guess—it's Pandora, isn't it?'

'It's Fleming,' she retorted, annoyed that he had not attempted to argue with her. 'Rachel Fleming. Goodnight.'

'One moment . . .' Once again he detained her, and she turned to look at him more coolly than she felt, irritatingly aware that her pulse rate had quickened. 'I would like to explain.'

'It's not necessary——'

'I think it is.' He inclined his head back to where the door of his car still gaped open. 'I was not unconscious, as you seem to think. The bottle was not mine. I—took it from someone else.'

'Oh, really?'

'Yes, really.' He shrugged. 'You will have noticed that it was uncapped. I intended to pour it away, but I was tired and I must have got into the car and flaked out.'

Rachel gasped. 'You mean you're saying you hadn't been drinking?' she exclaimed disbelievingly.

'No.' He lifted his shoulder. 'On the plane I drank a good deal of wine, I think.'

'On the plane?'

'From New York,' he explained levelly. 'That was why I was so tired, I guess. It is more than twenty-four hours since I saw a bed.'

Rachel sighed, tempted to point out that the journey from New York took a lot less than twenty-four hours. But to do so would imply that she required further explanation, and in all honesty he had had no need to explain anything to her.

'Well——' she said now, forcing a polite smile, 'it seems I made a mistake. I'm sorry. I'll be more wary in future——'

'On the contrary...' His attractive mouth lifted.
'You did what you thought was best, and indeed, had I
been—unconscious, your assistance would have been
most welcome.'

Rachel moved her shoulders. 'Think nothing of it.'
Her eyes sought the security of her car. 'I have to go.'

'You must allow me to drive you home,' he declared,
dogging her steps with his, apparently indifferent to the
fact that his car was just asking to be stolen. His hand
restrained her arm once more. 'Believe me, I am not
drunk. You will be quite safe with me.'

*Will I?* thought Rachel cynically, aware of the
strength in the hand curled about her flesh. Ridiculous
as it seemed, she was instinctively aware that this man
meant trouble, and although she had no reason to be
alarmed, she reacted automatically against his undoub-
ted magnetism. She was engaged to Roger. Just because
they had had a minor upset there was no reason to feel
this unwarranted attraction towards another man;
particularly when that man was self-assured and
wealthy and probably well-used to the adulation of the
opposite sex.

'I—my car is here,' she got out at last, gesturing
towards the Mini parked a few feet away. She freed
herself determinedly and took the steps necessary to put
some space between them. 'Thank you, but I don't need
a lift. Goodnight.'

He swayed back and forth on his heels and toes as
Rachel clumsily forced the key into the lock. Her
fingers were all thumbs, and she was half afraid he was
going to come and take the keys and do the job for her.
She could already see him squatting beside her, his lean
hands reaching surely for her keys, brushing her hands,
making her skin tingle as her flesh had tingled when he
touched her...

*God!* With a sigh of relief, the key fitted and turned,
and she wrenched open her door and scrambled inside.
Her legs seemed absurdly long all of a sudden, and she
had to coil herself behind the wheel, searching for the
ignition with the same hurried panic as she had used on
the door. She need not have worried, however. The man

did not move. He simply watched until she had
negotiated herself out of the parking space, and then
turned and walked indolently back to his vehicle.

'I thought you were home early last night,' remarked
Jane drily, setting down the cup of tea she had brought
on the table beside Rachel's bed. She viewed her
friend's darkly-ringed eyes with a wry grimace. 'Just
after midnight, wasn't it? I know I didn't expect you
until three, at least.'

'Oh——' Rachel dragged herself up on the pillows,
giving the other girl a bleary-eyed stare. 'I left the party
early,' she explained. 'Roger and I had a row, and I
walked out.'

'I see. So that's the reason why you haven't slept.'
Jane grimaced. 'What was it about this time? The usual
thing?'

'Mmm.' Rachel lifted her teacup and took a gulp of
the strong sweet liquid, wondering as she did so why
she felt so guilty. It was true. She and Roger had had
previous rows about their anticipated wedding, almost
always concerning his mother's role in it, and just
because that had not been the reason for her restless
night it didn't mean she owed Jane any other
explanation.

'But surely he's realised by now that you're not about
to let Mrs Harrington take charge of the arrangements,'
Jane exclaimed, moving about the room, drawing back
the curtains and lifting a discarded pair of tights from
the floor where Rachel had dropped them. 'I mean, it's
not as if you don't have any family, is it?'

'No.' Rachel shrugged. 'But with my parents being
divorced, she sees her opportunity to take control.
Besides which, she doesn't consider my mother as a
likely contender, and you know she disapproves of my
father.'

'Well . . .' Jane was reluctantly candid, 'your father
hasn't exactly endeared himself to your future in-laws,
has he?'

'No.' Remembering the night of her engagement
party, Rachel had to be honest, too. 'But paying for a

staff of caterers isn't exactly beyond his abilities, and I can handle all the details.'

'I suppose she wants a terribly swish affair,' said Jane thoughtfully. 'To be charitable, she's probably only wanting to save you the trouble. After all, you have a job; she doesn't. Which reminds me, it's a quarter to eight.'

'Quarter to eight?' Rachel's eyes turned in horror to the clock on the bedside table, and swallowing the rest of her tea in a gulp she thrust her legs out of bed. 'Why didn't you tell me?'

'I did,' Jane pointed out wryly, leaving the room. 'Don't panic! I'll go and make the coffee while you get dressed. Do you want some toast?'

'I won't have time,' exclaimed Rachel, throwing off her cotton nightgown and grabbing a clean pair of panties from the drawer. 'Mr Black is leaving for Chelmsford at half-past nine, and I promised I'd go in early so we could deal with his mail before he left.'

'Oh, well,' Jane was philosophical, 'it's not as if he's likely to fire you. I sometimes wonder what he'd do without you.'

Rachel grimaced. 'So do I, but I'd rather not find out,' she retorted as she disappeared into the bathroom.

Fifteen minutes later, she appeared in the kitchen of the flat, and Jane looked up from the morning paper with a faintly admiring smile. 'Well,' she said, 'you made it. And with five minutes to spare.'

Rachel shook her head. 'Do I look all right?'

'Don't you always?' Jane's comment was not without a trace of envy. 'Next time I come into this world, I'm going to be a blue-eyed brunette!'

Rachel laughed. 'Not with this hair, I hope.' She touched the unruly mass of dark-brown silk that refused to adhere to any current fashion and tumbled riotously to her shoulders. 'I sometimes think I should have it all cut off, only Roger likes it this way.'

'I bet he does!' Jane pulled a face as she viewed her own mousy crop. 'Besides, with your height you can carry it. Now, stop fishing for compliments and drink your coffee. I want to get washed up before I leave.'

'Do you have an early class?' asked Rachel, between sips. Jane taught history at the local comprehensive school, and did not have to face the morning rush into the city that her flatmate had ahead of her.

'Not until ten,' Jane replied comfortably, helping herself to more toast. Unlike her friend, she always ate a good breakfast, and her ample girth was proof of her weakness for food. 'Are you sure you don't want anything to eat? You know what they say about eating breakfast . . .'

'I'll get a sandwich from the machine at break,' Rachel assured her, putting down her cup and picking up the jacket of her suit. 'Thank heavens it's not raining. At least the buses shouldn't be too full.'

Five minutes later, Rachel was walking along Oakwood Road to the bus stop. She never used her car for work; it was simply too impractical in the rush-hour traffic. Nevertheless, she was often tempted, particularly when the buses were packed and went by the stop without doing so.

It was a fine, sunny morning, with the promise of spring in the air. The daffodils were nodding their heads in Oakwood Gardens, and the grey squirrel that darted across the grass in search of food gave her spirits an unexpected lift. It would be March next week, she thought with some amazement, and the wedding was barely ten weeks away. Once she and Roger were married, his mother would have much less say in his affairs, and Mrs Harrington would have to accept that she was no longer the most important woman in her son's life. At present, she found it far too easy to divert Roger from the plans they had made, but once the wedding was over and Rachel was living at the apartment, Mrs Harrington would not be so welcome there.

Recalling how she had stormed out of Roger's apartment the night before, Rachel was reluctantly reminded of what had happened after. She had not found it easy to dismiss the incident from her thoughts the night before, and even now she felt herself tensing at the memory. Of course, she had soon recovered from

the sense of panic that had gripped her at the time. Her
unwilling interest in the man had been the natural
sequel to the row she had had with Roger, and after all,
their meeting had been highly unconventional. It was
natural that she should have felt some curiosity about
him, particularly bearing in mind his unquestionable
good looks. Not that he had been handsome, as Roger
was handsome, of course. The stranger's features had
been much more irregular, harder, possessed of a harsh
beauty that was more distinctively masculine. He had,
she supposed, what was commonly known as sex-
appeal, and that dominated his dark-skinned appearance . . .

Irritated at the trend of her thoughts, Rachel joined
the queue at the bus stop, her burst of lightheartedness
evaporating. For heaven's sake, she thought impatiently,
what was the matter with her? Why couldn't she forget
about what happened the night before? It wasn't as if
she was ever likely to see the man again. He was a
stranger and he was not English, and she didn't know
why she hadn't told Jane, so that they could have a
giggle about it.

The solicitor she worked for, Arthur Black, was
waiting for her when she arrived at the firm's offices in
Fetter Lane, and his bustling presence succeeded in
driving all other thoughts out of Rachel's head.

'You're late,' he remarked dourly, massaging the bald
patch on the top of his head. 'I did ask you to get here
by a quarter to nine, Miss Fleming. It's now five
minutes past, which leaves us only twenty-five minutes
before my departure.'

'I'm sorry,' Rachel took off her jacket and hung it on
the hook by the door, 'but the traffic was——'

'—hectic, I know,' he interrupted her shortly,
disappearing into his own office. 'It always is,' he
called, as she extracted her shorthand note pad from a
drawer and gathered up several pencils. 'I should have
thought you could have anticipated that by now.'

'Yes, Mr Black.'

Rachel grimaced and followed him into his office,
shivering a little as the gas fire sputtered to reluctant

life. The old building badly needed renovating, but the firm of Hector, Hollis and Black was unlikely to undertake it. They seemed to thrive on its sagging floors and dusty corridors, and even the offices of the principals were like Mr Black's office: poorly lit and shabby. Nevertheless, they were never short of briefs, and Rachel could only assume their clients imagined the exorbitant fees they paid were all swallowed up in their defence. Certainly they employed some of the best brains in the legal profession, and when Rachel first joined the firm as a junior typist she had been excited at the prospect of meeting such people. Now, however, the initial spark of enthusiasm had been somewhat doused. Working as Arthur Black's secretary for the past two years had helped her get things into perspective, and she no longer viewed the profession through rose-coloured spectacles. A law practice was not particularly exciting or romantic, as she had first imagined. It was mostly dull and repetitive, and only occasionally did she meet one of those charismatic characters, whose advocatory skills had made their names famous.

'I shall be in court most of the morning,' Mr Black was saying now, after having dictated half a dozen letters and consigned an equal number for Rachel's personal attention. 'But I shall ring the office immediately afterwards, in case there are any urgent messages. You will be here, I take it? You're not planning to go out for a meal?'

Rachel shook her head. 'No. Roger's playing golf this morning, and I've no plans to see him until this evening.' *If he turns up*, she added to herself silently. After last evening's fiasco, he might conceivably expect her to make the next move.

'Oh, well——' Mr Black shrugged his rounded shoulders, 'that's all right, then.' He paused. 'Though I must say that young man of yours seems to have a great deal of free time. Does he work at all?'

'Of course he does!' Rachel was indignant. 'But, as he works for himself, he can choose his own hours.'

'Hmm.' Mr Black sounded unimpressed. 'Running women's clothes shops, I suppose.'

'Roger supervises the management, yes.' Rachel rose to her feet. 'Is this all, Mr Black? Do you want me to contact Mr Perry about the Latimer case?'

Mr Black's nostrils flared as he accepted the rebuff, but he made no comment. 'Yes,' he said. 'Fix an appointment for me to see him on Friday. Oh, and arrange to send Mrs Black some flowers tomorrow, will you? It's our anniversary, and I shan't have the time.'

'Yes, Mr Black.' Rachel's mouth grew wry. 'Is that it, then?'

'I think so.' Mr Black looked at his watch. 'And with fifty seconds to spare. I suppose I should congratulate you.'

Rachel's lips twitched. 'That won't be necessary, Mr Black. I'll see you this afternoon, shall I? Or won't you be back?'

'It rather depends what happens,' replied her employer thoughtfully. 'I'll give you my answer at lunchtime. I should know by then.'

Sophie Tennant appeared soon after Mr Black had left the building, slipping into Rachel's office with a conspiratorial smile on her face. 'Guess what?' she said, perching on the side of Rachel's desk. 'Mr Rennison's asked me to have lunch with him. Do you think I should accept?'

Rachel pulled the letter she had been typing out of the machine and viewed it critically. Then she looked up at the girl draped decoratively over the corner of her desk. Sophie was eighteen, four years her junior, and just as young and susceptible as Rachel had been when she first came to work here. A pretty blonde, with blue eyes and a pink and white complexion, Sophie had attracted the eye of one of the junior partners, and Rachel wondered how she could tell her she had had to negotiate that particular obstacle herself four years ago.

'He is married,' she pointed out now, shuffling the letters waiting to be typed together. 'I've met his wife. She's very nice.'

Sophie pouted. 'You're telling me not to go, aren't you?'

'No.' Rachel shook her head. 'That's for you to

decide. I'm only saying that—well, it's not the first time he's tried to date one of the typists.'

'So what?' Sophie swung her heel impatiently against the side of Rachel's desk. 'I came to tell you because I thought you might understand. Everyone else around here is ancient!'

'I wouldn't exactly call Mary Villiers ancient,' replied Rachel tolerantly, and Sophie grimaced.

'She's twenty-six if she's a day! All the secretaries are old, except you. And once you've left, I'll have no one to talk to.'

'Well, I'm not planning on leaving just yet,' remarked Rachel drily. 'I'm not giving up work when I get married, you know that.'

Sophie shrugged. 'So you say. But what if you get pregnant? You won't have much choice then, will you?'

'N-o.' Rachel acknowledged the point, but she refrained from adding that it was unlikely. Roger had said several times that he didn't want to start a family immediately, and in any case, they had no proof that such a contingency was even possible. In spite of his modern outlook on make-up and clothes and furnishings, Roger was singularly old-fashioned when it came to relationships, and although he had taught her ways to please him without their going to bed together, they had never actually made love.

'So what do you think?' Sophie persisted. 'I mean, it's only lunch. It's no big deal.'

Rachel shrugged. 'So long as he remembers that.'

'What do you mean?'

'Well, would you like it, if you were his wife? Is it fair to encourage him to cheat on her?'

Sophie sighed. 'He is very attractive, isn't he?'

'If you like ex-rugby players, I suppose he is.'

'Oh——' Sophie's smile came and went, 'you're not much help. Haven't you ever been tempted to cheat on Roger? I know you've been going out with him for ages! Surely there've been occasions when some other man has attracted you.'

'I don't think so.' Rachel was crisp, her tone sharper because of the unwanted memory Sophie had stirred.

'Look, I've got to get on. You'll have to make up your own mind. It's your life, not mine.'

She felt a little mean when the younger girl had gone, realising her attitude had been governed by that unwelcome recollection. It was difficult for someone like Sophie to cope with the practised charm of a man like Peter Rennison. How could boys of her own age compete with his sophistication—and his Jaguar XJS?

It was almost lunchtime when the switchboard rang through to say there was a call for her. 'Oh, that will be Mr Black,' said Rachel at once, reaching confidently for her notepad, but Jennifer, the telephonist, demurred.

'If it had been Mr Black, I'd have put him straight on to you,' she exclaimed. 'Or Roger either, for that matter. But this man won't give his name, and I thought I'd better ask you before putting him through.'

Rachel's mouth felt suddenly dry. 'He—won't give his name?' she echoed, and the telephonist went on:

'He says it will mean nothing to you. Do you want to speak to him? Or shall I ask him to call back when Mr Black is there?'

Rachel was silent for so long that Jennifer asked whether she was still there, and pulling herself together she said she was. 'Did—did he ask to speak to Mr Black?' she asked at last, aware of a sudden tightness in her stomach, and Jennifer's response did nothing to alleviate her discomfort.

'No. No, actually, he asked for you,' the telephonist declared, obviously just comprehending that fact herself. 'So what do I do? Shall I put him on? I must admit, he does sound rather dishy!'

Realising that whoever was calling, it was likely to cause a talking point in the office for days, Rachel came to a decision. 'Tell him—tell him I'm out,' she said quickly, feeling a hot flush run up her cheeks at the deliberate lie. 'He's probably one of those freaks that call from time to time. Just get rid of him, will you, Jennifer?'

'He did know your name,' the other girl reminded her

doubtfully. 'He could be a friend of your father's. Or of Roger's.'

'Then he'll have to get them to ring me,' said Rachel, trying to sound unconcerned. 'Don't worry about it, Jennifer. I'll find out later.'

'Oh—all right.' Clearly Jennifer was disappointed that she was not going to take the call, and Rachel was glad she had refused. She could just imagine Roger's reaction if he found out some strange man had been trying to ring her. And he might, bearing in mind the grapevine at Hector, Hollis and Black.

Mr Black himself rang a few minutes later and Rachel listened to his instructions with some abstraction. She was still trying to convince herself that the previous call had had nothing to do with what had happened last night, and it was difficult to concentrate on legal matters when her brain refused to function normally. It couldn't have been him, she told herself fiercely. He had no reason for getting in touch with her again. And in any case, how had he known where to find her? There must be dozens of Rachel Flemings in the greater London area.

'Did you get that?'

Realising Mr Black was still speaking to her, Rachel was relieved to see that her hand had automatically taken down his instructions, even while her mind was occupied with other things. 'You want me to take the Oliver file to Mr Rennison, and then go to Willis and Potter to collect some documents. Is that right?' she ventured, and her employer agreed rather grudgingly that it was. 'So long as you remember to tell Rennison I want that file back tomorrow,' he added brusquely, before clearing his throat. 'Damn this chest of mine! I think I'm getting a dose of bronchitis. Call Mrs Black, will you, and ask her to get a repeat prescription of my tonic from the chemist. I'd ask you to get it for me, but the chap in Cricklewood knows what I need.'

'Yes, Mr Black.' Rachel acknowledged his request and jotted it down. 'Anything else?'

'No, I don't think so. I should be back around four. Do you think you could stay until six this evening? I'd like these reports typing up before I leave the office.'

Rachel hesitated. Roger was supposed to be calling for her this evening and they were going to have dinner with some friends of his. But he wasn't coming until seven-thirty, and she would have plenty of time, even if she didn't leave the office until six. If he rang before she got home, Jane could explain.

'Okay,' she said now, 'I'll stay until six. Is that everything?'

'That's it,' he agreed dourly. 'Goodbye.'

Sophie appeared in the doorway as she was plugging in the electric kettle to make herself a cup of coffee in lieu of a meal, and Rachel arched dark brows in her direction. 'What, no lunch?'

'No.' Sophie sidled into the room. 'I told him I had another date. Can I stay in here with you? Just until he's left the building?'

'You can have some coffee, if you like,' Rachel offered casually. 'I'm not going out today. I promised Mr Black I'd be here in case there were any urgent messages.'

Sophie grimaced, and after surveying the room for somewhere to sit, she found herself a comfortable place in the leather armchair in the corner. 'Thanks,' she said, taking the earthenware beaker Rachel handed her. 'This is cosy, isn't it? I wish I worked for one of the partners. Our office is as draughty as a wind tunnel!'

'I know—I used to work there,' Rachel sympathised, resuming her seat at her desk and propping her feet up on the waste paper basket. 'Mmm, coffee: the saviour of the twentieth century!'

Sophie relaxed. 'How long is it to the wedding? Your wedding, I mean. Didn't you say you were getting married at the beginning of June? Lucky thing! Have you decided where you're going to spend your honeymoon?'

Rachel looked down into her coffee cup. 'Nothing's properly decided yet. Oh, we're getting married at the beginning of June, you're right about that. But Roger doesn't know whether he'll be able to get away at that time. We may have to postpone the honeymoon.'

'What a shame!' Sophie gave her a commiserating

look. 'Still, I suppose being together is the important thing, isn't it? Are you going to move into his apartment?'

Rachel nodded. 'That's the idea.'

'It is his own apartment, isn't it?' Sophie was youthfully inquisitive. 'His mother doesn't live there, does she?'

'No.' Rachel's smile was tolerant. 'She has her own house in St John's Wood.'

'I envy you, you know,' remarked Sophie sighing. 'Being able to give up work, if you want to. And not just because you're marrying Roger either. It must be nice to be rich.'

'I'm not rich,' exclaimed Rachel, laughing. 'And I do have to work, believe me!'

'But your father——'

'My father doesn't support me,' declared Rachel firmly. 'If that's what you think, forget it.'

'But he would if you asked him,' said Sophie irrepressibly. 'My father couldn't, even if he wanted to. He finds it hard enough to support the rest of the family!'

Rachel had no response to make to this, and for several minutes the two girls sat in silence, each busy with their own thoughts. For Rachel's part, she was thinking that Sophie had something she had never had, and that was a proper home life. Her own parents' divorce when she was barely eight had left her at the mercy of aunts and boarding schools. Her mother had taken herself off to Australia with the salesman she had fallen in love with, and Rachel's father had found various excuses why he could not take care of his child. In consequence, until she was eighteen Rachel had seen very little of either parent, and only when her father discovered what a beautiful young woman she had turned out to be did he begin to appreciate the asset she might prove to his business dealings. But by then it was too late. Rachel had found employment with Hector, Hollis and Black, and her subsequent meeting with Jane Snowden, an older girl, who used to attend the same school, culminated in their taking the flat together as soon as Jane had completed her course at university.

'Well, anyway,' said Sophie at last, 'I wish something exciting would happen to me!'

'Like Peter Rennison?' suggested Rachel drily, and the younger girl grimaced.

'Well, he is handsome, you must admit. And I love that car of his, don't you?'

Rachel shook her head. 'It's all right.'

'*All right?*' Sophie was beginning indignantly, when without warning the door opened and a man's tall figure appeared in the aperture.

For the space of a moment, Rachel thought it was Peter Rennison, come to check up on Sophie's immature excuse. She was in the process of finishing the coffee in her mug and her first glimpse was of a man's dark pants and suede boots set some inches apart. But as she lowered her cup and her eyes moved up over an expensive leather jacket covering an equally costly silk shirt and tie, her conviction weakened, and by the time she reached the determined curve of his jaw she was certain she knew who it was. Her eyes flew to his, to clear grey eyes set beneath brows several shades darker than his hair, which in this light revealed the streaks of sun-bleached lightness in its wheat-gold vitality, and her stomach contracted.

'Good morning,' he said, with cool assurance. 'Or should I say good afternoon?' He consulted the slim watch, whose leather strap encircled his wrist. 'It is almost one o'clock.'

## CHAPTER TWO

RACHEL exchanged a look with Sophie and seeing the avid expression on the other girl's face she inwardly groaned. Much though she liked her, Sophie was the last person she would have wished to be here at this moment, and she could already hear the gossip which would ensue from this encounter.

Realising she had to say something, Rachel put her feet to the floor and stood up. 'Er—can I help you?' she asked, hoping against hope that he might get the message and not compromise her. Why on earth had he come here? What did he want? And how had he found her in such a short time?

'I hope so,' he said now, the grey eyes moving intently over her flushed face, and Rachel ran her moist palms down the seams of her skirt. She had forgotten how penetrating his gaze had been, and seen in daylight he was infinitely more disturbing. 'Allow me to introduce myself,' he added, moving into the room and immediately dwarfing it. 'My name is Roche,' he said it with a French accent, 'Alexis Roche. Completely sober, as you will have observed.'

Rachel closed her eyes for a moment and then, aware of his sudden move towards her, quickly opened them again. 'I—well—Mr Roche,' she said awkwardly, casting another glance in Sophie's direction, 'what can we do for you?'

He was silent for a moment, as if gauging the import of her question, but then, with a careless shrug of his shoulders, he said: 'I telephoned you this morning. You refused to speak to me.' He paused. 'So—I am here. In person, as they say.'

Rachel moistened her dry lips. 'Er—how did you get in? How did you find this office?'

The grey eyes narrowed between short thick lashes, whose ends were tipped with the same silvery bleach as his hair. 'It wasn't difficult to get in,' he essayed smoothly. 'I merely came through the door, like everyone else. As to how I found this office—I asked.'

'Who?'

Rachel was playing for time, desperately trying to find a way out of this without betraying their association to Sophie, who was listening to the exchange with ever-increasing interest. His explanation of finding her was too reasonable to be false. It was comparatively easy to walk into the building, particularly if one acted as if one was familiar with its rabbit-warren of halls and corridors. And anyone could have told him which office was hers. It wasn't a secret, after all.

'I don't know who,' he said now, with some impatience. 'Some elderly man I met on the stairs. Is it important? I did not come here to find out where you worked, merely to invite you to have lunch with me.'

Rachel heard Sophie's sudden intake of breath and felt suddenly angry. He had no right to come here and behave as if they were old friends, she thought frustratedly. Just because he had told her his name it did not give him the prerogative to ask her out to lunch. She knew nothing about him. He knew nothing about her. She could be married for all he knew, and with this in mind, she raised her left hand to her throat to expose the obvious glitter of her engagement ring.

'I'm sorry,' she said—though if he had any perception, she thought aggressively, he would know that she was not—'I'm afraid I can't accept your invitation. My—fiancé—wouldn't like it.'

Alexis Roche's gaze did not falter. 'My invitation was to you, not your fiancé,' he said, with impassive arrogance. 'I should like to thank you, more fully than I did last night.'

His words were deliberate, Rachel was sure, and she wanted to die of embarrassment. She could just imagine how this was going to be relayed around the office, and every incriminating syllable was deepening the interest in Sophie's round blue eyes. The way he had used their encounter, they might have spent the night together for all the younger girl knew, and Rachel couldn't believe he was unaware of it.

Realising her only means of defence lay in attack, she gave up the unequal struggle to keep the facts of their meeting quiet. Turning, she gave Sophie a frosted smile before saying crisply: 'Mr Roche and I met last evening, as I was leaving Roger's party. He—he wasn't feeling very well, and—and I offered to help him.'

'Really?' Sophie slid off her chair, her eyes never leaving Alexis Roche's face. 'How exciting!' She drew a little nearer. 'Do you live in London, Mr Roche?'

He withdrew his gaze from Rachel with evident reluctance, and surveyed the younger girl with polite interest. 'For the present,' he replied, without explaining any further. Then: 'Would you mind leaving us? I should like to speak to Miss Fleming privately.'

'Oh, sure,' agreed Sophie, nodding, just as Rachel burst out: 'Don't go!'

But, after lifting her shoulders a little apologetically, Sophie hesitated only momentarily before obeying Alexis Roche's instructions, and Rachel watched with compressed lips as she edged towards the door. 'I'll see you later,' she murmured, pulling a rueful face, and Rachel stood there helplessly as her only protection disappeared.

*Protection!* The word had insinuated itself into her mind almost without her consciously seeking for it, and she clenched her fists impotently. *She* didn't need protection; *he* did. She felt so angry, she could have done him physical injury.

'Will you please leave?' she demanded now, walking towards the door and putting her fingers on the handle. 'My boss will be back from lunch shortly, and he doesn't approve of us entertaining guests on the premises.'

Alexis Roche made no move to leave. Instead, he looked around the shabby office, his lips curling as he remarked: 'I can't imagine you wanting to entertain anyone here. Is it always as dirty as this?'

Rachel caught her breath. 'It's not dirty,' she defended, even though she had thought the same many times. 'It's—dusty, that's all. Law offices are like that. Solicitors often have to refer to cases from the past, and the records get old and musty sitting on the shelves. We know where things are, when we need them. That's the important thing.'

'Haven't you heard of computers—and micro-technology?' he enquired wryly, and Rachel expelled her breath on a gasp.

'This is an old established firm,' she replied shortly. 'Our clients might not approve of their case histories being recorded on a computer. Besides,' she added, not quite knowing why she was bothering to explain, 'computers cost money, and——'

'—and your clients would prefer their fees to be spent in their defence,' he put in smoothly. 'Very well, you've convinced me. Now will you allow me to buy you lunch?'

Rachel stared at him. 'Mr Roche——'

'You may call me Alex.'

'Mr Roche, do you want me to call for assistance to have you ejected from this building? I can, you know. And I will, if you don't leave.'

Now he sighed, and pushed his hands into the pockets of his jacket. The jacket was honey-coloured and complemented his dark tan, and she couldn't help the unwilling curiosity of wondering what nationality he was. He spoke French, and yet he didn't look French, if such a thing was possible. He was too tall, for one thing, and those cool grey eyes . . .

Abruptly she halted her speculation, aware that he was still watching her with that narrow-eyed catlike appraisal. She hoped he wasn't able to read her mind. Its turbulent upheaval was in complete contrast to the calm and collected façade she was endeavouring to maintain.

'Why won't you have lunch with me?' he asked quietly. He glanced towards her desk. 'You've eaten, perhaps? Very well, I will buy you a drink——'

'Mr Roche, I don't accept invitations from strange men.' Rachel hesitated, then added stiffly: 'Now, will you leave?'

He frowned, his well-marked brows descending over eyes that were distinctly cooler now. 'I am not a strange man, Miss Fleming. I have told you who I am. If you wish to know a little more of my family background, I can tell you that my father is in shipping and my grandfather owns land in Bahdan——'

'I don't wish to know your family background, Mr Roche,' exclaimed Rachel impatiently, though his final words had intrigued her somewhat. *Bahdan*. That was in the Middle East. It was one of those sheikdoms that had recently come into prominence, and if his father owned land there, he must be in oil.

Nevertheless, it was nothing to do with her, and drawing a deep breath, she pulled the door wide. 'Good afternoon, Mr Roche,' she said pointedly, evidently waiting for him to leave, and with another brooding frown, he finally accepted his dismissal.

But he paused in the doorway, close enough for her to smell the faint scent of some shaving lotion that hung about him, and to feel the heat of his body. 'Until we meet again,' he murmured, the fresh odour of his breath stirring the hair on her forehead and making her overwhelmingly aware of his alien attraction.

She didn't answer him, but with the door closed and her shoulders pressed against it she gave way to a sudden fit of shivering. It was the draught from the corridor, she told herself. The cold from outside came straight up the stairs. Yet she had never noticed it before, and although the door was closed, she was still shaking.

Sophie didn't appear again that afternoon, and Rachel was relieved. She supposed that sooner or later she would have to give a more detailed explanation, but the longer that was put off, the easier it would be.

Mr Black arrived back soon after four as he had predicted, and the rest of the day was spent in typing up the reports of the hearings he had attended. With her hands flying busily over the keyboard and her brain engrossed with other people's problems, Rachel had little time to worry about her own, and it was not until she was leaving the building that she felt a certain sense of apprehension. But no one was waiting for her. She made her way to the bus stop without incident, and on the journey home she occupied herself with wondering whether Roger had called in her absence.

Jane had a cup of tea waiting for her when she entered the flat. Rachel had rung her friend earlier to explain that she was working late, and now Jane regarded her sympathetically as she kicked off her boots and flopped on to the couch in the living room.

'Rough day?' she asked, automatically picking up the boots and putting them away. 'You look tired. Did Roger ring?'

'I gather from that he hasn't rung here,' commented Rachel, bending to rub her aching instep. 'No, he didn't ring. I suppose if he doesn't turn up, I'll have to ring him. Steve and Laura are expecting us this evening.'

'He'll turn up,' said Jane carelessly. 'Particularly as Steve and Laura are his friends, not yours. He won't want them to think there's anything wrong.'

'You could be right,' Rachel grimaced. 'Er—there haven't been any other calls for me, have there?'

'Who? Your father?' Jane shook her head. 'No.'

'I wasn't thinking of my father, actually,' said Rachel, deciding to confess. 'I—er—I had a visitor at the office today. A man I met late last night. I just wondered how he'd found out where I worked.'

'A man? What man?' Jane was intrigued. 'Someone you met at Roger's party? Hey, that's not why he's mad at you, is it? Because you went off with someone else?'

'No.' Rachel sighed. 'It was after I left the party I met him.' Briefly, she explained what had happened, omitting to mention her own disturbing reactions to Alexis Roche. 'He—he turned up at lunchtime. I thought perhaps he might have rung here first.'

'Not that I know of.' Jane pulled a wry face. 'So who is he? What's he like? You say he's French?'

'I said he spoke French at first,' said Rachel, not wanting to go into details. She had thought quite enough about Alexis Roche as it was. 'I don't know anything about him.'

'But why did he go to the office?'

Rachel bent her head. 'To ask me to have lunch with him.'

'He did?' Jane whistled. 'And did you?'

'Of course not.' Rachel looked up at her friend half indignantly. 'How can you ask?'

Jane shrugged. 'Well, he's obviously made an effort to find out all about you.' She paused. 'Is he good-looking?'

'I really couldn't say.' Rachel got to her feet abruptly and deposited her empty cup and saucer on the nearest table. 'I'm going to have a bath. If Roger rings, let me know, will you?'

Jane's eyes twinkled. 'All right. And what if anyone else rings?'

'I'm out,' said Rachel brusquely, walking towards the door. 'And stop looking like that! It wasn't at all funny, believe me. Sophie Tennant was in the office when he turned up, and you know what she's like! It'll be all round the office tomorrow.'

Jane's expression softened. 'So what? You've done nothing wrong, have you? Oh, go and get your bath. I don't want to have to entertain Roger because you're not ready.'

Soaking in the bath, Rachel managed to get things into perspective. She was overreacting, she knew it. It was perfectly reasonable that Alexis Roche should come to thank her for what she had done, even if he had been less than grateful the night before. No doubt he had regretted his behaviour and wanted to make amends. And as for asking her out to lunch—well, men had asked her out to lunch before without arousing such a strong sense of indignation. It was her awareness of his physical attraction that had made her behave as she had, and he could not be held responsible for that.

Nevertheless, there remained the niggling worry as to how he had found her. As she dried herself and dressed, in the cream shirt and slacks she had laid out before her bath, she could not explain that particular puzzle, however the sound of the doorbell dispelled all other considerations. Holding her breath, she waited for Jane to answer the door, and presently she heard the familiar sound of Roger's voice in the living room. Only then did she relax, putting a final touch of eyeshadow at the corners of her eyes before putting down her brush and going out to meet him.

Her first, *infuriating* impression was of how pale Roger looked compared to Alexis Roche, but hard on the heels of this came the more apposite realisation that he was nervous. He was a little above medium height and stockily built, and it was unusual to see him in anything but a confident position, however right now he looked distinctly uneasy.

'Hello, Ray,' he said, running uncertain fingers

through the dark strands of his hair, and although she
normally disliked his diminutive use of her name,
Rachel was too relieved at his apparent diffidence to
give it a second thought.

'Hello, Roger,' she responded, as Jane melted away
into the kitchen, and shaking his head he moved
towards her.

'I'm sorry,' he exclaimed, taking her shoulders and
drawing her unresistingly towards him. 'About last
night, I mean. I was rotten, wasn't I? I've thought about
it all day, wondering if you got home okay, wondering
if you forgave me . . .'

Suppressing the thought that if he had been so
worried about her, why hadn't he rung, Rachel allowed
him to cover her mouth with his. His kiss was warm,
affectionate, a balm to her troubled emotions, and she
responded to it eagerly. But although she linked her
arms about his neck and parted her lips invitingly,
Roger drew back after the briefest of caresses,
murmuring: 'Jane,' with irritating insistence.

'Jane's not in the room,' protested Rachel impatiently,
but although Roger assured himself of this fact, he did
not pursue their embrace.

'Laura and Steve are expecting us,' he reminded her
firmly, tightening the knot of his tie and adjusting the
jacket of his suit. 'We can talk later. Are you ready?'

Rachel shrugged and went to collect a warm tweed
jacket to wear over her shirt and slacks. If only Roger
wasn't so conscious of what other people might think,
she thought irritably, checking the silky swirl of curls
about her shoulders. Still, at least they were not at odds
with one another. She ought to be grateful for that.

The evening spent with the Curtises should have been
pleasant enough, but Rachel found she wasn't enjoying
herself. Perhaps if she and Roger had been alone it
would have been better, she thought. As it was, she was
conscious of what had been said the night before, and
conscious also of the fact that although Roger had
apologised for his behaviour, he had not said anything
about retracting his words. There was still the prospect
of who was to arrange the wedding to resolve, and she

wished she had put her pride aside and rung him this morning before he left for Sunningdale.

Driving back to the flat later, she determined to have it out with him, and taking a deep breath, she said: 'We've been avoiding the subject all evening, but we have to talk about the wedding, Roger.'

'I know.' He took his eyes off the road for a moment to glance her way. 'I suppose that's why you've been so quiet, isn't it? I just wish you wouldn't involve other people in our affairs.'

Rachel blinked. 'Involve other people?' she echoed faintly. 'I don't understand.'

'I think you do.' Roger was precise. 'Last evening you walked out of the apartment, without even wishing our guests goodbye, and tonight you've done your best to make Steve and Laura feel uncomfortable.'

Rachel gasped. 'How?'

'Well, you've hardly opened your mouth all evening.'

'You and Steve were talking. I was listening.'

'You could have talked to Laura. Steve and I were talking about work. It can't have been of much interest to you.'

'On the contrary,' Rachel was indignant, 'I was interested. After all, when we're married I'll expect you to discuss your work with me. Just as you do with your mother.'

'My mother is my business partner,' exclaimed Roger impatiently. 'That's hardly the same thing.'

'So you would rather I talked about knitting and cooking with Laura?'

'Of course. They are the things women usually talk about, aren't they?'

'No.' Rachel dug her nails into her palms in an effort to control her temper. 'Not these days, anyway. We talk about all sorts of things, and knitting and cooking are not my strong points.'

'Laura's an excellent cook.'

'I know it.'

'So perhaps you should get some pointers from her.'

Rachel trembled. 'Laura Curtis is an anachronism, Roger. She has no conversation at all outside domestic

matters. All she thinks about is her home and her
husband, and the child she's expecting.'

'So?' Roger was not prepared to concede. 'What's
wrong with that?'

Rachel tried to calm herself. 'I thought you said we
wouldn't be having any children—not immediately,
anyway.'

'We won't.' Roger shrugged. 'But that doesn't mean
you can't show an interest in such things.'

'Roger, I did show an interest. We talked about
quotes female matters close quotes for fully an hour!
After that, I just dried up.'

'And you showed it.' Roger snorted. 'I was
embarrassed.'

'Were you?' Rachel's lips tightened. 'I'm afraid I
didn't notice.'

'Obviously not.' He swung off the main thoroughfare
into Oakwood Road. 'Still, that's not really relevant to
the real bone of contention between us, is it?'

'No.' Rachel looked down at her hands clasped
tightly together in her lap. 'Have you made up your
mind about the wedding arrangements?'

Roger sighed, drawing the TR7 in to the kerb outside
the Victorian apartment building where Rachel and
Jane had their flat. 'I should be asking you that
question,' he said levelly. 'It really is up to you, I
suppose. I just wish you would consider my mother's
offer, that's all.'

'I have considered it.' Rachel made a determined
effort to appeal to him. 'Darling, can't you understand?
I don't want your mother interfering in something
which is essentially the bride's prerogative.'

'I think it's supposed to be the bride's parents'
prerogative,' remarked Roger pedantically. 'And as we
both know, your parents are unlikely to care how it's
carried out.'

Rachel pressed her lips together. 'Roger, if it's only a
question of paying for a reception, my father can do
that. As to the other arrangements—my dress, and so
on—I do have friends, you know.'

'But Mother wants this to be a special occasion,'

persisted Roger. 'She wants to make it easy for you, can't you see that? She could book the reception, organise the food, arrange about the cake; and as for yours and the bridesmaid's dresses—well, we are in business, aren't we?'

Rachel took a deep breath. 'I only want one bridesmaid, Roger, and that's Jane.'

'Jane!' Roger was scathing. 'For heaven's sake, Ray, do you want to make the whole affair look ridiculous? Jane's fourteen stone if she's an ounce! What kind of a bridesmaid would she make?'

Rachel seethed. 'The very best kind,' she declared tautly. 'I wouldn't dream of leaving her out—simply because your mother has some idea of having a troop of little flower girls to follow me out of church!'

'There you go again!' Roger's jaw jutted. 'Just because Mother wants you to look your best, you're determined to thwart her. Why? Why, for heaven's sake? Sandra's little girls would look delicious in pink satin!'

'Delicious!' Rachel's lips curled. 'Can you hear yourself, Roger? I don't want our wedding to be remembered because of its pretty appearance! Marriage is a serious commitment. It's a serious occasion. And I want Jane to be a witness, because she's the best friend I've got.'

'Perhaps you should be marrying Jane, then,' declared Roger childishly, and Rachel knew a blinding moment of anger.

'Perhaps I should,' she retorted, thrusting open her door and getting out. 'Don't bother to come in. There's no point in us discussing this any further.'

'Aw, Ray——' Roger leant across the front seat, calling after her. 'Ray, I didn't mean it. Come back! We haven't even kissed goodnight.'

'Call me tomorrow,' replied Rachel, over her shoulder, and she heard the car roar away as she inserted her key in the door.

The following day was Friday, and Rachel went to work with a feeling of resignation. Still, she consoled herself, whatever was said, the weekend was close enough to dispel any rumours, and perhaps by Monday someone else might have done something noteworthy.

As luck would have it, Sophie was absent, and one of the other typists, who came to deliver a message from Mr Hollis, explained that her mother had called to say she was full of cold.

'It's that draughty office,' agreed Rachel sympathetically, nevertheless relieved to be free of any further explanations for the present, and the other girl nodded in agreement.

Even so, it was not one of Rachel's better days. Mr Black was in a foul mood, due no doubt to the fact that his wife had forgotten to collect his tonic from the chemist, and his chest had worsened accordingly, and Peter Rennison's appearance just before lunch did not improve matters.

Putting down the file Rachel had had one of the typists deliver to him the previous afternoon, he leant familiarly over her desk, inhaling the clean fragrance of her hair. 'Do I have you to thank for Sophie's sudden aversion to my presence?' he enquired, bending to switch off her machine so that she could not continue typing. 'It seems the poor girl has really taken fright. She hasn't even turned up to work this morning.'

Rachel bent and determinedly switched on her typewriter again. 'Sophie is sick, Mr Rennison,' she replied politely. 'Was there something else you wanted? I'm afraid Mr Black has a client with him at the moment.'

Peter Rennison straightened. 'Cool collected Rachel,' he remarked sarcastically. 'Do you ever let your hair down? Emotionally, I mean?'

Rachel did not answer him, and infuriated by her lack of attention, he exclaimed: 'I pity that poor devil you're marrying! Does he know what a frigid little madam you are? Or maybe he doesn't care. I hear he's quite a mother's boy. Is that true?'

Rachel looked up at him then, the wide blue eyes sparkling with contempt between their fringe of silky black lashes, and the man knew a frustrated sense of contrition. 'Hell, I'm sorry, Rachel,' he muttered, leaning on the desk again. 'But you drive me crazy, do you know that? I wouldn't give a damn about any of the girls if you'd agree to go out with me.'

Rachel sighed and shook her head. 'You're married, Mr Rennison. And I'm engaged. I—please don't ask me again.'

'Don't bet on it,' he responded, conceding defeat for the present and walking towards the door. 'You tell that bloke you're marrying he'd better make you happy, or he'll have me to deal with!'

Rachel couldn't suppress an unwilling smile as he left the office, and she cupped her chin on one hand and stared disconsolately into space. She couldn't help thinking that if Roger had been more like Peter Rennison she might feel more sure of him, instead of harbouring the suspicion that his mother's feelings would always come first.

She was still sitting there in a daydream when the door opened again, and this time Mr Hodges, the caretaker, came into the office. To her surprise, he was carrying a long white box which he set down on her desk, and she gazed at it in wonder as he gave her his grudging smile.

'This came for you, Miss Fleming,' he said, touching the white ribbon which encircled it. 'Aren't you going to open it? Looks like flowers to me.'

'And to me, Mr Hodges,' said Rachel eagerly, abandoning her daydream for an unexpectedly welcome reality, and tearing off the ribbon, she displayed the box's contents.

It was full of roses, pure white roses, as fresh as the moment they were picked from the bush. Long-stemmed, some starting to open their petals, others little more than ivory buds, they spilled their fragrance into the dusty atmosphere of the office, and as Rachel gazed at them, a lump came into her throat.

'They must have cost someone a pretty penny,' remarked Mr Hodges drily, bending his head to enjoy the bouquet. 'Must be more than a couple of dozen of them in there. Roses in February! What next?'

Rachel lifted all the roses out, looking for the card

which she was sure must accompany them. But there was none. Just the pure white roses in their pure white box, eloquent enough of the meaning behind them, she decided.

Mr Hodges was lingering, and eager to get on the phone to Roger, Rachel thrust one of the delicate blooms into the old man's hand. 'A buttonhole,' she said, smiling, and the caretaker took his dismissal happily, tucking the stem through his lapel.

Her first attempt to reach Roger was not successful. He was not in his office, his secretary told her, and realising it was lunch time, Rachel agreed to call back. Then, collecting a couple of empty milk bottles, she filled them with water and deposited the roses in them, discovering as she did so that he had indeed sent her twenty-four.

'Two dozen,' she murmured to herself, as she made her lunchtime cup of coffee. He had never done anything like that before. Which made it all the more appealing, revealing as it did his desire to really mend the breach between them.

She eventually got through to Roger at a quarter to three, and although he came on the line, she could tell at once that he was not pleased to be disturbed.

'Rachel, I've got the buyer from Streetline with me at the moment,' he exclaimed, evidently involved in making a sale. 'Could we talk tonight, do you think? Come to the apartment. We can talk there.'

'All right.' Rachel squashed her disappointment that she was not to have more time to thank him right now. 'I—I just wanted you to know, I love them.'

There was a pause, and then Roger asked half irritably: 'What was that?'

'The roses,' said Rachel urgently. 'I love the roses. Thank you for sending them. It was a—a wonderful thought.'

'Wait a minute . . .' Clearly Roger was fighting a losing battle with his curiosity, 'what are you talking about? What roses? I didn't send any roses. They must be for somebody else.'

Rachel noticed he didn't say *from* somebody else, and

for the first time she wondered how Mr Hodges had known they were for her. There had been no indication on the box, no card, as he had seen. She shook her head bewilderedly. If Roger hadn't sent them, who had?

The answer was too outrageous to be true. In spite of his professed affection for her, Peter Rennison would never do something as incriminating as send flowers, and in any case, what other man of her acquaintance could afford to spend so much money on two dozen roses? It had to be someone to whom twenty-five or thirty pounds meant very little; someone who wore Italian leather jackets and Cartier watches, and treated a Lamborghini Countach with casual indifference . . .

'Is that all?'

Realising Roger was still waiting for her response, Rachel pulled herself together. 'What? Oh, yes—yes,' she murmured unhappily. 'Sorry to have disturbed you, Roger. Goodbye.'

'Until later,' he inserted, reminding her of her promise to go to his apartment, and nodding her head, she added: 'Until later,' in a low unenthusiastic voice.

When she rang Mr Hodges' small office to enquire about the roses, he was quite definite that they were hers. 'A gentleman brought them,' he said, sniffing down the phone. 'For Miss Fleming, Miss *Rachel* Fleming. Now you know there are no other Miss Flemings in the building, let alone a Miss Rachel Fleming.'

Rachel sighed. 'The man——' She paused. 'What was he like?'

'I dunno. Foreign-looking. Tall and dark——'

'Dark, did you say?'

'—wearing a kind of chauffeur's uniform.'

'Oh!' Rachel's brief moment of uncertainty fled. 'Oh, well, thank you, Mr Hodges. I'm very grateful.'

With the receiver restored to its rest, there remained the problem of what she was going to do with them. Her first instincts were to leave the roses in the office, but to do so would evoke exactly the kind of interest she most wanted to avoid. And besides, Mr Black would not appreciate their presence. He would probably say they aggravated his asthma, and with the weekend coming, it wasn't fair to leave them to die. She would have to take them home and hope to goodness Roger did not question her too thoroughly as to their sender's identity. She could always pretend they had been delivered by mistake, but no one knew to whom they really belonged.

In consequence, she emerged from the building that afternoon carrying the white box in her arms. Against the dark material of her double-breasted jacket, it was distinctly noticeable, but happily it was raining and the other girls were in too much of a hurry to get home to pay her any attention. It was a little cumbersome, too, coping with its length and the copious wedge of her shoulder bag, but she gasped indignantly when it was suddenly lifted out of her grasp.

'*Permettez-moi, mademoiselle,*' said a rather gutteral French voice, and she looked round in surprise to find a man in chauffeur's uniform at her elbow.

'I beg your pardon——' she began, more because she was astounded at his effrontery than at his use of another language, and the man, whose harsh features were not altogether reassuring in the half light, bowed his head apologetically.

'Forgive me,' he exclaimed, his English overlaid by a heavy accent, 'but I am here to escort you, *mademoiselle*. You wish me to carry your bag, also?'

'No.' Rachel was vaguely alarmed by his intrusion. In the fading light of an early evening, it was disconcerting to be accosted when there was no one she knew to come to her assistance, and while she suspected Alexis Roche was behind this, she didn't want to get involved with him either. 'I——' She looked regretfully at the box of roses in his arms, and then, realising she could hardly claim them in the circumstances, she shook her head. 'No, I don't need any help, thank you. Excuse me, I have a bus to catch.'

'Ah, *mais non.*' To her dismay, his hand curled round her sleeve, gripping her gently, but firmly, in the kind of grasp she knew would tighten like a vice if she tried to get free. 'Monsieur Roche is waiting for you, *mademoiselle*. Come with me. It is not far.'

# CHAPTER THREE

RACHEL gasped. 'Will you let go of me!'

'Please, *mademoiselle*, do not make a fuss.' The chauffeur started propelling her along the street without any apparent effort. 'Monsieur Roche would not wish for you to cause any embarrassment. See, the car is there.' He pointed to a vehicle parked some yards further along the narrow thoroughfare. 'It is parked on your yellow lines, *non*? Let us not keep my master waiting.'

'I don't give a damn about your master,' protested Rachel fiercely. She really couldn't believe this was happening, and she looked at the faces of passers-by wondering why none of them was trying to help her. But, amazingly, no one seemed to be taking the slightest notice of her, and she assumed that with the cold and the wet they were more concerned with their own comfort than hers. No doubt they believed she was being escorted to her car by her chauffeur, she thought, a sob of hysteria rising in her throat. The box of roses tucked beneath his arm seemed to confirm this, and no would-be kidnapper had ever had a more powerful ally. The chauffeur was huge, easily six feet three or four, with massive shoulders and the kind of build more in keeping with a professional wrestler. It would take a brave man to tackle him indeed, and Rachel couldn't imagine any of the umbrella-carrying brigade they were passing doing such a thing.

As they neared the car, which she identified as being the most recognisable status symbol of them all, the door was pushed open from inside and a man emerged. Although he was warmly garbed in a thick fur-lined overcoat, his pale hair was unmistakable, and Rachel stared at him frustratedly.

'How dare you?' she exclaimed, as soon as they were near enough for him to hear her words. 'How dare you abduct me like this? I don't know what they do in your country, but in England men do not go around kidnapping young women!'

'Did you do that, Hassim?' Alexis Roche enquired lazily, his hands pushed deep into the pockets of his coat. He lifted his shoulders carelessly, without waiting for a reply. 'My only intention was to offer you a lift, Miss Fleming.'

'Well, I don't need a lift,' retorted Rachel, finding herself free at last and rubbing the arm which Hassim had gripped so purposefully. 'And you had no right to send me those roses. When I want flowers, my fiancé will buy them for me!'

Alexis Roche shrugged, a gesture which seemed to imply a mixture of indifference and regret, and taking the box from Hassim, he tossed it carelessly to the ground. 'My apologies,' he said, as Rachel gazed aghast at the scattered blooms. 'I thought you might like them. But it is of no matter.'

Rachel caught her breath. 'You're not going to leave them there?'

'Why not?'

Drops of rain were sparkling on the artificially-silvered lightness of his hair, and as she looked up at him, Rachel knew an unwelcome quickening of her pulses. He was the most sexually disturbing man she had ever met, as well as being the most unpredictable. For a heart-stopping moment she wondered what he would have done if she had thanked him for the roses, and the prospect of bringing an unguarded smile to those thin lips caused a sudden painful constriction in her stomach.

'They'll die,' she said now, forcing herself to think only of the flowers, and he pulled a wry face.

'As do we all, Miss Fleming,' he responded, without expression. 'You are getting wet. Don't let me detain you.'

Contrarily, Rachel hesitated. 'The roses . . .' she ventured uneasily. 'You won't leave them like this?'

'No?' Alexis Roche swung open the car door behind him. 'Don't concern yourself. They are nothing.'

'But they are!' Rachel sighed. 'Please . . .'

Alexis Roche paused. 'I will make a bargain with you. Hassim will rescue the roses if you allow me to take you home.'

Rachel gasped. 'You're not serious!'

'*Deadly* serious,' he retorted mockingly, and she looked down at the wilting roses with a helpless sense of impotence.

'Why should you want to take me home?' she exclaimed at last. 'We hardly know one another.'

'That can be remedied,' he remarked, his grey eyes holding her with disruptive consequences.

'I—no! I mean—you can't. We can't.' She licked her dry lips. 'Why are you doing this?'

'I wanted to see you again,' he replied simply. Then: 'What is your decision?'

'I—I——' Rachel looked down at the roses again, and then up into his dark face. Unbidden came the memory of Roger's voice on the phone, the impatience he had exhibited, his supreme arrogance in believing that no other man was likely to send her flowers, or indeed, that she might be willing to accept them. And suddenly she found herself saying: 'All right. All right, you can take me home. So long as you rescue the roses.'

Inside the car, she immediately regretted her impulsive action. The flowers were not that important. What she was really doing was something which she knew would make Roger extremely angry if he found out. And she had no wish to examine any other motives which might have elicited her reckless behaviour . . .

Hassim quickly restored the scattered roses to their box and Alexis Roche climbed into the back of the Rolls-Royce beside her after giving the chauffeur his orders. 'Flat 3, Oakwood Road, Kilburn, isn't that right?' he remarked, brushing a film of rainwater from his sleeves, and Rachel remembered that she still didn't know how he had found her.

'That's correct,' she agreed, edging away from the depression his weight had made in the soft leather. 'How did you find out? I didn't give you my address, and the telephone is in Jane's name.'

'Jane?'

'My flatmate.' Rachel was glad of the darkness to conceal her expression. 'I assume you didn't contact the police.'

'Well, only indirectly,' he assured her casually. 'I took the number of your car and a friend of mine identified you.'

Rachel stared at his profile, and now she wished she could see *his* expression. 'You took my number! But——'

'——you thought I was drunk, I know.' He turned his head towards her. 'I told you I wasn't.'

Rachel shook her head. 'Even so, they wouldn't know where I worked.'

'Ah——' His lips parted, and she guessed he was amused by her persistence. 'In that instance I had to rely on Hassim. He visited your apartment and spoke to a—Mrs Bently, am I right?'

Rachel sighed. Of course! Mrs Bently. Why hadn't she thought of that? The woman who came in twice a week to clean the flat was always there on Wednesday mornings, which would account for the fact that Jane knew nothing about it.

'She had no right to give your—your—Hassim that information,' she said now, and he inclined his head.

'I would agree with you. She had no way of knowing what his intentions might be.'

'No.' But Rachel could imagine the middle-aged charlady, faced with a man of Hassim's proportions, having little desire to argue with him. 'I—I shall speak to her.'

'Do that.' Alexis relaxed against the upholstery beside her. 'But don't entirely blame her. Hassim can be very persuasive.'

'Hassim . . .' Rachel couldn't prevent the question. 'Is that an Arabic name?'

'Hassim was born in Bahdan,' Alexis agreed smoothly. 'His father was my grandfather's bodyguard for many years.'

Rachel frowned. 'And—and is he your bodyguard?'

'My grandfather likes to think so.'

Rachel drew her lower lip between her teeth. 'Your grandfather?' she probed, unable to resist. 'Not your father?'

'No.' He expelled his breath lazily. 'My father does not have so many enemies.'

Rachel was intrigued, but realising she was allowing herself to be diverted, she turned determinedly to the window. It wasn't her concern, she told herself severely. His background was nothing to do with her. After this evening, she was unlikely to see him again. Men like Alexis Roche did not waste their time with girls who showed so overtly that they were not interested.

'Will you have dinner with me?'

His unexpected request brought her head round with a start, and she gazed at him disbelievingly. 'Have—dinner with you?'

'This evening,' he confirmed, without emphasis. 'I'm familiar with various eating places in London, or alternatively we could eat at my house.'

'Your house?' Rachel felt incredibly slow-witted, but somehow she had never expected him to have a house in London. Paris, perhaps; or Nice; but not London.

'My house,' he conceded smoothly, unbuttoning his overcoat. 'My chef is quite efficient. The food would be good, I assure you.'

'I'm sure it would.' Rachel knew a helpless feeling of unreality. 'However,' she endeavoured to speak normally, 'it's completely out of the question. I'm having dinner with my fiancé.'

'Tomorrow evening, then,' he said flatly, lifting his shoulders in an indifferent gesture. 'Hassim will pick you up at seven o'clock and bring you to Eaton Mews. We can decide then what to do.'

'No!' Rachel gazed at him frustratedly now. 'No, you don't understand. I can't—I won't have dinner with you, ever. I'm engaged. I don't do that sort of thing.'

'What sort of thing?' She could see the pale glitter of his eyes even in the shadows of the car.

'You know,' she persisted. 'Go out with other men. It—it wouldn't be fair.'

'Not even if you want to go out with another man?'

he queried softly, and her skin prickled. 'Not even then?'

'But I don't—I haven't—oh, this is Oakwood Road. I'm home.'

'Wait.' His hand stayed her as she would have got out of the car, and she quivered as Hassim left his seat to walk round the bonnet and swing open her door. 'Your roses,' he murmured, putting the box into her hands, and Rachel was still trembling when the luxurious limousine drew away.

Rachel's father rang on Sunday morning.

'How about having lunch with me?' he suggested, after learning that Jane had gone to Worthing to spend the day with her parents, and Rachel was happy to agree. Spending time alone was not good for her in her present frame of mind, and she was ready and waiting when Charles Fleming rang the doorbell.

Her father was a man in his late fifties, to whom the years had not always been kind. His propensity for the good life had finally made a permanent mark upon his fleshy features, and the pouches beneath his eyes seemed more pronounced than when Rachel had last seen him.

Nevertheless, as they went down to his car, she decided he had not deserved the way her mother had treated him, and although she knew there had been faults on both sides, his age and accessibility had tended to influence Rachel in his favour.

They drove out to Windsor and had lunch at a hotel overlooking the river. At this time of year the waterway was not particularly attractive, but the customers taking lunch were more interested in the food. They had home-made pâté, and roast beef, and finished the meal with cheese and coffee, and it was not until they had reached this stage that Charles betrayed the real reason for his invitation.

'How is that boy-friend of yours getting along?' he enquired, surprising Rachel by his question, as he and Roger had never had much liking for one another.

'He's fine,' she said now, ignoring the slightly hollow

feeling her words evoked. 'But we—er—we're having some difficulties over the arrangements for the wedding. Roger's mother wants to take over everything, and I've explained you and I can organise the reception.'

'Organise?' Charles frowned. 'You mean pay, I suppose?'

'Well—yes. And arrange where it's to be, of course. And choose my dress and Jane's.'

'Hmm.' Her father nodded, pouring the last dregs of the bottle of wine he had ordered into his own glass and viewing it thoughtfully. 'Well, you know, my sweet, it might not be a bad idea to let Mrs Harrington have her way——'

'What?'

'—as she's so set on it. I mean, it's not as if your mother was here to take offence. I'd have thought you'd have welcomed a—a woman's touch. It's obvious Roger's mother thinks the world of you.'

'It's not obvious at all!' Rachel was indignant. 'I don't know why you're saying this. You don't like Mrs Harrington—you've said so. And you've never shown any particular love for Roger, if it comes to that!'

'Now, now . . .' Her father patted her hand, glancing about them half anxiously, as if afraid their conversation might have been overheard. 'Don't go getting upset. All I'm saying is that perhaps you should consider it. They are going to be family, aren't they? Families should stick together.'

Rachel gasped. 'You mean you won't give me your support?'

'Well . . .' Charles drew out the word consideringly, 'it isn't as simple as that, Rachel. Things are pretty tight at present. Money's scarce. We're in the middle of a recession, and it isn't always possible to do all the things we'd like to do.'

'What are you saying?'

Charles Fleming sighed. 'Don't look at me like that! I'm your father, Rachel. It's not my fault if certain investments I've made haven't yielded the profit I expected.'

'You mean—you're having financial difficulties?'

'Temporarily. Only temporarily,' her father assured her firmly. 'But you can see, can't you, that this isn't exactly the right time to come to me for money. As a matter of fact—well, I did wonder—that nest-egg your grandmother left you—is there any chance of you being able to lend me a couple of hundred?'

Rachel sucked in her breath. 'Lend you——'

'Just for a week or two,' put in her father earnestly. 'I've got what they call a "cash flow" problem.'

'And two hundred pounds will help?' said Rachel incredulously.

'For the time being,' agreed her father. 'It's just a little problem, but I need cash for entertaining and so on.'

'I thought you used credit cards,' said Rachel, frowning, and her father gave an impatient exclamation.

'Don't you trust me, Rachel?' he demanded. 'I've never asked you for anything before, have I? Surely it's not such a momentous decision.'

Rachel bent her head. It was true; he had never asked her for money before. But until she was twenty-one, the five thousand pounds her grandmother had left her had been held in trust, and it was only six months since her birthday.

'How much did you have in mind?' she asked now, and her father breathed a sigh of relief.

'Could you make it—five hundred?' he suggested tentatively, and Rachel lifted her head to gaze at him in disbelief.

'You said a couple of hundred,' she reminded him, but Charles Fleming was not deterred.

'Two hundred, five hundred, what's the difference?' he exclaimed carelessly. 'You'll have it back in a few days. Shall we say five per cent?'

Rachel blinked. 'Five per cent?'

'Interest,' said her father, patting her hand. 'Can't have you losing by this, can we?'

Rachel flushed. 'I don't want any interest, Dad. I—when do you want it? I can write you a cheque now, if you like.'

'Oh, no,' his hand imprisoned hers, 'not a cheque. I—er—I'd prefer cash, if that's all right with you.' He gave her a winning smile. 'Easier all round, don't you know? Don't want the old tax man getting his nose into this transaction, do we?'

Rachel took a deep breath. 'I'll get the money tomorrow lunchtime. Do you want me to bring it to your office?'

'No. No, I'll meet you.' Charles looked thoughtful. 'Shall we say—on the Embankment, near Temple Station, at one o'clock?'

Rachel shrugged, feeling suddenly depressed. She had thought her father had asked her out for lunch so that they could be together, but now it seemed all he had wanted was a handout. She sighed, remembering the things Roger had said about her father; that he was a fool and a womaniser, that his business dealings were not always honest, and that she was lucky her parents had split up when they did, thus removing her from his corrupting influence.

She sighed then, determinedly putting these thoughts aside. She was being silly, she told herself. The fact that her father was asking her for a loan was no reason to jump to the conclusion that Roger had been right all along. It *was* the first time he had come to her, and she was his daughter, after all. Who else should he turn to?

'Temple Station,' she agreed now, reaching for the meal check. 'And I suppose I'd better handle this, too.' She managed a smile. 'As you're having a cash flow problem!'

For several days the subject of their wedding was carefully avoided by both Rachel and Roger. Rachel met her father on Monday lunchtime and handed over the five hundred pounds, and this was something else she did not discuss with her fiancé. She knew Roger would make some scathing comment if she confessed the truth to him, and she didn't want to create any more dissention when matters were so strained between them.

At the office she had to run the gauntlet of a certain

amount of teasing. Sophie was back at work, and had lost no time in coming to see her friend to ask about the mysterious stranger. The fact that Rachel had refused to discuss the affair had not made a scrap of difference to her. She had her own ideas concerning Alexis Roche, and although Rachel refused to participate, Sophie perpetually found some way to bring his name into her conversation. In consequence, the female washroom buzzed with gossip, and when the story of the roses somehow found its way to feminine ears, Rachel had no choice but to concede that it was true.

'White roses!' exclaimed Sophie reverently, clasping her hands to her throat in a deliberately melodramatic gesture. 'Oh, Rachel! Isn't it romantic?'

'It's not romantic at all,' retorted her friend, pushing papers into a file. 'And I wish you'd forget about it. I have.'

'Have you, Rachel?' Sophie rested her hands on the other girl's desk and gazed disbelievingly into her face. 'Aren't you just the tiniest bit sorry he hasn't come here again? I mean, he was—fascinating, wasn't he?'

'No. I mean—of course I'm not sorry he hasn't come here again!' Rachel spoke impatiently. 'Sophie, I have to get on. Mr Black is waiting for these reports.'

Nevertheless, after the younger girl had gone, Rachel had to admit she had emerged from the office rather apprehensively these last few nights. Not for any reason of anticipation, she reminded herself firmly, but simply as a precautionary measure. She had not imagined Alexis Roche to be a man who gave up easily, and it had crossed her mind that he might try to intercept her again. However, nothing had happened, and she had come to the conclusion that her feelings of unease had been totally unwarranted.

On Thursday Roger rang just as she was leaving the office for lunch. She had some odds and ends of shopping to do, and she had arranged to meet one of the other girls at the Wimpy bar for a snack, and the timing of Roger's call was inopportune at least.

'Could it wait until this afternoon, darling?' she asked, glancing anxiously at her watch. 'I'm meeting

Isabel in half an hour, and I have some shopping to do first.'

'No, it can't wait.' Roger ignored the appealing note in her voice. 'This is important, Rachel. We've been invited to a reception at the Metropolitan Hotel this evening, and I'm ringing to ask you to be ready at seven o'clock.'

'Tonight?' Rachel gave a helpless wail. 'But, Roger, you know we didn't plan to see one another this evening. I've arranged to go to the cinema with Jane. She wants to see that French film at the Rialto——'

'Never mind that.' Roger sounded irritable. 'Rachel, I don't think I'm making myself clear. This reception at the Metropolitan is something special. It's a pre-season fashion show, and there are to be buyers there from all over Europe. I can't usually get an invitation to these affairs, but this morning Sancha Forrest rang me and——'

'Then you go, Roger,' said Rachel quietly. 'It's obviously not just a social affair——'

'No, it's not. It's an event.' Roger sighed. 'But, Rachel, the invitation was for both of us . . .'

'Take your mother, then.' Rachel knew she was being offhand, but she couldn't help it. The idea of spending the evening at a fashion show was not attractive to her, particularly as she knew Roger would take every opportunity to further his own ends.

'Rachel!' he exclaimed now, evidently getting angry. 'I'm asking you. What was it you said the other night? That after we were married, you expected me to share my work with you? How do you equate that with your attitude now?'

'Oh, Roger!' Rachel sighed. 'It's very short notice.'

'For me, too. But, like I said, Sancha Forrest only rang me this morning.'

'Who is Sancha Forrest?'

'Don't you know?' Roger took a deep breath, and then, as if explaining the situation to a child, he went on: 'Sancha Forrest is just one of the most important dress designers in England. Surely you remember reading about that evening gown she made for one of the members of the Royal Family!'

'Oh—yes.' Rachel could remember reading something about it. 'But why would she invite you? You don't design clothes, Roger.'

'I know that.' Roger made a sound of impatience. 'But I suppose she realises that it's people like me that keep the fashion industry moving in Britain.'

Rachel bit her lip. Considering Roger bought most of his stock overseas, she thought this was a slight exaggeration, but perhaps he was right. After all, most people couldn't afford the kind of clothes designed by the Sancha Forrests of the fashion world. They generally depended on boutiques like Roger's to copy the designs and produce them in a more affordable form.

'All right,' she said at last, giving in. 'I'll phone Jane and explain the situation.'

'Good girl!' Roger's irritation vanished. 'I knew you wouldn't let me down. Until later, then.'

Getting ready to go out that evening, Rachel half wished she had not allowed herself to be persuaded. She wasn't in the mood for meeting people or for impressing the clients Roger hoped to attract. She felt curiously dull and dejected, and Jane's acceptance of the situation was little consolation.

'You should be mad at me,' Rachel declared, when she emerged from her bedroom to find her friend curled up on the couch in front of the television set. 'And I'd much rather be going to see *Les Trois* with you than attending this reception.'

Jane shrugged philosophically. 'The way I see it, your relationship with Roger is going through a pretty sticky patch at the moment. Far be it from me to upset the balance. Besides, we can go and see a film at any time, and Roger did say that this was important, didn't he?'

'Well, yes.' Rachel was grudging.

'So—stop looking so depressed about it,' said Jane drily. 'Or your fiancé will begin to suspect you've found another man.'

Rachel turned away to pick up the warm velvet-lined cloak she was planning to wear over the silk shirt and pants suit she was wearing, glad of the brief respite to hide her expression. Jane's words were disturbing for a variety of reasons, not least the uneasy conviction that she was allowing their dispute over the wedding to assume too much importance. What did it matter really? she rationalised. The ceremony was only the outward expression of their feelings for one another. Did it really matter who organised it? Who paid for it, for that matter? One way or another, they were going to get married, and after the wedding was over they had the rest of their lives to share. *The rest of their lives. . . .*

Just for a moment, the enormity of that statement rocked her carefully controlled emotions, and then she hurriedly slipped the cloak about her shoulders. This was definitely not a night for introspection, and she determinedly squashed the memory of what Sophie had said the day before. She was not even the tiniest bit piqued that Alexis Roche had not made another attempt to see her, she told herself. And she was not allowing her frustration over that to influence her behaviour towards Roger. She was relieved that Alexis had not continued to pursue an association that had been futile from the onset. But she was tired—tired of making excuses for Roger's vacillation, tired of competing with his mother for his attention, and tired of marking time until they could get married. Long engagements were always a strain, or so she had heard, and it was natural that she should have periods of self-doubt. But tonight things would be different, she promised herself. Tonight she would tell Roger that if his mother still wanted to organise the wedding, she could, bridesmaids and all, so long as Jane was not left out.

With this decision made, Rachel felt much better, and when Roger rang the doorbell she went to greet him with more enthusiasm than she had done for weeks. 'Love you,' she said, ignoring his halfhearted response to her kiss, and he looked at her strangely before acknowledging her admission with a mumbled: 'Me, too.'

# CHAPTER FOUR

ALEX Roche moved rather impatiently from one foot to the other and immediately drew the attention of the hovering floor manager.

'Can I get anything for you, Mr Roche?' he enquired, with the obsequiousness of one who was not ignorant of the importance of his superior, and the younger man moved his velvet-clad shoulders in weary distaste.

'Thank you, no,' he responded, accompanying his remark with a tight smile. 'I am waiting for someone,' he added, realising his presence here in the lobby was arousing a certain amount of unrest. 'Carry on. My guests will arrive shortly.'

'Yes, sir.'

The floor manager reluctantly moved away, and Alex withdrew behind one of the tall veined-marble pillars that supported the balcony above. In spite of what he had told the other man, he did not wish to be observed before he was ready, and a glance at his watch had told him that he should not have to wait much longer.

As he waited, Alex focussed his wandering attention on his surroundings, acknowledging, with a faintly rueful air, that contrary to his father's opinion, the old man had succeeded in restoring the old hotel to its former grandeur. Although it stood in Piccadilly, in recent years the Metropolitan had lost much of its charm, owing to the ravages of time and machinery. Its elegant façade had become blackened by smoke and petrol fumes, and inside, its run-down appearance had proved too expensive for its former owner to renovate. When Alex's grandfather had bought the hotel in 1980, it had cost the better part of a million pounds to redecorate and restore, but now the immaculate face-lift was complete, and it had resumed its place as one of the most exclusive venues in London.

At present, a steady stream of guests was entering the

enormous foyer, shedding their coats in the downstairs cloakroom, and mounting the shallow, carpeted staircase to the first floor. The reception which had been arranged was being held in the ballroom, and Alex could hear above him the steady hum of sound as uniformed major-domos attended to the new arrivals. A buffet was being served and the liveried staff had been instructed to move among the guests with trays loaded with glasses of champagne—an informal gathering before the real business of the evening began.

Observing some of the more outrageous outfits being worn, Alex's lips curled. Why was it Western women persisted in dressing themselves like men, or worse? he wondered. One girl was wearing a multi-coloured cat-suit, liberally laced with zips, and she had dyed her hair in stripes to match. Alex could see nothing feminine in her appearance at all, or in the girl dressed all in white who accompanied her. Her white clown's face did not amuse him, and his expression tightened contemptuously as he intercepted an admiring glance cast in his own direction.

Yet more people were arriving, and Alex's jaw relaxed as he recognised the slim dark girl who was being helped off with her cloak. Although he had expected her to wear a dress, she was not—she was wearing beige silk trousers and a loose-sleeved matching shirt, that tied at her waist in a knot—but his eyes narrowed in approval of her attractive appearance, and he had to drag his eyes away to look at the man with her.

So that was Roger Harrington, he reflected, from the concealing shadow of the pillar. A rather pompous-looking man, whose attitude to his fiancée was inclined to be patronising. Alex didn't like the way he hurried Rachel out of her cloak, or the comments he was addressing to her as they made their way up the softly-woven carpet of the staircase.

'Really,' Roger was saying disgustedly, 'Some people will go to any lengths to draw attention to themselves! I'd like to know how they got here. What qualifications do they have to attend an affair like this?'

Alex inclined his head in mocking acknowledgment of this particular comment, but the irony of his humour was unobserved. Already the dark-haired man and his beautiful companion had disappeared from his view, and he emerged from his shadowy alcove to gaze after them with considering eyes.

'Alex!'

Sancha Forrest's shrill voice assailed his ears, and although he regretted the interruption, his expression was politely smiling as he turned to greet the show's organiser.

'Sancha,' he essayed smoothly, taking the hand she proffered, and bowing his head over it. 'You are looking quite magnificent. I did not realise ostrich feathers were still in fashion.'

Sancha Forrest smiled without artifice at the man facing her. 'They're not,' she replied carelessly, dismissing the milk-white plumes bobbing at her shoulder. 'But I'm too old to be regarded as anything but eccentric. And don't pretend with me, Alex. I can see from your expression that an affair like this is not to your taste. So why are you here? Don't blame me if you're bored already.'

'How could I be bored in your company, Sancha?' exclaimed Alex gallantly, but his companion was not deceived.

'I could hardly believe it when you rang and asked me to invite Roger Harrington,' she continued. 'I almost rang and asked Nadine whether she knew of this Miss Fleming and her fiancé.'

Alex released her hand abruptly. 'But you didn't?' he queried tensely, and Sancha's carefully made-up features assumed an indignant expression.

'Of course not,' she denied, the faint, middle-European accent she had almost succeeded in erasing from her voice appearing suddenly. 'Your mother would be most concerned to hear that you were concerning yourself with someone other than Mariana, and we have been friends for too long for me to lie to her.'

Alex's expression relaxed. 'Good. You have no need to feel concerned. My mother is not involved here.'

'And Mariana?'

Sancha's painted brows arched as she deliberately mentioned the girl's name, but Alex was not perturbed. 'Mariana is not here,' he said, with infuriating logic. He offered her his arm. 'Come and have some champagne. I can guarantee it is excellent.'

Realising she was not about to learn anything further at this point, Sancha leant heavily on his arm as they mounted the stairs. 'I am getting too old for these affairs,' she muttered, as they reached the first floor. 'Why do I go on with them? Does anyone really thank me for it?'

'You know they do,' replied Alex placatingly, allowing her to precede him through the double doors of the ballroom, which had been thrown wide for the occasion. 'How else would these young designers get to show off their talents? Besides,' he cast her an affectionate glance, 'you know you really love it.'

'I wonder?' Sancha looked up at him doubtfully for a moment, and Alex had the distinct feeling it was not her own philanthropy that occupied her thoughts at that moment.

The ballroom was looking particularly beautiful this evening. There were flowers everywhere, great masses of blooms occupying every available space, and filling the air with their various perfumes. Their colours were highlighted by the three magnificent chandeliers suspended overhead, and between the long reflective mirrors that lined the walls, the handpainted murals, which had recently been restored, had been draped with bows of gold velvet. This evening the polished floor had been covered by a thick cream and gold carpet, whose softness and thickness cushioned the many feet which were presently walking upon it.

'Delightful,' was Sancha's immediate reaction to her surroundings, and to Alex's relief, her dramatic exclamation drew a score of welcoming guests to surround her. Their presence enabled him to move away, and he looked about him half impatiently, seeking one familiar face.

'Alexis—Alexis *darling*!'

Yet another unwelcome voice arrested him, and as he turned reluctantly to acknowledge its owner, he caught sight of the person he was looking for. Rachel Fleming was standing less than ten feet away, part of a group that contained her fiancé, who was talking animatedly to a man on his left. Alex guessed it had been the use of his name which had attracted Rachel's attention to him, but he was surprised at the look of shocked consternation that crossed her face at the sight of him. First of all she went bright red, then quite pale, and Alex had to hide his irritation at the unwanted delay in the execution of his plans the girl beside him now presented.

'I couldn't believe it was you,' she was saying, laying a possessive hand upon his arm. 'I said to myself, Alexis Roche wouldn't be interested in a fashion show. Not unless Mariana had brought him, of course. She is here, isn't she? You can't have come alone!'

'I'm afraid Mariana is not with me,' Alex replied flatly. 'It's good to see you again, Lucille.' He controlled the impulse to glance over his shoulder with a supreme effort. 'Are you well?'

Lucille Gautier pouted prettily. She had been at finishing school with Mariana and it was unfortunate that she should be here this evening. But no matter, he thought grimly. Mariana knew exactly how he felt. It would have served her right had he chosen to use someone like Lucille for his purpose. But Lucille was too easy—and she was not engaged to an Englishman.

'I am very well,' Lucille was saying now, her expression revealing the curiosity she was no doubt feeling. But, conquering her desire to pursue the topic of Mariana, she chose to take advantage of the situation. 'All the better for seeing you, darling. And if you're alone——'

'I'm not.' Alex's clipped denial was just a little too quick, even for Lucille's doubtful sensitivities, and her lips tightened perceptibly. 'If you'll excuse me, I must go and offer my respects to—to a friend of the family,' he added crisply. '*Au revoir*, Lucille. *A bientôt!*'

He was aware of the French girl's eyes following him

as he turned to make his way to where he had seen
Rachel standing, and his shoulders moved in a barely
noticeable gesture of dismissal. It was done; the
decision had been made, he reminded himself harshly.
Maybe, in time, he would learn to regret his actions,
but for now, revenge was sweet . . .

Getting Roger to circulate, when he had obviously been
enjoying his conversation with Klaus Stronheim, had
not been easy. Roger was not the easiest person to
manipulate in any situation, but after exchanging that
startling moment of identification with Alexis Roche,
Rachel had been desperate. Without really knowing
how, she had succeeded in convincing Roger that there
were probably other people here he should meet, and
while the Frenchman paused to speak with a very
attractive blonde, Rachel had managed to put Roger's
bulk and several chattering groups between herself and
imminent disaster.

Even so, she was not happy. Seeing Alexis like that
had awakened all the disturbing emotions she had
convinced herself were the result of too much
introspection. And in addition to this, she could not
altogether dismiss the belief that Alexis's appearance
was not wholly coincidental. Yet it must be, she argued,
making an effort to listen to what Roger was saying.
She was flattering herself if she imagined that a man
like Alexis Roche might attend a function like this on
the offchance of seeing her. It was pathetic and
ludicrous for her to think that way. She really must stop
living in a daydream. It *was* a coincidence: nothing
more, nothing less.

'That's Sancha Forrest over there,' Roger indicated
now, nodding towards an elderly woman dressed
incongruously in the style of a pre-war debutante, and
Rachel forced herself to show interest.

'She's not at all as I expected,' she remarked in
surprise. 'I assumed she'd be very chic—and much
younger.'

'Mmm.' Roger swallowed the last of his champagne
and helped himself to another glass from a passing tray.

'I agree—she isn't exactly a good representation of our industry. But she's filthy rich, and most of these people wouldn't stand a chance of being noticed without her patronage.'

Rachel shook her head. 'I'm afraid I don't know anything about fashion. But I like the way she looks. It's rather— sweet.'

'And every designer in the country will be using that line before the season's over,' remarked a woman's voice beside them. 'Hello, Roger. What are you doing here? Since when did your boutiques begin to sell anything original?'

Roger rode the insult rather better than Rachel expected, and his expression was wry when he turned to respond to her challenge. 'Vicky Young, as I live and breathe,' he declared laconically. 'I haven't seen you for donkey's years!'

'Not quite that long, Roger,' the young woman replied with sweet sarcasm. 'And I don't measure by those methods, not being an ass myself!'

Roger laughed. 'Your tongue's as sharp as ever anyway,' he conceded lightly. 'Hey, let me introduce you to my fiancée. Rachel, meet Victoria Young. We've known one another from—well, from way back.'

Rachel noticed that the other girl's expression faltered briefly as Roger made the introduction, but Vicky had recovered herself by the time they shook hands.

'I never thought Roger would get married,' she exclaimed, curbing the sharpness of her words with a faint smile. 'Are you a model, by any chance? He always had a soft spot for girls in bikinis.'

'I'm afraid not.' Rachel was not offended by her outspoken approach. 'But you surprise me.' She cast her fiancé a teasing smile. 'Does Mrs Harrington know of her son's predilection for half-naked women?'

Vicky relaxed somewhat. 'Mrs Harrington? Is she still around?'

'Of course she's still around.' Roger spoke somewhat huffily now, evidently finding Rachel's attempt at humour less to his taste. 'Er—Vicky met my mother some years ago, Rachel. As a matter of fact, they got on very well together.'

'Really?' Rachel was intrigued. Roger had never spoken of the girls he had known before their association, but looking at Vicky now, Rachel guessed that she and Roger were much of an age. Even though she was wearing a short skirt and an Afro hair style, the other girl had to be in her early thirties, and for the first time Rachel found herself speculating on a previous relationship.

'Anyway,' went on Roger with some irritation, 'it's good to see you again, Vicky. I heard you'd gone to the States. I never expected to see you here.'

'No.' Vicky shook her head. 'Well, I was living in New York for a time, but I got homesick. I just arrived back last month. I'm looking for a job, actually. Do you have anything to offer me?'

Roger frowned consideringly, and Rachel wondered whether she ought to be feeling something more than mere interest that a girl he had once obviously known rather well was presently trying to insinuate herself back into his life. Although Vicky was exhibiting no antagonism towards her right now, it was obvious that they were unlikely to be friends. But all Rachel could feel was a sense of relief that apparently Alexis Roche had taken the hint.

She didn't know what caused her to glance sideways at that moment. She had finally succeeded in convincing herself that she had been unnecessarily apprehensive, and although she was only listening to Roger's comments with half an ear, she was not seeking any diversion. On the contrary, she was perfectly aware that he was going to offer Vicky some kind of occupation, albeit that of a temporary salesperson, but somehow it didn't seem important any more. In a little while they would all sit down on the beautifully upholstered cream and gold chairs that had been set out at the other side of the ballroom and watch the fashion show. Then, a little while after that, she and Roger would be alone, and she could tell him her decision about the wedding. That was infinitely more important than anything else, and in consequence she was feeling quite relaxed when she saw the tall blond Frenchman making his determined way towards them. There was no question that he was heading for anyone else. His eyes met and held hers with an intentness that was almost paralysing, and although it was a clichéd idea, she was reminded of the hypnotising gaze of a cobra.

Panic spread through her, but there was nothing she could do. Roger was still talking to Vicky, and even if she could drag him away there was no doubt that Alexis Roche would follow them. Why? she asked herself wildly. Why was he doing this? And close on the heels of this thought came the treacherous comparisons between his sun-browned skin and powerful leanness and Roger's paler indulgence.

'Miss Fleming!' His voice was like his skin, warm and brown and subtley textured. 'How delightful that you could come. And may I say that, as always, you look quite stunning!'

The sleek silver bonnet of the Lamborghini drew to a halt outside Rachel's apartment building and her hand reached thankfully for the handle of the door. At least she was home, she realised unsteadily, not wanting to think of how she had got there, but the catch wouldn't move, and she guessed that it was locked.

'Will you please open this door?' she demanded, turning to glare at the man now engaged in turning off the car's engine, and Alex inclined his head with infuriating slowness before adhering to her request.

'One moment,' he added, as she was about to scramble out of the car. 'Don't go yet. I want to talk to you.'

'Well, I don't want to talk to you,' retorted Rachel, her breathing shallow as she gathered her cloak about her. 'Goodbye, Mr Roche. Please don't try to contact me again.'

'You object?'

His quiet words arrested her movements briefly, and she turned to stare at him incredulously. 'Of course I object,' she exclaimed. 'I just don't know why you're doing this. I've explained my situation, not once, but several times. I'm engaged to be married, Mr Roche— although this evening you've done your best to undermine those arrangements.'

'I?' Alex regarded her through narrowed lids, and her pulse raced in spite of herself.

'Yes, you,' she pressed on, ignoring the trembling feeling deep inside her. 'You know you did!'

'Can I be blamed for the fact that your fiancé apparently doesn't trust you?' enquired Alex smoothly, and Rachel's nails pressed into her palms.

'You encouraged him not to do so,' she accused, wanting to leave him, and yet compelled to convince him once and for all of her sincerity, and Alex's thin lips curved into a mocking smile.

'What did I say?' he queried. 'Did I imply a relationship between us?'

'You let Roger think we'd met before!'

'We had——'

'No, you know what I mean.' Rachel expelled her breath raggedly. 'You deliberately led him on to believe that our association was more—was more intimate than it is.'

'Did I?' Alex half turned in his seat towards her. 'Perhaps that was an innocent mistake. Perhaps, because I find you so—attractive, I speak of you more warmly than I should. Is that it?'

Rachel quivered. Within the limited confines of the car, his nearness was very disturbing, the gleam of his eyes darkened to dull brilliance as the thick lashes narrowed to concentrate his appraisal.

'Why?' she got out unsteadily. 'Why me?' and then turned her head abruptly from that cool-eyed penetration.

She knew she ought to get out of the car. She knew that every second she stayed here, she was inviting a development more dangerous than anything she had encountered thus far. But the anger she had felt only moments before had been neutralised by his questionable logic, and the emotions stirring inside owed more to a sense of forbidden excitement than to the indignation she ought to have been kindling on Roger's behalf.

'I think you know the answer to that,' he responded now, though he made no move to touch her. 'That's why you were so panic-stricken when I appeared this evening.' He paused. 'Are you going to tell me I'm wrong?'

'I—yes. *Yes.*' Rachel forced herself to look at him again before continuing unevenly: 'I was—alarmed when I saw you this evening. And as it turns out, I had good reason to be. Why else would I be here with you, when Roger should have brought me home?'

Alex shrugged his shoulders. 'Your fiancé chose to allow me that privilege.'

'He was angry,' exclaimed Rachel helplessly. 'Surely you understood that!'

'He is a fool,' responded Alex carelessly, evoking a gasp from Rachel's parted lips. 'Whatever the provocation, I should not have allowed the situation to develop as it did.'

'You admit there was provocation, then?' she persisted, flinching nervously when Alex lifted his arm to rest it along the back of her seat.

'What was it one of your famous playwrights wrote once?' he murmured, his fingers brushing the neckline of her cloak. 'I admit nothing? Something like that, anyway. My lawyers always tell me one should wait to be accused.'

'Your lawyers?' Rachel tried to speak normally, but her voice came out several degrees higher than it should. 'You mean you're used to this kind of situation?'

'This kind of situation—no,' he answered her softly. 'I have to confess, it is a novelty to find a female who is apparently unmoved by the fact that I desire her.'

Rachel gulped. 'You're crazy!'

'Am I?' His straying fingers threaded the tumbled softness of her hair. 'Yet you must know it's not your conversation that attracts me, delightful though it is.'

'Stop it!' Rachel caught herself in time, shaking her hair free of his caressing fingers. 'I don't want to hear

this. I want you to go away and leave me alone. Now—
this instant! Before—before——'

'Before what?' he asked softly, his thwarted fingers
seeking another goal. Finding the entry to the neckline
of her cloak, his thumb probed inside, touching her
nape and arousing an unwanted film of goosebumps
over her soft flesh.

'Al—I mean, Mr Roche!' she protested fiercely,
turning her head towards him, and then wished she
hadn't when she discovered he was much closer than
before. 'You must—stop.'

'Stop?' he questioned, his voice a little uneven now.
'Stop what? Stop tormenting you? Or stop this
unnecessary delay——' and bending his head, he
replaced his fingers with his lips.

'No——'

Desperately, Rachel tried to get away from him now,
but the hand which had been so tantalisingly playful
before was firmly about her shoulders. His other hand
disposed of her efforts to press against his chest, and in
any case, the hard strength beneath her protesting
fingers was disturbingly appealing. She wanted to touch
him, she realised, as his teeth tugged sensually at her
earlobe, and she wondered how it was that he could
disrupt her so when he had not even kissed her lips.

'You taste as good as the fragrance you exude,' he
murmured against her ear. 'Stop fighting me. You want
this, too. We are two adult people, and our bodies'
needs are not unknown to us.'

'No——'

Rachel managed to articulate the word before his
mouth found hers, but its negative reason was lost
beneath the experienced pressure of his lips. Alex Roche
was no amateur at making love to a woman, and
Rachel's senses swam as he plundered her unprepared
sweetness. With a sureness totally lacking in any other
man Rachel had kissed, including Roger, he took
possession of her mouth in a hungry assault that left her
weak and gasping and completely devastated. Hers was
hardly a response; she was too shocked by the
rapacious intimacy of his mouth to do anything but not

resist. Nevertheless, the searching passion of his
embrace was a startling revelation. She had never
experienced such a physical reaction, and her lips felt
bruised and a little numb when he finally lifted his
head.

For several seconds he just stared at her, the grey
eyes too shadowy for her to make out any expression,
and in those taut seconds she became aware of other
factors. Her cloak had fallen apart while he was kissing
her, and now the hand which had fought off her
protests rested at her waist. Through the thin silk of her
trousers she could feel its heat and its strength, and a
hurried appraisal of her appearance elicited the
embarrassing knowledge that he could not be unaware
of her body's arousal, even if she had not responded to
his mouth. There was other, more evident, proof of her
reaction to his passion, and as if aware of her thought,
he allowed his palm to brush tantalisingly against the
crest of one swollen breast.

'Don't!'

His action brought her paralysed limbs to life, and
she struck his hand away with a violent motion. The
fact that he should consider himself free to touch her as
he willed made her feel humiliated and cheap, and she
gathered her cloak about her again with hands that
shook uncontrollably.

'Incredible,' he remarked, lounging back in his seat as
she made her unsteady preparations. 'So mature—and
yet so innocent. I think your Roger Harrington is no
expert when it comes to making love.'

Rachel's face burned. 'And you are, I suppose!'

Alex shrugged. 'You did not think so,' he commented.
'But then you need a little educating.'

Rachel thrust open the door of the car and scrambled
out. Even now, she couldn't quite comprehend what
had happened. Even though her lips were burning and
there was a most unwelcome ache in the pit of her
stomach, she found it extraordinarily hard to accept
that the evening had ended the way it had. That Roger
should have allowed Alex Roche to bring her home was
hard enough to stomach; that Alex Roche should have

taken advantage of her in that way was completely unbelievable.

Fumbling in her bag for her key, she was reaching up to put the sliver of metal in the lock when it was taken from her, and Alex completed the operation. 'After you,' he said softly, as the door swung open, but Rachel turned to him fiercely, determined not to be thwarted this time.

'You're not coming in,' she said huskily, pressing herself back against the frame of the door. 'This is my home. I want you to leave.' She took a deep breath. 'Or do I have to scream?'

Alex lifted his shoulders in a dismissing gesture, and obediently dropped the key into her still-open purse. 'I was only going to escort you to your door,' he protested lightly. 'No matter. I will call you tomorrow instead——'

'*No!*' Rachel almost choked on the word. 'If you call me, I shan't answer you. I never want to see you again, do you understand? I intend to tell Roger the truth—the *whole* truth. He'll believe me, once I tell him what kind of a man you are.'

'And if he doesn't?' he queried softly. Then he sighed and shook his head. 'Oh, Rachel, you don't know what you're talking about. I don't know much about your fiancé, but I do know he won't make you happy.'

'You don't know anything of the kind——'

'I know how inexperienced you are. That's enough.'

Rachel clenched her fists. 'Will you please go away?'

Alex shrugged. 'If you insist. But if you change your mind, you can always reach me here.'

He handed her a card, but Rachel refused to take it. The slip of pasteboard fluttered unheeded into the right angle created between the wall of the house and the step Rachel was standing on, and without waiting for him to say anything more, she shouldered her way inside and slammed the outer door behind her.

Jane met her at the door to the flat, her plump face exhibiting the anxiety she had evidently been feeling. 'So that was you down there,' she exclaimed, as Rachel walked wearily into the living room. 'I thought it was too early. For heaven's sake, what's happened? You look awful!'

'I feel awful,' said Rachel miserably, sinking down on to the couch and unfastening the cloak. 'Do we have anything to drink? I could surely use something.'

'Just sherry,' admitted Jane doubtfully. 'Do you want that? Or would you rather have a cup of tea?'

'Sherry,' said Rachel, leaning back and closing her eyes. 'Make it a stiff one.'

'There you are.' Jane returned a few moments later with a tumbler half full of the amber-coloured liquid. 'What's happened? Who was that who brought you home? I heard the car and looked out, and I thought I recognised you, although I couldn't be sure. It was some car!'

'Wasn't it?' Rachel opened her eyes and fixed them on her friend. 'It belongs to Alexis Roche.'

'The man who sent you the roses?'

'The same.'

'But—how——'

'Don't ask.' Rachel pushed herself into a sitting position and swallowed a gulp of the sherry. 'He was at the reception. As a matter of fact, he was responsible for us being there, only Roger doesn't know that yet.' She took another drink and then looked helplessly up at Jane. 'He won't leave me alone. He says he—wants me. He's trying to drive a rift between me and Roger.'

'You're not serious?' Jane perched on the side of the couch beside her. 'Come on: what really happened?'

'I'm telling you the truth.' Rachel looked at her friend blankly. 'Honestly, that's what he says. I don't know what to do.'

Jane's lips twitched as if she found the affair almost humorous, but then, meeting Rachel's desperate eyes, she sobered. 'I'm sorry,' she said. 'I can see you're serious, but really, love, you must see there is a funny side to it. I mean, I can't help the unworthy thought that Roger must have had his nose put out of joint by what's happened.'

'Roger!' Rachel rested her elbow on her knee and

lodged her chin in one hand. 'Oh, Jane, Roger was absolutely furious. I've never seen him so angry.'

'With good reason, by the sound of it,' remarked Jane charitably. 'Go on. What did happen?'

Rachel sighed. 'Well, we went to the reception, as you know. At the Metropolitan Hotel. It really was a sumptuous affair, and the ballroom where the fashion show was held was really beautiful.'

'And Alexis Roche organised it.'

'Oh, no.' Rachel shook her head. 'Sancha Forrest organised it. You've heard of her, haven't you?'

'She's a kind of patroness of the arts, isn't she?' asked Jane thoughtfully. 'No matter. Go on with the story.'

'Well, she is part of the story really,' said Rachel unhappily. 'It was she who invited us. Al—*Roche* only got her to add Roger's name to the list.'

'How intriguing!' Jane grimaced, but then straightened her face again at a look from Rachel. 'How did you meet him, then?'

'Tonight?' For a moment Rachel forgot she had told Jane of their earlier encounters, and the older girl pulled a face.

'Of course tonight,' she exclaimed shortly. 'Hurry up! I'm dying to know how he got you away from Roger.'

'Well, he didn't. At least, not exactly.' Rachel gave an agonised shake of her head. 'Oh, Jane it was awful! Roger had met this girl he used to know years ago and they were exchanging small talk, you know how you do? And—and Alex Roche just came up to us.'

'And that was the first you knew that he was there?'

'N—o.' Rachel admitted the truth grudgingly. 'I had glimpsed him earlier—at least, I'd thought it was him——'

'You didn't *know*?' Jane looked sceptical, and Rachel bent her head.

'All right,' she said, 'I suppose I did know it was him, but I couldn't believe it was anything other than a coincidence, until he came to talk to me.'

Jane suppressed a gurgling sound. 'And?'

'Oh? he was so—*familiar*. You know—as if we'd known one another for ages. And intimately! I had to

introduce him to Roger and—and Roger's friend, and I
know *she* thought it was most peculiar. It couldn't have
been worse really, from Roger's point of view. It was
bad enough for him to think that—that I'd been lying
to him, without this Vicky Young witnessing his
humiliation!'

'I see.' Jane nodded. 'So what happened next?'

'Well——' Rachel wearily expelled her breath, 'we all
stood together for a while—not talking, just sort of
looking at one another. And then Vicky saw someone
she knew who she thought Roger might like to meet
and they went off together.'

'Just like that.' Jane was appalled.

'Just like that,' agreed Rachel, lifting her shoulders.
'Oh, I suppose if I'd followed them, Roger would have
had to acknowledge my presence. But he just ignored
me, and I do have some pride, you know.'

'Not to mention the fact that Alexis Roche was
standing beside you,' put in Jane mildly, and Rachel's
eyes flashed to hers.

'What do you mean?'

'Well . . .' Jane shrugged, 'humiliation works both
ways, doesn't it?'

Rachel's shoulders sagged. 'What am I going to do,
Jane?'

'I gather that was when you decided to leave.'

'Not immediately.' Rachel frowned. 'Alex—I mean,
Roche—he suggested we had another drink, and short
of causing an ugly scene, there wasn't much I could do.'

'You could have left him and come home,' pointed
out Jane reasonably, and Rachel's pale cheeks deepened
with colour.

'I thought Roger might come back,' she protested
weakly. 'And besides, you don't know Alex Roche.
He's not like Roger. He doesn't take no for an answer.'

'So you came home with him.'

'Eventually.' Rachel gazed at her friend appealingly.
'It wasn't my choice, believe me! Jane, you've got to
believe me! My God, I'm beginning to think I'm going
out of my head! I didn't want him to bring me home; *I
didn't.* I intended to get a taxi—I told him so. The

fashion show was starting, you see, and Roger seemed
to have disappeared off the face of the earth, and I just
wanted to get away.'

'So why didn't you?'

'Take a taxi?' Rachel's wide blue eyes were accusing.
'Jane, I tried to. I came downstairs—the ballroom was
upstairs, you see—but by the time I'd persuaded the
woman in the cloakroom to let me have my cape
without handing over the ticket, Alex's car was at the
door.'

'So you just got meekly into it?'

'I had to.' Rachel spread her hands frustratedly.
'Jane, he knew *everybody*! The receptionists, the
bellboys, the commissionaire; even the woman in the
cloakroom! Once she realised I was with him, there was
no problem. Jane, he *owns* the hotel. Or at least his
family does.'

Jane blinked. 'The Metropolitan?'

'Yes.'

'But——' Jane made a helpless gesture, 'Rachel, the
Metropolitan is owned by an *Arab* consortium! I was
only reading about it in the newspaper the other day.
They've spent over a million pounds renovating the
original structure and modernising the interior.'

Rachel quivered. 'You're not—you're not implying
that—that Alex Roche is an Arab, are you?' She
uttered a slightly nervous laugh. 'He—he's fair; or, at
least, his hair is. Arabs aren't fair!'

'Nevertheless,' Jane was insistent, 'I did read it,
Rachel.'

Rachel pushed herself up from the couch, pacing
across the floor on decidedly unsteady legs. Jane must
be mistaken, she told herself severely, but even as she
thought this, she remembered what Alex had said about
his grandfather owning land in Bahdan. And the
chauffeur, Hassim, she recalled with growing unease.
There had been no doubt about his identity.

'What's the matter?' Jane looked up at her in some
concern. 'It doesn't matter, does it? You're not
planning on seeing him again, are you?'

'No!' Rachel was vehement.

'Well then . . .' Jane got to her feet now. 'Don't worry, love. Roger will come round. And when you tell him the truth . . .'

'You think he'll believe me?'

'If he doesn't, he's a fool,' declared Jane staunchly. 'Now, how about some supper?'

Rachel shook her head. 'I don't want anything.'

'Okay.' Jane looked at her sympathetically. 'We'll have another drink, then. Now, stop worrying about Roger. I've no doubt he's taking Vicky home right at this moment.'

'Do you think that's any consolation?' exclaimed Rachel bitterly, and Jane sighed regretfully as the younger girl slammed the bedroom door behind her.


## CHAPTER FIVE

RACHEL rang Roger's apartment at nine-thirty the following morning, but could get no reply. Guessing he had probably left for his office, she phoned there instead, but once again she was unlucky. His secretary hadn't seen him, she said, and Rachel had no reason to doubt her. Leaving a message, asking him to call her when he did come in, she rang off, and spent the rest of the morning tensing every time the phone pealed.

At a quarter to twelve the phone rang again, but although this time the call was for her, it was her father, and Rachel could hardly hide her disappointment.

'You sound depressed,' he remarked, detecting her mood, and Rachel made a concerted effort to hide her real feelings.

'Not really,' she said, forcing a lighter tone. 'It's been a rough morning. How are you? Did you sort out your cash-flow problems?'

'Well——' The slight hesitation was intentional, Rachel suspected, with new-found cynicism. 'That's really what I wanted to talk to you about, Rachel. Could we have dinner this evening?'

'Dinner?' Rachel bit her lip. 'Oh, Dad, I don't know . . .' She sighed. 'Look, if it's about the money, forget it. Just pay me back when you can. I'm not waiting for it.'

'No. Well——' her father was evidently having some difficulty in sorting out his words, 'that isn't exactly what I meant, darling.' He paused. 'It isn't that simple.'

'What do you mean?' Rachel took a deep breath. 'You can't pay me back?'

'Rachel, I'd rather not talk about this on the telephone. You never know who might be listening.' He hesitated. 'How about if I came to your flat this evening? Say about six—or six-thirty. That way, if you've got plans for the evening, I won't be interfering with them. Hmm? What do you say?'

Rachel felt the first faint stirring of anxiety. 'You're not in any kind of trouble, are you, Dad?' she asked. 'I mean, if you are——'

'Not now, my dear, not now.' Charles Fleming refused to be drawn any further. 'This evening, hmm? Six o'clock?'

'Oh—all right.'

Rachel had little choice but to agree, and with a nonchalant 'Ciao!' her father rang off. But long after she had replaced her receiver, Rachel was still thinking about his call, and wondering why, in such a short space of time, her life seemed to have acquired so many complications. Still, she reflected dourly, she could hardly blame Alex Roche for her father's shortcomings, and dismissing that particular problem from her mind she determinedly applied herself to the report she had been typing before he rang.

Roger didn't ring before lunch, and swallowing her pride, Rachel phoned the Harrington offices again at three o'clock. This time Roger was in the building, but not in his office, and after waiting for ten minutes while his secretary tried to find him she had to ring off when Mr Black demanded her services.

'Ask him to phone me back in half an hour, will you?' she begged his harassed secretary, and picking up her notebook, she hurried into her employer's office.

In the event, Roger did not take up her invitation, and Rachel left the building that evening feeling decidedly frayed. It had been a horrible day, she thought, turning up her coat collar against the chill breeze that was blowing. Mr Black had been in one of his least endearing moods, and he had not been best pleased when he discovered she could not work late that evening.

'You young people and your interminable demand for entertainment!' he declared, rather unjustly, but Rachel had restrained the retort which had sprung to her lips. She had been half afraid she might say something she would regret later, and instead she had allowed him to think it was Roger, and not her father, who was responsible for her lack of dedication.

Walking along Fetter Lane towards the bus stop, she was reflecting rather bitterly on life's adversities when a tall figure fell into step beside her. She had been completely unaware of his presence until that moment, but now her head jerked round in baffled frustration.

'*You!*' she exclaimed, seeing in Alex Roche the epitome of all her troubles, and his dark features twisted into a wry smile.

'I'm still not welcome, I gather,' he remarked, his faint accent giving the words an unwanted attraction, and Rachel had to quell a sudden urge to give up the struggle against him. How much easier it would be if she admitted his attraction for her, she found herself thinking weakly, and quickly squashed the unworthy notion.

'I thought I told you——'

'—to keep away from you—I know,' he interrupted her smoothly. 'And I intended to. But you looked so— so *miserable* when you came out of the office building, and I had to find out if your fiancé has decided you are no longer to be trusted.'

'Roger?' Rachel's eyes darted up to meet his. 'What do you know about Roger?'

'Nothing.' Alex lifted his shoulders carelessly and then let them relax again. This evening he was wearing a fine-grained black leather jacket over matching suede trousers, and his lean good looks were attracting several curious glances from the girls emerging from the offices nearby. 'What should I know?' He paused. 'What do you know?'

Rachel looked away from him and shook her head. 'I haven't heard from him,' she admitted, not quite knowing why she was telling him this. 'He's been—busy—all day.'

'I see.' Alex glanced about him. 'So—I'll take you home.'

'I can get the bus——'

'What do you have to lose?' he exclaimed flatly. 'Come on.' He indicated the side street Rachel was about to cross. 'My car's parked just along here.'

'And if I refuse?'

'That's your prerogative.'

Rachel sighed. She was tired and fed-up, and it was a great temptation just to give in and let him take her home. Only the fear that he might take advantage of the situation as he had done the night before caused her to shake her head, and Alex made a resigned gesture.

'Would you like me to speak to him?' he asked instead, with unexpected perception, and Rachel gazed at him aghast.

'Speak?' she echoed faintly. 'Speak to whom?'

'Your fiancé,' said Alex drily. 'Harrington. Who else? I will if you want me to. I could explain how we really came to know one another. He might believe me, mightn't he?'

'You'd do that?' Rachel was astounded.

'Why not?' Alex grimaced. 'It's the least I can do, in the circumstances. I didn't intend for you to get hurt. I—care about you.'

Rachel's face burned. 'I don't know what to say.'

'Don't say anything. Just tell me where Harrington lives, and I'll go and see him.'

Rachel blinked. The idea of Alex Roche approaching Roger with what virtually amounted to an apology had left her feeling weak, and she could only gaze at him blankly.

'I—I don't understand you,' she confessed at last. 'I thought you were completely unscrupulous!'

'And now you find I'm not,' he responded softly. 'So, will you let me try and make amends?'

'He—he lives in Kimbel Square, where we first met,' Rachel told him with curious reluctance. 'Number 11, Park Court. It—it's a block of apartments just past the Embassy buildings.'

'I'll find it.' Alex paused. 'Now, are you sure you don't want me to take you home.'

'I'd rather you didn't.'

'Okay.' Alex accepted her decision with good grace. 'Some other time, maybe,' and without trying to change her mind, he turned away and was soon swallowed up in the rush-hour press of people.

Contrarily, as soon as he had gone, she wished he hadn't, and when she had to stand all the way home on the bus, she wondered why she had refused. After all, Roger already thought the worst of her, and recalling Alex's words, she guessed he knew exactly what had been going on. And why not? she reminded herself fiercely. It was all his fault. But somehow, even this knowledge did not have the power to regenerate her hostility towards him this evening. She only hoped Roger would listen to him. Surely, if Alex explained he had deliberately misled him, Roger would understand that she had had no part in it.

Jane had a cup of tea waiting when she arrived at the flat, and sipping it gratefully, Rachel was glad of the imminent arrival of Charles Fleming to distract her thoughts from other things.

'My father's calling about six,' she offered, reluctant to mention her encounter with Alex Roche. 'Don't ask me why. He says he wants to talk to me.'

'That's okay.' Jane nodded. 'I've got some marking to do. I'll get out of the way when he arrives.'

'Thanks.' Rachel put down her empty cup. 'I—er—did Roger call?'

'Ring, you mean?' Jane shook her head. 'I guess that means he hasn't rung you either. Don't worry—he will.'

'I wish I could feel as confident,' sighed Rachel unhappily. 'I did ring his office twice today, but he didn't return my calls.'

'Oh—oh, well, I'm sure there must have been a reason for it,' said Jane reassuringly. 'Maybe he's been busy. Didn't you say he wanted to attend that reception last night because he thought he might make some useful contacts?'

'Well—yes.'

'There you are, then.' Jane carried their two cups through to the kitchen. 'And if you made him jealous, so what? It might do him good to realise he shouldn't take you for granted.'

Their doorbell rang as Rachel was about to go and change out of her office suit, and pressing the button to open the door downstairs, she went to greet her father. Charles Fleming came into the flat with decided over-confidence, and Rachel, submitting to his embrace, wondered if she was overly sensitive when it came to her father's moods.

'Hello, Jane,' he exclaimed, greeting his daughter's flatmate in the same breezy manner. 'You're looking well. I gather those rascals you're teaching haven't got you down yet.'

Jane smiled politely. 'Not yet,' she responded, gathering up a pile of exercise books. 'If you'll excuse me, I've got some work to do.'

When Jane's bedroom door had closed behind her, Charles turned back to his daughter. 'What a nice girl Jane is, isn't she?' he remarked, and Rachel wondered why she found his comment so objectionable. Why couldn't she accept his compliments without suspicion? Why did she have this hollow feeling that laid doubt on everything he said?

'Won't you sit down?' she invited now, indicating an armchair, but her father waved her suggestion aside.

'You sit down, darling,' he exclaimed gratuitously. 'You look as if you've had a tough day. You know, you need a holiday. I hope that fiancé of yours has something exciting lined up for the honeymoon.'

'We may not be having a honeymoon,' said Rachel tersely, remaining on her feet. 'Look, Dad, could you come to the point of your visit? I don't want to be rude, but I do want to take a bath, and——'

'Of course, of course, I know.' Charles was full of understanding. 'And I'm holding you up.' He sighed. 'Not my scene at all, I do assure you.'

'Dad!' Rachel restrained herself with difficulty. 'Dad, if it's about that five hundred pounds——'

'It's not.'

'It's not?' Rachel blinked. 'Oh—but I thought——'

'I can guess what you thought.' Charles made an extravagant gesture. 'Dear me, if only that was all it was!'

Rachel's lips tightened. 'Do you mean you want to borrow some more money?'

'Borrow?' Her father shook his head. 'Not borrow, no, Rachel. I—er—I have a business proposition I want you to put to Roger.'

'A business proposition?' Rachel stared at him. 'What are you talking about?'

Charles Fleming sighed. 'Don't look at me like that! I'm not suggesting anything illegal. It's a perfectly reasonable suggestion. I need some ready cash, and the only solution I can see is to offer Roger a partnership.'

'To offer Roger a—Dad! You know Roger would never agree to that. Besides, why can't you get a loan from the bank? Other people do.' She paused. 'Or is this just a roundabout way of asking for the rest of Grandmother's legacy?'

'Rachel!'

'Well,' Rachel sighed, 'if it is, you can have it. I've managed so long without it, I expect I can manage a little longer.'

'It's not that simple, Rachel.'

Her father paced restlessly across the floor, and his daughter's eyes narrowed anxiously. Surely the several thousand pounds left in her deposit account were sufficient to allay his immediate expenses. And if not, exactly how much had he proposed to ask Roger for?

'Are you in financial difficulties?'

The question sprang almost involuntarily from her tongue, and Charles Fleming turned swiftly to look at her. For a moment Rachel saw the truth in his expression, but it was quickly veiled by an exaggerated

show of indignation. 'Financial difficulties?' he exclaimed, moving his neck as if his collar was too tight.
'Of course I'm not in financial difficulties. This is a
minor setback, that's all. A temporary embarrassment
due to unpaid accounts.'

'Whose unpaid accounts? Yours?' queried Rachel,
feeling suddenly much older than her father. 'Come on,
Dad, why don't you be honest with me? You need
capital. But how much?'

'Fifty thousand pounds,' declared her father flatly,
abruptly abandoning his pretence, and Rachel gasped.

'Fifty—thousand—pounds——!'

'It's not a lot,' Charles exclaimed, half impatiently.
'A flash in the pan to someone like Harrington. Why, at
one time I was handling deals for many times that
amount.'

'Fifty thousand pounds,' Rachel repeated disbelievingly. 'Oh, Dad, how could you let such a thing
happen? Where on earth do you expect to get that kind
of sum?'

'I've just told you—from Roger.'

'No.'

'What do you mean, no?'

'I mean Roger won't help you.'

'How do you know until you've asked him?'

'Because—oh, because Roger and I aren't exactly on
the best of terms at the moment.'

Charles Fleming blanched. 'You've not split up?'

'I don't know,' Rachel sighed. 'We—we've had a—
disagreement. I can't——'

'Not about the wedding again!' snapped her father,
his good humour evaporating fast.

'No.' Rachel shook her head. 'Not about the wedding
this time. It was—something else. Right now, I don't
even know when I'm going to see him again.'

'Damn!' Her father swore softly, his balled fist
thumping into the palm of his other hand. 'Why didn't
you tell me this this morning?'

Rachel sank down on to the couch now, curling her
legs up beside her. 'I'm sorry.'

'Yes, I'm sorry, too,' muttered her father bitterly.

Then, after a moment: 'Well, you'll just have to go to
him and ask him to forgive you for whatever it was that
split you up. Tonight, if possible. I can give you a
lift——'

'No!' Rachel gazed up at him disbelievingly. 'You
can't ask me to go to Roger to beg his forgiveness just
so I can get money from him——'

'Why not?' her father snorted. 'You love him, don't
you?'

'Well—yes.' Rachel was dismayed by her momentary
hesitation before admitting that she did. Of course she
loved Roger. Of course she wanted to marry him, she
told herself. It was only his prudish attitude that caused
her to doubt his feelings for her.

'There you are, then,' said Charles sharply. 'Or would
you rather your father went to prison? I might, you
know. If I can't convince my—creditors—that I'm still
solvent.'

Rachel cupped her hot cheeks with her equally hot
palms.

'All right, all right,' she said tremulously. 'I—will
speak to Roger. But not tonight. Not unless he comes
here.'

Charles Fleming pushed his hands into his jacket
pockets. 'When, then? Tomorrow evening?'

'Some time tomorrow,' Rachel conceded, with
reluctance, and with that her father had to be content.
But he looked decidely strained when he left, and she
could only assume he had found their interview as
difficult as she had.

The remainder of the evening was something of an
anticlimax. Roger did not ring, and as the night wore
on, Rachel found an increasing apprehension in his
continued silence. Had Alex Roche gone to see him? she
wondered anxiously, and if so, what had Roger's
reaction been? What if he had resented the other man's
involvement in their affairs? What if he hadn't believed
him? And what possible interpretation might he have
put on the fact that she had evidently seen Alex since
the previous evening?

She went to bed feeling very uneasy, and although

she slept, her dreams were punctured with bouts of panic that did not make for restful slumber. For once, she was up first in the morning, and Jane, detecting the reason, gave her a sympathetic look.

'Go and see him,' she suggested, sipping the cup of tea Rachel had brought to her bed. 'After all, you are still his fiancée. He hasn't asked for his ring back, has he?'

'No.' Rachel was grudging. Jane didn't know about her meeting with Alex, and right now, Rachel wished she had left well alone. Obviously, Roger had not believed him, and who knew but that he might see Alex's confession as another attempt to deceive him.

'I'd better get ready,' she said now, getting up from the bed and Jane stared at her in surprise.

'Get ready?' she exclaimed. 'Isn't it rather early to go and see Roger?'

'To go and see Roger?' said Rachel blankly. 'I mean, get ready for work.'

'It's Saturday,' said Jane mildly, and Rachel's lips parted.

'Saturday!'

'The day after Friday,' agreed Jane drily. 'I should go back to bed, if I were you. You're still half asleep.'

Rachel shook her head. 'Oh—I'm sorry.' She glanced at the clock. 'I've wakened you, and it's only half past seven.'

'Don't worry, I can easily get back to sleep again,' said Jane, putting down her cup on the bedside table and sliding beneath the quilt once more. 'I'd advise you to do the same.' But Rachel had had enough sleep, and after closing Jane's bedroom door, she went to get bathed and dressed. It was a bright sunny morning, and she had the idea of walking to Roger's apartment. It would take her the best part of an hour to get there, and the fresh air was exactly what she needed.

Fifteen minutes later, she left the building, warmly attired in woollen harem pants and a matching woollen anorak in an attractive shade of apricot. With her hair loose about her shoulders, she looked young and appealing, the absence of any but eye make-up giving her a faintly vulnerable appearance.

She reached Kimbel Square as the nearby church clock was striking nine o'clock, and smiling at the startled commissionaire, she entered Roger's apartment building. The lift took her up to the ninth floor of Park Court, and glancing out of the window, Rachel tried to distract herself with the view. Roger's apartment occupied half the top floor of this modern complex, and although she had never asked him how much the rent was, she knew it was considerable.

Mrs Hennessy, Roger's housekeeper, opened the door to her, and her eyes widened in surprise when she saw who it was. 'Why, Miss Fleming!' she exclaimed, stepping back to allow the girl into the apartment. 'You're an early caller. Is Mr Harrington expecting you? Because if he is, I'm afraid he's overslept.'

'It's all right, Mrs Hennessy.' Rachel endeavoured to behave naturally. 'Roger isn't expecting me. I thought I'd—surprise him.'

'I see.' Mrs Hennessy looked slightly perturbed now. 'Well, miss, you'd better come into the living room, and I'll tell him you're here.'

'No. No, don't do that.' Rachel put her hand on the housekeeper's arm, then drew back awkwardly. 'I mean, leave it to me. I'll announce myself.'

Mrs Hennessy hesitated. 'I don't know about that, miss. I—well, I have to tell you, Mr Harrington left instructions that if you rang I was to say he wasn't home.'

The housekeeper flushed as she said this, and Rachel could feel her own cheeks going red also. 'Oh—well,' she said, at last, adopting a casual tone, 'don't you worry, Mrs Hennessy. It's all been a—a misunderstanding. Leave it to me. I'll accept all responsibility, don't worry.'

Mrs Hennessy sighed. 'If you're sure . . .'

'I am.' Rachel forced a smile. 'You make some coffee, Mrs Hennessy. I'll handle this.'

With more confidence than she was feeling, she preceded the housekeeper along the elegantly-carpeted hall and halted outside Roger's bedroom door. 'Wish me luck,' she murmured, with more feeling than the housekeeper knew, and determinedly opened the door and went in.

Roger was already stirring. No doubt, their conversation had disturbed him, and now he was shifting beneath the green-striped coverlet. As Rachel crossed the room to draw back the heavy damask draperies, he opened his eyes, blinking indignantly in the unwelcome glare of sunlight.

'What time is it?' he mumbled, raising his fists to knuckle his eyes, and Rachel reluctantly approached the bed.

'It's a quarter past nine,' she told him, and his pyjama-clad elbows dug into the mattress as he propelled himself upward.

'Rachel!' he muttered, his jaw hardening into an uncompromising line. 'What the hell are you doing here? I told Mrs Hennessy——'

'I know what you told Mrs Hennessy, but I had to see you, Roger,' declared Rachel, feeling suddenly flat. 'We have to talk. Now or after you're dressed. It's up to you.'

Roger's lips tightened. 'Really? Well, if you've come to apologise, forget it. It will take more than an apology to heal the breach between us. I don't know how you have the nerve to come here. What's the matter? Has Roche given you the hard word?'

'No.' Rachel spoke wearily. 'Alex Roche means nothing to me. You must know that——'

'I know the pair of you made me look like a damn fool on Thursday evening,' Roger snapped coldly. 'How could you, Rachel? How could you? I trusted you. I thought we cared about one another. I never dreamed you were meeting another man behind my back!'

'Oh, don't be silly!' Rachel gazed at him impatiently. 'For heaven's sake, Roger, be sensible! How could I be meeting anyone else behind your back? We've seen one another almost every evening since Christmas. What chance have I had to conduct a secret liaison?'

Roger sniffed. 'What about during the day?'

'Oh, yes,' Rachel uttered a harsh laugh, 'Mr Black would let me do that, wouldn't he? Roger, most days I don't even leave the office at lunchtime!'

'Well, what the hell did he mean then?'

'How should I know?' Rachel sighed, realising with sudden insight that Alex Roche had not visited Roger after all. Perhaps it was just as well, she mused, not altogether sorry now that she seemed to be making some headway. 'You took it all too literally, Roger. All right, I did meet him one night after I left your apartment, but it wasn't like you think. It was only last week—the night of the party. You remember, we had—well, we had had words.'

'I remember.' Roger was still suspicious. 'So you picked him up?'

'No.' Rachel was indignant. 'Oh, it sounds unlikely now, I know, but—well, he was asleep in his car and I thought he was ill.'

Roger gazed at her. 'Go on.'

Rachel moistened her dry lips. 'There's not much else to tell. Once I discovered I was mistaken, I got into the Mini and went home.'

Roger frowned. 'So he was lying when he said you'd seen one another several times?'

Rachel flushed. 'Well—no——'

'What do you mean—no?'

'He's tried to date me since then.' Rachel decided to tell him everything. 'He's phoned me at work, he's sent me flowers; he even came to the office once and—and drove me home.'

Roger's mouth thinned. 'You let him take you home?'

'Yes.' Rachel shook her head. 'Look, it meant nothing, honestly. You've got to believe me. But can I help it if he won't take no for an answer?'

'It seems to me you must have given him some encouragement,' said Roger pedantically. 'Who is he anyway? Vicky said she'd never seen him at one of those affairs before.'

'No.' Rachel took a deep breath. 'He's French, I think. At least, his accent is. But I really know very little about him.'

'Mmm.' Roger was looking a little less tight-lipped now. 'And that's all there is to it?'

'Yes. Yes.'

'So why did you walk out of the fashion show?'

'Roger, you walked out on me! When—when I saw you intended staying with Vicky Young, I—well, I just left.'

Roger nodded rather more graciously. 'Yes, I can see I did rather leave you to your own devices. But Vicky and I are old friends.'

'I know that.' Rachel felt an immense sense of relief. 'So—you forgive me?'

Roger's smile was rueful. 'I suppose so.' He paused and then held out his arms to her. 'Come here. Let's kiss and make up.'

She went to him willingly, returning his kiss with rather more effort than enthusiasm. But at least the forceful pressure of his mouth was reassuringly familiar, and if she didn't feel that numbing devastation of her senses she had felt when Alex Roche kissed her, so much the better. With Roger, she could retain her own identity, not be absorbed by his.

'Oh, sweetheart, I've missed you,' he murmured, drawing her reluctant hands to his body. 'Hmm, that feels good. Go on, go on: make love to me . . .'

Some time later, Rachel emerged from Roger's bedroom to find Mrs Hennessy had laid the table for two in the dining room. 'I guessed you must be staying for breakfast,' she declared, setting a pot of coffee over a small burner. 'Will you have bacon and eggs, too? Or I've got some kippers, if you'd rather.'

'Just toast, thank you, Mrs Hennessy,' Rachel responded, forcing a faint smile. 'Mr Harrington is just taking a quick shower. He won't be long.'

'Right you are, miss.'

The housekeeper went away and Rachel seated herself beside the coffee pot. The table was set by the window, and below her she had an expansive view of the roofs of the immediate area, and the park just a few yards away to her right. But although she poured herself a cup of coffee and told herself she was glad she and Roger had made amends, she couldn't dispel a lingering sense of dissatisfaction that had no real foundation in their reconciliation. It had to do with their association, something that had not changed over the months they had been together. It concerned the— from her point of view—totally unsatisfactory sexual relationship they shared, and Roger's apparent indifference to her needs. Most girls of her age had already had at least one physical experience with a man, and although she didn't want to think about Alex Roche, she couldn't help remembering what he had said. She was innocent, and immature. And Roger seemed to be quite content to keep her that way.

When Roger joined her at the breakfast table, he was looking decidedly pleased with himself, and Rachel couldn't help the uncharitable supposition that he wouldn't be feeling that way if he had had to be satisfied with her kisses.

'Well,' he said, bending to bestow a moist caress on her forehead before taking his seat, 'this is nice, isn't it? A sort of forerunner of things to come. If only you and Mother could solve your differences so easily!'

'We can.' Remembering her earlier promise to herself, Rachel took a deep breath before admitting that she had decided to let Mrs Harrington handle all the arrangements for the wedding. 'So long as I can have Jane as my chief bridesmaid,' she conceded at last. 'That's my only reservation. Other than that, she can have a free hand.'

'Thank goodness!' Roger's relief was heartfelt. 'Oh, you've no idea how pleased she'll be to hear this. How about us going over there after breakfast? The sooner she gets things in motion, the better.'

'All right.' Rachel saw no reason to refuse, and Mrs Hennessy's arrival with Roger's breakfast and Rachel's toast put an end to any further discussion of the matter.

Even so, Rachel found it very hard to relax. She had still to broach the subject of her father's problems, and even in this new-found wave of optimism, she was unconvinced of Roger's understanding. She waited until the plates had been cleared, and they were having a final cup of coffee before bringing the matter up, and as soon as her father's name was mentioned, she saw Roger's expression change.

'That reminds me,' he exclaimed. 'You didn't tell me you'd lent him some of your grandmother's money. I think you might have done, in the circumstances.'

'You know?' Rachel was confused. 'But how?'

'Your father told me,' retorted Roger, adding several spoons of sugar to his cup. 'He came to see me on Thursday afternoon. Didn't I tell you? Oh, no, of course not—I didn't get a chance. Well, he did.'

Rachel swallowed. 'He came to see you?' she echoed disbelievingly. Then, to herself: 'Why didn't he tell me?'

'I imagine he was too ashamed,' remarked Roger disparagingly. 'He expected me to lend him some money, can you believe it? And when I said I couldn't consider it, he confessed that he'd already borrowed five hundred from you.'

'He asked you for money!' Rachel whispered faintly. 'Oh, lord! He must be in serious trouble!'

'Rubbish! He's overreached himself, that's all,' declared Roger uncharitably. 'I heard he's been gambling pretty heavily over the last few months. I suppose he needs some cash to try and recoup his losses.'

'Gambling!'

Rachel sounded appalled, and Roger expelled his breath impatiently. 'Surely you knew,' he exclaimed. 'What do you think he did with your five hundred?'

'He said he was having a cash-flow problem,' said Rachel unwillingly, and he uttered a mirthless laugh.

'Oh, that's rich!' he chortled. 'A cash-flow problem! Well, yes, I suppose that is what he's having. Bookmakers don't like to take cheques.'

Rachel shook her head. 'I can't believe it. I thought he needed the money for the company.'

'The company? What company?' demanded Roger scathingly. 'Fleming Engineering is on the verge of collapse, or so I hear. Like I said, your father's been spending too much time at the track.'

Rachel groaned. 'But why didn't he tell me? Why didn't *you* tell me?'

'I didn't think you'd want to know,' said Roger, with a grimace. 'I didn't know then that he was coming to you begging for handouts.'

'Oh, Roger!'

'What's the matter? Has he asked you for some more? Is that what all this is leading up to?'

Rachel got up from the table, unable to sit still under his unsympathetic appraisal. 'He did come to see me, yes,' she admitted, walking across to the stone-faced chimney breast. 'And he did want to borrow money,' she added, keeping her back to him. 'But not from me. From you. He—he wants me to offer you a—a partnership.'

'In Fleming Engineering?' Roger sounded incredulous. 'My God, the man's got no shame, has he?'

'He's in trouble,' said Rachel unsteadily, turning to face him. 'Real trouble this time. Fifty thousand pounds' worth of trouble!'

'What?' Roger thrust back his chair and got to his feet, as if he too was unable to take this news sitting down. 'Fifty thousand pounds!' he echoed. 'Is he crazy?'

'Just scared, I think,' Rachel ventured. 'He—he wanted me to speak to you last night, but I wouldn't.'

'So that's what brought you here today, is it?' asked Roger tautly. 'And I thought I was the attraction!'

'You were. You *are*!' exclaimed Rachel tremulously. 'Oh, Roger, don't be angry. I promised I'd ask you, and I have. But I'd have come anyway. I care about you!'

His expression softened. 'Yes,' he said, coming towards her now. 'Yes, I know you do. I'm sorry, love. I suppose I was just so stunned to hear about—well, about your father. God!' He smote his forehead with the base of his palm. 'He must be pretty desperate!'

'He is.' She gazed at him appealingly. 'Oh, I'm not defending him. I've got no sympathy for him, none at all, but he is my father, and I couldn't just let him go to prison when there was something I could do——'

'*Prison?*' Roger blinked. 'Is that likely?'

'It's not only likely, it's probable,' said Rachel shakily. 'Whoever his debtors are, they're not prepared to wait much longer.'

He shook his head. 'The old fool!'

'Yes—well,' she was not prepared to argue over that, 'there's no fool like an old one, so they say. So—what can we do?'

'We?' Roger stepped back from her. 'You can't expect me to pay his debts for him.'

'Well, not all of them, maybe, but if we pool our resources. I've still got four and a half thousand pounds of the money Grandmother left me. If—if you could cover it, I'm sure we could buy a bit of time——'

'Buy more racing slips, no doubt,' exclaimed Roger harshly. 'Come off it, Rachel! I'm not financing your father's gambling. If he's got himself into debt—well, hard luck! But don't expect me to put my hard-earned money into his pocket.'

Rachel's lips parted. 'He's my father, Roger——'

'So what?'

'So—I don't want him to go to prison.'

'I don't suppose he wants it either,' remarked Roger scornfully. 'He should have thought of that before he threw his money down the drain.'

'Roger——'

'No.'

'Five thousand, Roger. That's not so much, surely!'

'It's exactly five thousand too much,' retorted Roger, without hesitation. 'No, Rachel. Even if we have to get someone else to give you away, I am not giving that waster a penny!'

She couldn't believe it. She had thought Roger might not want to help her, she had thought he might be difficult. She had never actually contemplated his refusal to do anything to alleviate the situation.

'Come on,' he said now, 'get your jacket on. We'll go and see Mother and tell her the good news. With a bit of luck, she might be able to arrange for you to see the dress designer this weekend.'

'No.' Now it was Rachel's turn to stand firm, and Roger expelled his breath on an impatient sound.

'Rachel, you're not going to change my mind——'

'No?' Rachel's features felt frozen. 'Well, we seem to have reached an *impasse*, don't we?'

'Rachel, stop this——'

'Stop what?' she asked unsteadily, reaching for her jacket. 'Roger, I sometimes wonder if I really know you. Perhaps I've attributed you with characteristics you don't even possess. I don't expect you to condone what my father's done. I don't expect you to like this situation. But he is my father, and I do expect you to understand my feelings.'

Roger grunted. 'You're not being practical, Rachel.'

'Aren't I?' Rachel put on her jacket and fastened the zip. 'Well, perhaps you're too practical.'

'What do you mean?'

She drew in her breath, then said tautly: 'Perhaps what we're really talking about is generosity, Roger. Heaven knows, you're not exactly generous with anything—including your emotions.'

He stiffened. 'What the hell are you implying?'

How, or indeed if, Rachel would have answered him was never put to the test. The sudden ringing of the doorbell precluded any continuation of their conversation, and they were both silent as Mrs Hennessy went to answer the door.

'It's a Mr Roche, Mr Harrington,' she said, somewhat flustered, coming to the dining room door, and before she had finished speaking, Alex Roche had appeared behind her.

'Good morning,' he said, putting the protesting housekeeper aside and strolling into the room as if he owned it. 'I'm sorry for this intrusion, Harrington. Do forgive me. But I promised Rachel I'd come and put your mind at ease.'

The moment those cool grey eyes alighted on Rachel's face, she felt the betraying surge of colour sweep into her cheeks. It didn't matter that there was no reason for it. That revealing wave of heat was damning, and she could hardly blame Roger, she thought, if his suspicions were rekindled. Why on earth had the Frenchman chosen this moment to appear? His timing was appalling. And his innocent greeting did nothing to erase her consternation.

'Why, Rachel!' he exclaimed, with a convincing air of confusion. 'What are you doing here? I thought we agreed that I should handle this!'

## CHAPTER SIX

PRECEDING Alex Roche into his house in Eaton Mews some time later that morning, Rachel still possessed the firm belief that this could not be happening. What was she doing here? she asked herself. How had she got herself into such a position? And what was more important, how was she going to get herself out of it?

The house was one of those elegant London town houses, tall and narrow, and set between other houses of similar design. The buildings were deceptive, Rachel knew that from articles she had read in fashionable magazines about the fashionable people who lived in them, and Alex's house was no exception. The hallway they had entered into was oblong-shaped and extensive, stretching mysteriously into the shadows that lurked at the back of the house. A delicately-curved stairway gave access to the upper floors, and its cream and gold handrail matched the cream-panelled walls and cream and gold-patterned carpet on the floor. A fragile crystal chandelier was suspended at the foot of the staircase, and its mellow golden light added to the pale sunlight filtering through the fanlight above the door.

It was a beautiful introduction to the house, Rachel had to concede, the atmosphere redolent with the scents of a huge bowl of orange lilies residing on a polished table set in a niche of the stairwell. It was the kind of house only a millionaire could afford to furnish, she reflected briefly, before the muted tread of a manservant interrupted her troubled speculations.

'Sir?'

The man bowed low before Alex, and although he was dressed in Western clothes, his attitude was unmistakably servile. As he straightened, Rachel saw a narrow, middle-Eastern profile, thin lips curving back from large yellowing teeth.

'We will have coffee in the library, Karim,' Alex informed him with unconscious arrogance, and the manservant bowed again before withdrawing. There was no casual interchange between them, no familiarity between master and servant. Only an awareness of their individual positions, and the role they had each been chosen to play in life.

'It's this way,' Alex said now, pausing at the foot of the staircase, and Rachel lifted her head almost dazedly. 'The library,' he added, unnecessarily. 'It's on the floor above. Will you come?'

Rachel pulled herself together. 'I suppose so.'

Alex's eyes narrowed. 'Don't look so alarmed. I'm not in the habit of indulging in white slavery, however attractive it might seem in this case.'

'White slavery?' Rachel frowned. 'I don't know what you mean.'

Alex's lips twisted. 'No matter. Follow me. You'll feel better after you've had some coffee.'

She followed him up the curving staircase with some reluctance. This was the last place she should be after what had happened, she thought bitterly, but somehow she was loath to go back to the flat and have to explain to Jane that she and Roger were finished. That was too real, too painful to face just yet. So long as she remained in this partial state of inertia, nothing could hurt her, and why should she blame Alex Roche when the seeds of destruction had been sown long before his intervention?

A pastel-painted landscape gave the landing depth and space, and through double-panelled doors, a high-ceilinged apartment gave sanctuary to the hundreds of leather-bound volumes that lined its shelves. Here the carpet changed to a deeper beige, and hide-covered armchairs flanked a leather-studded desk of generous proportions. There were long rust-coloured velvet

curtains at the windows and a fireplace where a log fire
smouldered in sulky isolation, with a skin rug spread
before it, soft and long-haired and milky white

'Sit down.'

Alex gestured to one of the squashy leather chairs,
and Rachel silently obeyed his suggestions. In truth, she
was glad to withdraw into the depths of the armchair,
seeking, though she was hardly aware of it, an escape
from the sharpening prick of remorse.

The manservant, Karim, appeared before Alex could
do much more than settle himself on the corner of the
desk. Rachel was amazed at the speed with which the
man had prepared the coffee and laid a tray. But
perhaps he was used to such peremptory summonses.

'Thank you.' Alex spoke in English, Rachel was sure,
for her benefit, and the man bowed his head politely as
he served the aromatic beverage. Rachel, used to
serving herself in all circumstances, was a little taken
aback by such obsequious service, but evidently Alex
found nothing unusual in the proceedings.

After the manservant had completed his task and left
them, Alex leant across the desk to push her coffee
towards her. The rich liquid had been served in delicate
*demitasse* cups, and regarding their contents, Rachel
suspected half a cup would be enough. There was also a
plate of some sweet confection, sticky squares liberally
floured with sugar, that Alex ate with evident
enjoyment. Despite his obvious weakness for such
fattening food, there was not an ounce of spare flesh on
his body however, and Rachel couldn't help noticing
how, when he leant towards her, the muscles of his
chest and stomach tautened beneath the fine grey silk
of his shirt.

'What are you thinking?' he enquired, when she made
no move to join him in either the sweetmeats or the
coffee. 'Forget him! The man's a fool! Believe me, you
could do so much better.'

'Like you, I suppose?' commented Rachel, somewhat
tartly, taking the fragile cup and saucer into her hands,
as if to ward off any possible idea he might have of
putting his words into actions. 'Why did you wait until

this morning to go to Roger's apartment? I thought—I *assumed* you would try and speak to him last night.'

Alex poured himself more coffee, lifting his suede-clad shoulders in a dismissing gesture. 'I had other things to do last evening,' he replied, adding crystals of sugar to his cup. His eyes appraised her over its rim. 'How was I to know you would take matters into your own hands?'

Rachel had no answer to this, but she was still wary. She had no confidence that she should trust this man, and despite his apparent consideration for her feelings now, she couldn't forget how he had pursued her.

'I wish you hadn't interfered,' she said at last, sipping the coffee with more enthusiasm. It was surprisingly delicious, and it did have the effect of making her feel less depressed. Perhaps it was drugged, she thought suddenly, realising she would believe anything of Alex Roche.

'I only wanted to help,' he protested, his grey eyes intent. 'I told you—I care about you. More, I would suspect, than your friend Harrington could imagine.'

Rachel bent her head. 'I still wish you'd stayed away,' she insisted, ignoring his last remark, and Alex uttered a sound of impatience.

'Why? You could have cut the atmosphere with a knife when I came into the room! Don't pretend you had effected a reconciliation. No one could have been in any doubt as to what had been going on.'

'You're wrong!' Rachel put down her cup and got to her feet. But the action brought her too near to him, to the muscular length of his thigh occupying the curve of the desk nearest to her, and she quickly put some distance between them. 'We had made up. I'd told Roger the truth and he'd believed me—eventually.'

'So what went wrong?' Alex was very perceptive.

'Nothing!' She turned away, presenting her back to him as she struggled to sound convincing. Beyond the narrow windowpanes she could see an almond tree's pink-washed blossom, and the converted stables that had given the mews its name; but these attractive glimpses of normality could not divert her thoughts from the growing unease inside her. As the numbness

caused by her broken engagement gave way to piercing
recollection, she was painfully reminded of her father's
predicament, now that Roger could not be relied upon
to bail him out.

'Nothing?'

Alex's voice was right behind her, and she stiffened at
the awareness that in her confusion she had been
unconscious of his removal from the desk to the
window. His breath was warm against her neck, his
powerful frame emanating scents of shaving lotion and
tobacco, and the sharp clean fragrance of his skin. Were
she to move an inch, her body would brush his, and she
quivered in anticipation of his hands upon her waist.

'I think I ought to be going,' she murmured, unable
to hide her nervousness in the uneven quaver of her
voice. 'I promised I'd ring my father today, and it's
already almost lunchtime.'

'Have lunch with me,' Alex invited softly, and in spite
of her fears, he made no attempt to touch her. He
seemed to know exactly what she was thinking and how
to circumvent her protests. Was he aware, for instance,
that her fears were almost all self-induced, and that her
real dilemma lay in the fact that she was much too
susceptible to his lean good looks and unforced
sexuality?

'I can't,' she said now, compelling her legs to move
sideways to evade him. 'I—thanks for the coffee, but I
have to go. Jane will be wondering where I am.'

'Jane?' he queried, then his brow cleared. 'Ah, the
young woman you share your flat with.'

Rachel half turned. 'You know?'

'You told me,' he reminded her carelessly, casually
moving so that her escape route was cut off. With the
desk on one side and him on the other, she was
successfully cornered, and her pulse rate quickened as
adrenalin flooded her veins.

'Mr Roche——'

'Alex,' he corrected, lifting one hand to finger a
curling strand of chestnut silk that coiled on the collar
of her jacket. 'This colour suits you. But then most
colours do——'

'Mr Roche, please!' Rachel straightened her shoulders. 'I have to go. It was kind of you to bring me here, and to offer me coffee, but I realise now that by staying here I'm not solving anything. Roger—Roger may come to realise that he was wrong to jump to conclusions, and I'd hate for him to go to the flat and find me absent.'

'Harrington is unlikely to do any such thing,' Alex told her flatly. 'He has no sense. Anyone with a grain of intelligence could have seen you were telling the truth.'

She pressed her lips together. 'Do you think so?'

'I've said so, haven't I?' He raised the strand of hair to his lips. 'You're better off without him.'

Rachel trembled. 'I wish you wouldn't do that.'

'Do what?' Alex's eyes were disturbingly soft. 'Tell you that you're better off without him? You are—you know it.'

She took a deep breath. 'That's not what I meant.' She moved her head. 'You're not playing fair.'

'Why not?'

'Because—well, because you know I'm upset and confused; because you're playing a game with my emotions.' She shivered, as a chill feeling feathered along her spine. 'I don't even know what you want with me.'

'No?' His brows arched. 'I should have thought that was painfully obvious by now.'

Rachel moistened her dry lips. 'To—to make love to me?'

Alex's lips twisted. 'A simplistic assessment, but true. Yes, I want to make love to you. Will you let me?'

She was aghast. 'No——'

'Because you're still upset?'

'No. Because I don't—that is—I hardly know you!'

Alex shrugged. 'That can easily be remedied.'

'No, it can't.' She was growing desperate. 'I want to go home.'

'And if I don't let you?'

She gasped. 'You're not serious!'

'Why not?' His fingers brushed her cheek, his thumb probing the cheekbone that gave her face its shape and vulnerability. 'What makes you think I brought you here for any other reason?'

'You're crazy!'

'Why? Because I find you fascinating? Because I want to kiss you and touch you, and teach you all the things you'll never learn from Harrington?'

'Stop it——'

'Don't be afraid.' His hand slid surely beneath the weight of her hair, massaging her neck with calm deliberation. 'I won't hurt you, I promise.'

'No!' Rachel was horrified. 'What do you think I am? I don't—I don't get into bed with anyone who asks me. Roger's the only man I've ever—ever——'

'—been with, I know,' Alex supplied patiently, and she was too embarrassed to explain that even that was not entirely accurate. 'It's nothing to be ashamed of. It simply explains your attitude, that's all.'

'I'm not ashamed!' She caught her breath. 'You really think I want to go to bed with you?'

'Mmm.' With his eyes on her mouth, he nodded, and Rachel knew a helpless sense of indignation.

'Well, you're wrong!' she exclaimed, refusing to look at him, and she heard his soft laugh as her cheeks flamed with colour.

'Forgive me if I do not believe you,' he murmured, linking his hands behind her neck, so that now she was held securely at armslength. 'We were attracted to one another the first night we met. I knew it was only a matter of time before you realised it, too.'

Rachel gulped. 'Are you going to let me go?' she demanded, refusing to look into those caressing grey eyes, whose warm appraisal was causing a sharp constriction in her chest. 'I'm sure you don't usually have to force your attentions on unwilling females, Mr Roche. Or are you from that breed of men who get their kicks that way? I've heard there are such people——'

She was free before she had finished speaking, and glimpsing the tautness of his expression as he turned away, she wondered what particular nerve she had scraped. But she was too relieved to ponder this for long. Smoothing down the collar of her jerkin, she walked towards the door, only to halt unwillingly when once again he addressed her.

'I'll take you home.'

'It's not necessary.'

'Nevertheless, I will,' he averred, following her to the door and reaching past her to open it. 'Go ahead,' he directed, allowing her to precede him, and she did so jerkily, uneasily aware of the ambivalence of her feelings towards this man.

As she folded herself into the Lamborghini, Rachel couldn't help reflecting that her reasons for suspecting Alex Roche's motives were hardly convincing. He could be genuine, she supposed, but she found it hard to believe that a man with his advantages could be so compellingly attracted to a girl like her. And yet what else could it be? Until that night a little over a week ago, he had not even known she existed, and what other reason could he have for saying the things he did? Just because she was going to marry Roger there was no reason to disbelieve Alex's sincerity.

But at this point her calm reasoning gave way. *She* was not going to marry Roger, she acknowledged bleakly. This morning's outburst had finally destroyed all trust between them, and even the knowledge that she had misjudged Roger's character did not make the shattering of their relationship any easier to contemplate. For so many months, she seemed to have been living for the day when she and Roger became man and wife. It had become as natural as breathing, and it seemed incredible that she could no longer anticipate that event. Her life had seemed so set, so assured—and now, because of one man's intervention, her world had been turned upside down.

Yet was that entirely fair? she argued silently. How much differently might this morning's altercation have developed if Alex Roche had not chosen to appear? Could she really have forgiven Roger for the things he had said about her father? Could there have been any reconciliation with the burden of Charles Fleming hanging over their heads?

Rachel sighed. She loved Roger, she told herself fiercely. So why was she asking all these questions? Surely love itself should solve all problems. But what if the man she had loved was not the real Roger Harrington after all?

Alex was unusually silent as he drove the distance from his house to Rachel's flat. Her words in the library seemed to have succeeded in dousing his ardour, and glancing sideways at him, Rachel wondered what he was thinking. With his dark profile concentrating on the road ahead, she was able to observe him more overtly, and she couldn't help the treacherous surge of warmth that invaded her stomach at the realisation that there was no longer any real reason for her to repulse him. But that was ridiculous, she berated herself inwardly. After what had happened with Roger, how could she even think about getting involved with another man. Just because Alex Roche was rich, and good-looking, and *available*, there was no excuse for promiscuity.

There was a car parked in the road outside the flat, and as she recognised its significance, Rachel's heart dropped. What was her father doing here? she wondered, her agitation evident, and Alex drew in behind the car to give her a speculative glance.

'Harrington's?' he enquired flatly, misinterpreting her reactions, and she quickly shook her head.

'No,' she responded, unwilling to go into details, and Alex's mouth compressed as she scrambled out of the car.

'A boy-friend of your flatmate, perhaps,' he persisted, joining her on the pavement, and she gave him a worried look.

'What? Oh, no,' she answered absently, her mind already leaping ahead to its possible connotations, and Alex's hand descended on her arm as the door to the house suddenly opened.

'Whose car is it?' he asked, and she had the feeling that his fingers on her arm could easily become bruising. 'Tell me,' he advised, observing the movements of the man who had emerged from the house and remained just out of focus. 'I thought you told me there was no one else. Or was that row with Harrington over something more serious than our association?'

'Don't be ridiculous!'

Rachel tried to pull her arm away, but he wouldn't let her, and in the ensuing struggle, she became aware of the approach of the previously unseen spectator.

'Dad——' she began, as Charles Fleming held out a hand towards them, saying: 'Leave her alone. She has nothing to do with it. For God's sake, I said give me some time! That amount of money can't be conjured up overnight!'

Rachel stood at the window of the flat and watched her father's Ford accelerate away along Oakwood Road. He had gone; at least for the time being. But on Monday she had promised to withdraw the rest of her grandmother's legacy from her account, and Charles Fleming had arranged to meet her at the bank at noon, to collect her small contribution to his debts.Suppressing a shudder, she turned away from the window and encountered Jane's sympathetic expression. 'Oh, well,' she said, lifting her hands in a defeated gesture. 'You have good days, and you have bad days, and today has definitely been one of the latter variety!'

Jane shook her head. 'I would never have believed it of Roger.'

'I know,' Rachel grimaced. 'That makes two of us. But I wanted to die when my father mistook Alex Roche for one of Devlin's men.'

Jane nodded. 'I suppose it did look suspicious to him. I mean, he didn't even know you knew Alex Roche, and when he saw you apparently struggling with him——'

'It wasn't exactly like that.' Rachel flushed. 'Alex— that is——Roche had seen the car, and he thought it was Roger's.'

'Why would he think that?'

'Oh, I suppose because I looked so guilty,' muttered Rachel wearily, sinking into an armchair and crossing her legs. 'Anyway, he had no right to attempt to catechize me. What I do is nothing to do with him. Or Roger either, for that matter.'

Jane sighed. 'Roger will come round . . .'

'Will he?'

'You know he will.' Jane put a note of conviction into her voice. 'After all, aside from everything else, he loves you.'

'Does he?'

'Oh, stop being so negative, Rachel! You know he does. And you love him. Don't let your father spoil that.'

Rachel gave her friend a resigned look. 'If you loved someone, wouldn't you want to help them?'

'But it's not helping you, is it, Rachel? And you have to admit, your father hasn't exactly been truthful with you, has he?'

She shrugged. 'He is short of money.'

'But only because he's been spending too much money at the race track.'

'Don't you start!' Rachel hunched her shoulders. 'Oh, Jane, I don't know: I thought I knew Roger. Now I'm not so sure.'

Jane regarded her dubiously. 'Alex Roche wouldn't have anything to do with this, would he? I mean, what were you doing at his house anyway? You said he came to Roger's to try and explain, but you didn't explain how you came to be with him afterwards.'

Rachel felt the heat as a flush invaded her cheeks, and bending her head, she said carelessly: 'We left together. It was natural that he should offer me a lift.'

'But he didn't bring you home, did he? You went to his apartment.'

'House,' said Rachel wearily, resting her head against the back of the chair. 'We went to his house. I was—upset.' She pushed back the moist hair from her forehead. 'Wouldn't you have been? Alex—Alex Roche offered me coffee, and I accepted.'

'Just coffee?' asked Jane drily, and Rachel turned her head away.

'What else?' she replied, unable to meet the other girl's eyes. 'Now, can we leave this subject? I don't want to think about it any more.'

But of course she did. It would have been impossible
not to think about what had happened at Roger's
apartment and the subsequent developments at Alex
Roche's house in Eaton Mews. Rachel was so confused,
the two scenes tended to run together like some
fantastic interplay, and Alex's role swung from victim
to aggressor with uneasy feasibility. Why had he waited
until that morning to go to Roger's apartment? Was he
really as innocent of guile as he would have had her
believe? And why was she putting so much emphasis on
Alex's role, when it was Roger himself who had acted
out of character?

The remainder of the day passed without incident.
Roger did not phone, and remembering his anger when
she left the apartment with Alex Roche, she couldn't
entirely blame him. Nevertheless, she had hoped he
might have had more faith in her, and it was daunting
to discover how swiftly he had accepted her guilt.
Perhaps he hadn't wanted to believe her, she reflected
dully. Perhaps he had been having second thoughts
about their relationship. Whatever the reason, he had
refused to listen to her pleas, and she had been left with
the humiliating alternatives of either accepting Alex's
offer of a lift, or walking home with the tears still
glistening on her cheeks.

As for Alex . . . Her pulse stirred with unwanted
emotion at the memory of his behaviour. It was wrong
and it was crazy, but there had been moments in the
library at his house when she felt herself on the brink of
giving in to his demands. It was a purely sexual
reaction, of course, she told herself now, but
nonetheless powerful because of that. Alex knew exactly
how to play on her emotions, and in her low state, she
had been twice as susceptible to his demands. That she
hadn't given in had been due more to the sharpness of
her tongue than to a physical rejection. Somehow she
had got under his skin, and recalling his silence all the
way to the flat, she wondered what it was that had
angered him so. Something about forcing his attentions
on women, she remembered curiously, then forgot that
in the humiliating recollection of her father's inter-

vention when they reached the flat. What must he have thought when her father accused him of being one of Harry Devlin's debt-collectors? No doubt his opinion of her had taken a downward plunge at the realisation that her father was being hounded like a common thief.

On Sunday morning, Rachel didn't feel like getting out of bed at all, but self-pity was not something she had ever condoned, and dismissing her problems, she was up and dressed soon after nine. Surprisingly, she had slept, her body responding to the influence of the bottle of wine Jane had produced to drink with their supper the night before, and although she could feel depression lurking like a black shadow at the back of her mind, she refused to let it get her down. Something would turn up, she told herself firmly, as she prepared Jane's breakfast. After all, she still had her job, which most times she enjoyed, and her health, and time was a great healer, or so she had been told.

The phone rang just before lunchtime, and exchanging a glance with Jane, Rachel went to answer it. 'It could be your mother,' she remarked, as her friend disappeared into the kitchen, and Jane pulled a wry face before closing the door behind her.

'Rachel! Rachel, is that you?'

It was her father, and Rachel's heart, which had lifted at the use of her name, sank back into its normal position.

'Yes, it's me,' she agreed, trying not to let her feelings show, and he asked her if she was all right before plunging into the purpose for his call.

'It's about what happened yesterday,' he said, and she guessed he was feeling pretty guilty about what had occurred.

'It's all right, Dad,' she exclaimed, deciding there was no point in allowing him to shoulder the blame. 'I'm glad I found out in time. If Roger feels like that, then maybe we weren't meant for each other after all.'

'Roger?' For a moment there was a note of confusion in Charles Fleming's voice, but it was quickly disguised. 'Roger,' he said again. 'My dear girl, I could have told you what Roger Harrington was like six months ago! You're well rid of him, believe me! You'd never have been happy with that tight-fisted——'

'You haven't asked him for money before, have you?' Rachel broke in urgently, assailed by the dismaying thought that perhaps this wasn't the first time Roger had been approached, but her father's next words reassured her on this point.

'Of course not,' he exclaimed. 'As if I would! And without telling you? What do you take me for?'

'You did go to see Roger last Thursday without telling me,' Rachel reminded him drily. 'You shouldn't have done that.'

'Oh, I know. But I was desperate.' Her father put an appealing note into his voice. 'Darling, I didn't want to take your last few pounds from you. And Harrington could have afforded it, you know he could.'

'Yes, well——' Rachel didn't want to talk about what Roger could or could not have done. 'It doesn't matter, Dad. It's over now. You'll get the rest of Grandmother's money tomorrow, but after that, I'm afraid, you're on your own.'

'Well, that's what I wanted to talk to you about, actually,' said her father tentatively. 'I mean, we both know four thousand pounds isn't going to solve anything, don't we?'

'What are you saying? I thought you intimated that it would buy you some time——'

'It will. About two days,' replied her father quickly. 'But honestly, Rachel, that barely pays the interest.'

She sank down on to the arm of a chair, her knees weakening beneath her. 'Dad, if you expect me to approach Roger again——'

'I don't. I don't,' Charles sounded convincing, and Rachel's nerves loosened a little. 'I can accept defeat as well as the next man, and I know that it's no use approaching Harrington again.'

'Well then, I don't see——'

'That young man you were with yesterday,' her father interrupted her swiftly. 'Alexis Roche, wasn't it? Do you have any idea who he is? Who his father is?'

The colour rushed into Rachel's face and then drained out of it again. 'I—know—who he is,' she got out unsteadily. 'But if you think——'

'Wait! Wait!' Her father gave a nervous laugh. 'Really, Rachel, stop jumping to conclusions. I only asked if you knew who the man was. You never did tell me how you came to meet him. Is he a client of Hector, Hollis and Black?'

'No. No, he's not.' Rachel took a deep breath and got to her feet again. 'Dad, I've got to go. I'm right in the middle of preparing lunch, and I can smell something burning——'

'All right, all right, I can tell when I'm not wanted.' Her father had adopted an offended tone now. 'I realise it's a lot to expect, that you should feel any concern for my feelings. I know I haven't always been the best father in the world, but it hasn't been easy for me since your mother left. A man wasn't meant to bring up children alone—that's woman's work. But I managed as well as I could, sending money to Aunt Amy, paying for your education——'

'What do you want from me?'

Rachel's strangled plea arrested his words, and it was several seconds before he mumbled ungraciously: 'Nothing. I want nothing, Rachel. I shouldn't have rung. I'm sorry.'

'Oh, for God's sake!' Her fingers gripping the receiver tightened painfully. 'You can't expect me to ask Alex Roche to lend you the money! I—I hardly know the man!'

'That wasn't my impression,' said Charles Fleming quickly. 'I saw the way he looked at you. I saw the way you looked at him. No wonder you're not bothered about the way Harrington has behaved——'

'I didn't say that!'

'You didn't have to. But you're my daughter. You know which side your bread's buttered.'

Rachel gasped. 'You can't be serious! Alex Roche means nothing to me. I—I'll probably never see him again.'

'But you could.'

'What do you mean?'

'Oh, come on, Rachel. Who are you kidding? If you rang Roche and said you'd like to see him——'

'No!'

'Why not? What have you got to lose?' her father persisted. 'Oh, I'm not suggesting you ask him for a date outright. But you could say you'd left something in his car. A glove or something——'

'I wasn't wearing gloves.'

'A handkerchief, then.'

'No!'

There was a prolonged silence after this exchange, and Rachel was on the point of asking whether her father was still there when Charles Fleming spoke again.

'All right,' he said, a defeated note in his voice. 'I knew I shouldn't ask you, but I had to try. I've got to handle this myself, I realise that now. I'll give you a ring tomorrow, after I've had some time to think.'

'But what about meeting at the bank at noon?' exclaimed Rachel anxiously. 'I thought you wanted——'

'I'll get back to you,' responded her father shortly, and rang off before she could say anything in her own defence.


## CHAPTER SEVEN

ALL during Monday, Rachel expected her father to ring, but he didn't. The phone remained persistently silent, and even Mr Black, who had been expecting a call from a client in Manchester, asked her several times if there had been any messages.

'You haven't been out of the office, have you, Rachel?' he demanded testily at lunchtime, and she assured him with some fervour that she hadn't.

Without the appointment with her father to keep, she spent the lunch hour in the office, flicking through the pages of a magazine Sophie had lent her, and trying not to think about what he might be doing. The idea that he could conceivably contact Alex Roche as he had contacted Roger would not be displaced, and by the end of the day her nerves were raw with anxiety.

It didn't help when Sophie accompanied her to the bus stop, and with her usual lack of discretion asked Rachel if she had left her engagement ring at home. 'I noticed you weren't wearing it at lunchtime,' she said, 'but when you didn't say anything, I assumed you must have left it in the cloakroom or something. Nothing's wrong, is it?'

Rachel sighed. 'Nothing—except that Roger and I have split up,' she declared flatly. 'Now, do you mind? I'd rather not talk about it?'

'Of course.' Sophie was immediately apologetic. 'I'm sorry, Rachel. I didn't mean to be nosey.'

Rachel suspected she meant to be exactly that, but she didn't say so. Sophie's heart was in the right place, and if she was inclined to be inquisitive, that was no reflection on the warmth of her character.

'It's all right,' she responded now. 'I'll get over it. Oh, look, isn't this your bus? You do get this one, don't you?'

'Usually,' agreed Sophie airily, making no move to get on as other would-be passengers were doing. 'But I'm going to see my Aunt Hazel this evening, and she lives not far from where you have your flat.'

'Oh.' Rachel accepted this news without enthusiasm. If Sophie was travelling home with her there would be many more opportunities for her to ask pertinent questions, and she half wished she had said she had shopping to do and not involved herself this far.

The bus Sophie normally took pulled away and Rachel looped the strap of her bag back on to her shoulder. In the distance, she could see another bus approaching, and she hoped for once it would be full, and they might have to stand. At least standing there was little chance of private conversation, and they might even get separated in the crush of passengers.

But before the bus could reach them, the sleek grey

bonnet of a car Rachel was fast coming to recognise cruised to a halt beside the queue of people. 'Want a lift?' enquired Alex's lazy tones, as the electric window glided smoothly downwards, and she glanced at Sophie in an agony of embarrassment.

'Go ahead,' said Sophie enviously, eyeing the sleek sports car with covetous eyes. 'I'll see you tomorrow, you lucky cat!'

'I——' Rachel was conscious of the bus approaching, and of the fact that Alex was parked in its space. 'Er— can you give Sophie a lift, too?'

'If you like.' Alex was indifferent, adjusting the front seat so that the younger girl could get into the back as he pushed open the door.

'I'll sit in the back,' said Rachel at once, scrambling into the rear of the vehicle, and Sophie, too bemused to protest, got obediently into the seat beside the driver.

'I say, this is awfully nice of you,' she began, casting Rachel a discomfited glare. 'There was no need, you know. I could have caught the bus. It was following on right behind.'

'No problem,' said Alex carelessly, giving her a brief smile. 'Just tell me where you live, and I'll drop you off first.'

Encountering the grey eyes reflected in the rear-view mirror, Rachel wondered if she was imagining the calculation she saw there. It could have meant anything, she told herself, concentrating on the traffic outside. Her father couldn't have contacted him. *He couldn't!*

'You work for Hector, Hollis and Black, don't you?' Alex was saying now, directing his remark to Sophie. 'I saw you there, didn't I, when I came to see Rachel. Are you someone's secretary, too?'

'Unfortunately not.' Sophie had flushed, but it was evident from the way she was looking at him now that she had got over her first flush of embarrassment. 'I'm just a member of the typing pool. We're at the mercy of all the members of the practice.'

'I'm sure they appreciate the fact,' remarked Alex drily, giving her an amused look, and watching the

effect he was having on Sophie, Rachel felt an unwilling
resentment stirring inside her.

It was difficult at that moment to see him in any
other way than through Sophie's eyes, and it was
obvious she found him very attractive. In close-fitting
denim pants and a dark blue corded jacket, his ash-gold
hair brushing the collar of the cream silk shirt he was
wearing underneath, he was disturbingly masculine, his
lean good looks accentuated by the darkness of his skin.
Even the thickness of his lashes, as they narrowed the
swift appraisal he kept giving his uninvited passenger,
was an added fascination, drawing her attention to the
darkness at their roots.

'What part of London do you live in, Mr Roche?'
Sophie asked now, ignoring Rachel's sudden intake of
breath. 'I live in Streatham, which is south of the river,
but I'm going to visit my aunt in Kilburn.'

'I see,' Alex nodded. 'I thought I hadn't seen you
with Rachel before.' He cast a mocking glance over his
shoulder. 'Your aunt lives quite near Rachel, then.'

'In Laurence Avenue,' said Sophie, nodding. 'I'll
direct you once we get on to the Edgware Road.'

'Thank you.'

Alex inclined his head, and Sophie, seemingly starting
to enjoy this unexpected diversion, glanced round at the
other girl. 'Actually,' she remarked, 'you can drop me
off after Rachel, if you like. Oakwood Road is the
turning before Laurence Avenue.'

The unwelcome twinge of jealousy Sophie's outrageous suggestion evoked was quickly followed by an
equally frustrating feeling of indigation when Alex
declined her strategy.

'I think, as you're sitting in front, it will be easier if
you get out first,' he essayed politely, ignoring her eager
protests. 'Besides, I want to talk to Rachel. Privately.'

'Really?' Sophie couldn't quite keep the malice out of
her voice. 'Lucky Rachel!'

'She might not agree with you,' he responded, lazily,
his eyes seeking Rachel's once again in the mirror. 'But
no matter.' He paused. 'Now can you tell me which way
from here?'

After depositing Sophie outside her aunt's house, Alex suggested Rachel joined him up front. 'Unless you prefer to look at the back of my head,' he remarked drily, as she hesitated where she was.

'Oh, very well.' Realising she would only give Sophie more grist for her mill if she remained in the back, Rachel got out and in again. 'Now, will you take me home? I'm late, and I'm going out this evening.'

'Are you?' Alex gave her an assessing look as he slowed to negotiate the junction. 'Who with? Roger? Or your father?'

Rachel stiffened. 'What do you know about my father?'

'What should I know?' Alex accelerated out into the main stream of traffic. 'You introduced us on Saturday lunchtime. Or have you forgotten?'

Rachel looked at him with troubled eyes. 'He—he hasn't been—in touch with you, has he?'

He frowned. 'Why should he have been in touch with me?'

'Oh, will you stop answering my questions with questions of your own!' exclaimed Rachel tensely. 'Either you know what I'm talking about or you don't. Which is it?'

Alex hesitated. 'Your father has not been in touch with me,' he said at last. 'Did you think he might?'

She turned her head away. 'No. No, not really.'

'Now you're not being entirely truthful, are you?' he observed with disturbing perspicacity. 'And you still haven't told me who you're going out with this evening.'

'Oh—Jane,' said Rachel unwillingly. 'We're going to see a film we'd planned to see last week.'

'What film?'

'Does it matter?' She cast him a helpless look. 'It's a French film, as it happens. *Les Trois*.'

'I know it.' He inclined his head, and she remembered belatedly that he was French himself. 'Do you like the cinema?'

'Sometimes.' Rachel could see no point to this discussion, and turning her head, she looked out the window again. Why had he come to meet her if all he wanted to talk about was her taste in films? She'd be home in a few moments. Laurence Avenue was only a few minutes from the flat.

It was at that moment she realised they were going in the wrong direction. Instead of turning left out of Laurence Avenue, Alex had turned right, and they were already approaching the snarl-up of traffic before Marble Arch.

'Where are you going?' she demanded, turning to him angrily, and Alex's lips twisted as he appraised her furious features.

'Where I intended going before you so kindly offered my services as a chauffeur,' he responded smoothly. 'To my house in Eaton Mews. If we can make it through this traffic before tomorrow morning.'

Rachel stared at him. 'I'm not going to your house.'

'I'm afraid you're going to have to,' he replied, without taking his eyes from the road. 'I told you, I want to talk to you. And it is about your father, believe it or not. Does that pacify you?'

She caught her breath. 'So he has been in touch with you!'

'No.'

'But you said——'

'I said I wanted to talk to you about your father. End of explanation.'

She pressed her lips together. 'I suppose you've found out who Harry Devlin is,' she muttered. 'You can't blame my father for jumping to the wrong conclusions. He saw us together and he—well, he——'

'—thought I was molesting you,' Alex inserted, finishing the sentence for her. 'Nice individuals your father deals with, doesn't he?'

Rachel made no response, and for the next few minutes Alex was too involved in negotiating the powerful car through the press of other vehicles to handle any further conversation. But once they reached the comparative freedom of Park Lane, Rachel returned to the attack, saying bitterly: 'I suppose you've guessed why I thought he might have been in touch with you.'

'I didn't need to guess,' Alex responded obliquely, taking the opportunity to overtake a slow-moving Mercedes and getting a horn blown at him for his pain. 'Look, let's leave this until we can talk properly, hmm? It shouldn't take us too much longer now.'

But it did. Rachel was sure she could have walked to Eaton Mews quicker than the traffic was moving, and although she didn't want to think any kind thoughts of Alex Roche, she couldn't help remembering that he had driven several miles further than he had intended, just to take Sophie to her aunt's. Not that that was any justification for his behaviour, she reminded herself severely. If he had told her their destination before she got into the car, she would most certainly have refused his offer.

It was well after six before Alex brought the Lamborghini to a halt outside his London home. Looking up at its elegant façade, Rachel couldn't suppress the involuntary surge of excitement that gripped her at being here again, and she knew she would have to ring Jane and set her mind at rest.

'Can I use your phone?' she asked, as soon as they entered the gold-tinted beauty of the hall, and Alex, observing the obsequious approach of the manservant, gestured patiently towards the cream receiver that rested beside the bowl of flowers on the polished oak table.

Rachel, picking up the receiver rather doubtfully, discovered it had rows of press-button numbers on its underside, and that no further instrument was required.

While Alex spoke with the man she recognised as Karim, Rachel pressed the necessary numbers required to reach the flat, but when Jane came on the line, her courage faltered. 'I—er—I won't be home for at least another hour,' she told her, hoping Alex was not eavesdropping. 'Mr Black's just asked me to stay late. Do you mind?'

'No. No, I suppose not.' But Jane sounded rather surprised all the same. 'Do you realise what time it is, Rachel? I expected you home over half an hour ago.'

'I know.' Rachel cast another surreptitious glance in Alex's direction. 'Look, I can't explain now.'

'I thought you just did.' Jane was too astute. 'Rachel, there's nothing wrong, is there? You sound very strange.'

'Everything's fine,' declared Rachel firmly. 'But I'm afraid we're going to have to postpone that film again.'

'Never mind.' Jane was philosophical. 'I guess we weren't intended to see it, were we? And don't worry about dinner. It's only cold meat and salad, it won't spoil.'

'Thanks, Jane.' Rachel hated herself for not being honest with her, but she couldn't face that kind of explanation right now. 'See you later, then.'

'Be good,' responded Jane cryptically, and Rachel couldn't help wondering if her friend had guessed what had happened. It seemed that everyone she knew could anticipate what she would do next, she reflected, as she replaced the receiver. She wished she was as perceptive.

'Well? Does she object?' asked Alex in a mocking voice, and turning, Rachel found him propped against the baluster watching her. How long he had been watching her, she had no way of knowing. There was no sign of Karim now, and he was evidently waiting for her to accompany him upstairs.

'I didn't tell her,' she said now, deciding to be truthful. 'It was easier to tell her I was working. I'll explain when I get home.'

Alex gave her a wry look. 'You're not good at telling lies, are you?'

Rachel flushed. 'I wouldn't want to be.'

'No.' He conceded the point goodhumouredly. 'Well, take off your coat. I've asked Karim to prepare us a light dinner. I'm sure after all that emotional turmoil, you must be ravenous.'

'I didn't come here to have dinner with you!' she exclaimed, infuriated by his arrogance, but Alex came and purposefully lifted her navy blue jacket from her shoulders, and short of indulging in another of the futile struggles she had had with him in the past, there was nothing she could do but give in gracefully.

'Come along,' he said, directing her towards the stairs with a firm hand at her waist. 'The morning room is upstairs, and I've asked Karim to serve the food in there.'

'Is—Karim always prepared for every eventuality?' she asked shortly, preceding him up the stairs more quickly than she might have done to escape his possessive hold, and Alex smiled.

'He is very efficient,' he essayed easily, and then, more incisively: 'He wouldn't be in my employ if he wasn't.'

The morning room was across the landing from the library, and as its door was standing ajar, Rachel had a brief glimpse of plain, butter-coloured walls, and tapestry-backed chairs around a polished circular table. 'Perhaps you would like a drink before we eat,' Alex suggested, leading the way into the library, and she followed him more slowly, re-acquainting herself with her surroundings.

To her surprise, although she accepted a glass of sherry, Alex drank nothing alcoholic. Instead he poured himself a glass of Coke, perching on the desk as he had done before, overwhelming her by his presence. To counteract his nearness, she chose to sit on one of the ladderbacked chairs by the door, spurning the soft armchair beside the desk, and his eyebrow quirked interrogatively as she put some distance between them.

'So,' he said, after she was seated, 'this is not so bad, is it? Perhaps one day you will agree to have a meal with me without my having to abduct you. That way, you might wear something more in keeping with the occasion.'

Rachel glanced down at her dress. For once, she had worn something other than a business suit to the office, but the navy blue wool, with its prim white collar, was still determinedly formal. So what? she argued silently, she had no desire to impress Alex Roche. Nevertheless, his words had reminded her of her reasons for being here, and dismissing any thoughts of her appearance, she plunged once again into the attack.

'Why have you brought me here?' she asked, holding

on to the sherry glass with more strength than discretion. 'What can you possibly have to say about my father? His affairs are nothing to do with you.'

'You're wrong.' Alex spoke softly but insistently, swallowing the remainder of the Coke in his glass with evident relish before depositing it firmly on the desk. 'Charles Fleming's affairs—oh, yes, I made it my business to find out his full name—his affairs are everything to do with me. You see, he doesn't owe Harold Devlin any more, he owes me.'

Rachel sprang to her feet. 'You mean——'

'I mean I bought out your father's debts,' affirmed Alex quietly. 'The fifty-seven thousand pounds he owed to Devlin has been taken care of.'

'Fifty-*seven* thousand pounds!' Rachel was appalled. 'But why should you do a thing like that?'

Alex's expression became ironic. 'Why do you think?' he asked flatly. 'What do you want me to say? Do I have to spell it out to you?'

Rachel's tongue circled her lips. 'I don't believe you.'

'Why would I lie?' Alex spread his hands. 'How else could I know the extent of your father's foolishness.'

She shook her head a little blankly. 'I—don't understand——'

'I'm sure you do.' He slid off the desk and faced her. 'Fifty-seven thousand pounds means very little to me financially. Conversely, on a personal level, it means the difference between failure and success.'

Rachel's face contorted. 'You think—you think you've *bought* me?'

He lifted his shoulders. 'Haven't I?'

'*No!*'

She flung the denial at him as her fingers tightened recklessly around the fragile glass. She was scarcely aware of its dangers as the realisation of what Alex was saying struck her like a hammer blow, and when the stem snapped in her hand, her reactions were proportionately slower. The jagged edges sank into her flesh, and she looked down almost disbelievingly as a moist warmth spread over her palm and dripped on to the carpet. She was bleeding, she saw, as if from a distance, and then a black haze engulfed her and she knew nothing more . . .

She awakened to the awareness of silk against her cheek. As her eyes opened to a world of warmth and subdued lighting, she was instantly sensible that she was lying in a huge bed, her head cushioned on the softest of pillows, her limbs covered by a lightweight quilt. Apart from a slight throbbing in her hand, she could feel no discomfort, and a hurried exploration beneath the covers elicited the knowledge that she was still fully dressed.

'Are you feeling better, *mademoiselle?*'

The harsh tones were unfamiliar, and turning her head Rachel saw the man hovering beside the bed. It was Alex's manservant, Karim, she saw with sudden recognition, and she blinked rapidly as the recollection of what had happened returned with painful clarity.

'What am I doing here?' she exclaimed, struggling up in the bed, and Karim put out a hand towards her, as if to press her back again.

'You fainted, *mademoiselle*,' he told her quickly. 'You cut your hand on a glass, and passed out. My master carried you in here, and left me to attend to your injury.'

Rachel lifted the hand which was still throbbing so that she could see it. Someone—Karim?—had wrapped a piece of white linen around her palm, and just faintly, through its folds, she could see a trace of red.

'The wound is clean, *mademoiselle*, but if you are feeling well enough, I will bathe it with a lotion *antiseptique*. *Ensuite*, I will secure the cut with elasticated strips, to prevent a scar from forming.'

'Is that necessary?' All Rachel wanted to do was get out of the bed and out of the house, as soon as possible, and in all honesty, she still felt rather weak.

'Let Karim attend to it,' advised a lazy voice from across the room, and looking up, Rachel saw Alex himself had come to stand in the doorway, supporting himself with one hand against the lintel. 'He is well qualified, believe me.'

Rachel quivered, the uninjured hand which sought her throat discovering that someone had unfastened the neckline of her dress to expose the creamy column of her throat. 'I'd rather go to a hospital,' she averred unsteadily, but Alex only smiled.

'My—friends—do not go to hospitals, except in an extreme emergency,' he replied, straightening. 'Attend to it, Karim. I will wait in the library.'

Karim made some response in a language Rachel did not understand, then followed his master out the door. Left alone, Rachel contemplated the possible success of attempting an escape, but abandoned it. Apart from anything else, she didn't know where her shoes were, and her coat and handbag had been left downstairs. No doubt the efficient Karim would have put them out of sight until later, and she could hardly run through the streets without any outdoor covering. Besides, she didn't know if she had the strength. Aside from the amount of blood she had lost, the news about her father still had the power to sap her energies.

Recalling the amount of blood she had lost, she vaguely remembered its seeping on to the floor in the library. She could imagine Alex's reactions to his beautiful beige carpet being stained, and she knew a moment's petty satisfaction in the thought.

It didn't last. A man like Alex Roche, who could spend fifty thousand pounds—no, fifty-*seven* thousand pounds—without turning a hair would think nothing of replacing a carpet. No doubt, some other member of his staff was already ripping it up in readiness, and tomorrow morning a team of fitters would arrive with its facsimile.

Karim returned carrying a metal tray, and set it down on the table beside the bed. 'Will you hold out your hand, *mademoiselle?*' he requested deferentially, and after a moment's hesitation Rachel obeyed.

While the manservant removed the linen bandage to expose the small but ugly wound, and bathed it in a lotion that only stung in its initial stages, Rachel looked about her. The bedroom was generous in size, easily accommodating the huge bed and several chests of

drawers. There was a long mirror over one of the
chests, and several attractive paintings, as well as two
intricately-woven carpets suspended from the walls.
They gave the room warmth and colour, complementing
the bronze-coloured carpet, and the matching damask
curtains at the windows. She wondered whose room it
was, her mind skittering away from the thought that it
might be Alex's, and turned her attention back to
Karim as he was completing his task.

Amazingly, all pain had disappeared. Even the
throbbing had gone, and she looked down at the three
strips of elasticated nylon he had stretched in place to
act instead of stitches with some amazement.

'It doesn't hurt at all!' she exclaimed, flexing her
fingers, cautiously, and Karim bowed his head.

'I am happy,' he said, gathering his medical
equipment on to the tray and lifting it into his hands. 'It
should heal very quickly, *mademoiselle*. The flesh is
strong and healthy, there will be no scar.'

'Thank you, Karim.' Rachel shook her head in some
confusion. 'I'm very grateful. It was a foolish thing to do.'

The manservant said nothing more, but merely
bowed once again before making his departure.
Evidently his duty was completed, and deciding she
could now request to be taken home, Rachel slid her
legs over the side of the bed.

'You are ready to eat now?'

Alex's suggestion brought her head round with a
start, and she knew an unwelcome trepidation at the
sight of him standing in the doorway once again. He
had shed his jacket, she saw, and turned back the cuffs
of his shirt, its loosened neckline revealing a fine haze of
bleached hair below the bones of his throat. He looked
lean, and handsome, and—dangerous—she acknowledged tremulously, the muscles of her legs jerking as she
put her feet to the floor.

'I'd like to go home,' she got out at last, not looking
at him, searching with her feet for her shoes. But they
were not there, and as he came lazily across the room,
she was intensely conscious of the disadvantages of
stockinged feet.

'Not yet,' he said, with some finality, halting only inches away from her. 'We have to talk about our future. There are many things I want to say.'

'Our future?' echoed Rachel harshly. '*We* have no future. I—I'll get the money to pay you back somehow. But until I do, you'll just have to charge me interest.'

'Oh, I intend to,' agreed Alex softly, looking down at her with disturbing eyes. 'But a financial arrangement does not interest me. I can think of much, much easier payments.'

Her breathing quickened. 'I don't believe this——'

'Why not?' He ran the knuckles of one hand along the curve of her jawline and allowed his fingertips to trail against the skin exposed by her opened collar. 'You know what I want. You know I'm going to get it. What's so unbelievable about that?'

Rachel didn't attempt to try and push him aside. She had struggled with him before, all to no avail. Her only hope lay in trying to reason with him, and to this end she exclaimed: 'Please don't touch me—I don't like it. No matter what you say, I shall never give you what you want willingly.' And remembering what had worked before, she added passionately: 'You're not an animal! Surely you have more respect for yourself than that!'

But this time her words fell on stony ground. As she was speaking, Alex had moved closer, bending his head to touch the curve of her neck with his lips, and as her pulses raced to assimilate this new sensation, he found one palpitating spasm with his tongue and soothed its wild vibration.

'Relax,' he breathed, his hands at her waist now, drawing her against him, and as Rachel opened her lips to protest, he captured their trembling softness with his mouth.

A little moan escaped her as she was compelled against his muscled body, but the searching possession of his kiss stifled her objections. In the car, she had been shocked and unprepared, submitting to his lips without thought or feeling, but this was different. Instead of feeling numbed and disbelieving, now she was fully aware of the warm invasion of his mouth, that caused a palpable weakness in her legs and a sharp constriction in the pit of her stomach. She wanted to yield against him, she realised; she wanted to put her arms around his neck and open her mouth wider to his exploration. But the sudden awareness of a growing hardness against her stomach brought her to her senses, and she jerked back unexpectedly, taking him by surprise.

'No,' he said now, not allowing her to escape beyond the length of his arms. His eyes were heavy with emotion, and there was a sensuous curve to his lips as he surveyed her quivering panic. 'No,' he repeated huskily, 'I won't let you go. I want you—you know it. Look at me, Rachel. You can see I'm not lying.'

Her eyes flickered nervously from side to side, stubbornly avoiding the swollen evidence of his desire that he was making no attempt to conceal. She looked everywhere, but at him, and her alarm was audible in the breathy faintness of her voice. 'I—I think you're disgusting!' she choked, as his hands slid from her shoulders to her throat, his thumbs forcing her to look into his face. 'H-have you no shame?'

'What is shameful about making love?' he asked softly, unperturbed by her accusations. 'I wonder what manner of man Harrington can be to have made you so afraid of something which can be quite—beautiful.'

'I wish you'd leave Roger out of this——'

'I'm sure you do.' Alex's fingers caressed her neck, arousing reluctant little *frissons* of pleasure along her spine. 'His name does not fill me with any feeling of satisfaction either. You went to him, to ask him to help your father, didn't you? And I surmise he refused.'

'It's nothing to do with you.' Rachel didn't want to think about Roger now. It reminded her too acutely of her own guilt in being here, in allowing Alex Roche to touch her, in consorting with the enemy . . .

'It has everything to do with me,' he responded, drawing her inexorably closer. 'If Harrington had agreed to help you, we might not be here now, and that would have been a great pity.'

'For you. Not for me,' retorted Rachel unsteadily, putting out her hands to ward him off. Her injured palm twinged a little as it encountered the unyielding muscles of his chest, and she knew a sense of hopelessness at the inequality of the contest. 'Please . . .'

'Oh, you do—believe me,' he murmured fervently, his breath quickening over her heated skin, and taking one of her hands in his, he pressed it against the pulsating muscle that thrust against her fingers. *'Nom de Dieu,'* he groaned, reverting to his own language in these moments of stress, *'touche-moi!'*

This was something with which Rachel was more familiar, but Alex's mouth possessing hers was vastly different from Roger's weak caresses. The hunger in his kiss ignited a flame inside her, and her mechanical response to his demands was soon forgotten in the urgent desire to assuage her own feelings. Touching Alex was not like touching Roger. He was no passive partner in the exchange. On the contrary, his fingers had quickly disposed of the unopened buttons on her dress, and now his hands were on her shoulders, sliding the offending article of clothing to the floor.

Rachel dragged her mouth from his long enough to protest when he loosened the lacy bra which, together with her panties, was all that protected her from his avid gaze, but Alex's tongue probing the swollen nipples drowned her objections. 'You're beautiful,' he said, refusing to allow her any shred of modesty. 'Don't be ashamed. Let me touch you. Let me feel you—against me——'

His shirt joined the remainder of her clothes on the floor, and loosening the belt of his pants, he propelled her back on to the bed behind them. 'Karim——' she breathed faintly, as he joined her, and Alex's mouth twisted in sensual satisfaction.

'Karim knows better than to interrupt us,' he told her huskily, and when she felt the muscled strength of his legs against hers, she realised he was as naked as she was.

This was not at all like being with Roger, she thought hazily, as Alex's mouth beat a searing path across her

breasts, then followed downward, over the quivering
flatness of her diaphragm to the softness of her
stomach. Roger had never given any thought to her
pleasure, only to his own, and while she told herself
that Roger had had more respect for her, it rang a little
hollowly in her ears.

Even so, she flinched in sudden panic when Alex's
mouth sought a more intimate invasion, and he gave a
soft laugh as he slid over her to find her mouth again.
'You have a lot to learn,' he breathed against her lips.
'But we will come to that later. Right now . . .'

She had purposely avoided looking at him, but just
then it was impossible not to do so. Poised above her, he
was so huge and compelling, and she turned her head
swiftly from side to side as if to deny that ultimate
invasion. 'You can't—I don't——' she began, in a
panic-stricken voice, but it was too late. With a sigh of
submission Alex lowered himself upon her, and a searing
pain tore into her stomach as he took possession.

She saw the look of bewilderment enter his eyes as he
encountered that unmistakable proof of her innocence,
but his own emotions were such that he could not draw
back. The soft sheath closed about him, and he groaned
with pleasure as her tightness drove him to the brink of
satiation.

'*Mon Dieu*, Rachel,' he muttered, smoothing back the
sweat-moistened hair from her forehead, and as the pain
subsided she looked up at him through tear-drenched
eyes. 'Now I understand.' He shook his head. 'You
should have told me.'

'I did.' Rachel amost choked on the words, and as if
to soothe her trembling vulnerability, he bent his head
and covered her mouth with exquisite gentleness.

But it didn't end there. To her horror, she found her
lips parting to accommodate his, and the increasing
passion in his kiss was evidence of the effect she was
having on him.

'*Ne m'arrête pas!*' he breathed, cupping her face
between hands which were no longer as steady as they
had been, and as he started to move, her arms reached
up to link behind his neck with unknowing sexuality . . .

# CHAPTER EIGHT

IT was all over too soon. Rachel had scarcely begun to enjoy the pleasurable sensations Alex's thrusting body was evoking before she sensed his shuddering climax, and he slumped heavily on top of her. Not so different, after all, she reflected bitterly, remembering Roger's groaning convulsions, and the artificial mood of bonhomie that always followed them. And Alex had taken something from her that Roger never had . . .

As tears filled her eyes again, she shifted beneath him, and feeling her movements, Alex drew away from her. Rolling on to his back, he shaded his eyes for a moment with one upraised arm, but when she moved to get away from him, his arm descended to grip hers and prevent her escape.

Turning his head to one side, he looked at her, his features assuming a rueful expression when he encountered her tremulous gaze. 'I know. I'm sorry,' he murmured, turning on to his side facing her and imprisoning her arm with both hands. 'I—how do you say?—blew it, didn't I? But don't blame me too much. I have waited a long time.'

'I don't want to talk about it.' Rachel stared resolutely ahead, refusing to meet his eyes, and he lifted one hand to twine his fingers in the tangled coil of her hair.

'Poor Rachel,' he said softly. 'You still don't understand, do you? But you will . . . and soon.'

'Can I get up now?' she asked tautly, the choked request scarcely audible, and Alex's fingers slid down her throat to cradle the still-swollen fullness of one betraying breast.

'Not yet,' he responded a little harshly, moving closer, and when she turned her head to give him a startled glance, she saw the rekindled desire in his eyes.

'I—you're not—you wouldn't——' she got out in

121

alarm before his urgent mouth closed over one taut
nipple and suckled insistently.

'Why not?' he breathed, moving to the other breast,
and Rachel felt the recurring heat in her loins as they
responded to his.

'It's—not possible, is it?' she protested, although
already she could feel it was, and almost against her will
her limbs moved to accommodate his.

'Better?' he asked, as he moved upon her, and Rachel
could no longer deny her body's needs. With a little
groan, she spread her hands over his back, urging him
nearer, and his mouth opened over hers in hungry
consummation.

This time there was no drawing back, no disappointing sense of anti-climax. Even though, she fought the
insidious need he was creating inside her, half afraid
that once again she would be left wanting. She could
not fight her own emotions. Instead of lying passively
beneath him, she moved with him, shared with him the
mutual mounting of passion, and in the final act of
union, her senses shattered and splintered over a
devastating peak of ecstasy.

She floated down to earth again through vibrating
clouds of feeling, and only then did she become aware
of the dampness of their bodies, the sweat-moistened
skin of Alex's back that she could feel was scored with
her fingernails. When he lifted his head, her embarrassment was such that she could hardly meet his eyes, and
her muffled: 'I'm sorry,' was said against the curve of
his shoulder. 'I hurt you,' she added, keeping her eyes
averted. 'You must think I'm very naïve.'

'Naïve?' he murmured. 'Oh, no, my darling, I do not
think you are naïve. Not any longer,' he amended drily.
And then, seeing her total confusion, he went on: 'You
are beautiful—more beautiful than I had imagined.'
His lips twisted. 'Do you forgive me?'

Rachel quivered. 'I'd never——'

'I know.' Alex interrupted her wryly. 'That was not
what I asked.'

She licked her lips. 'Was I—did I do it right?'

'Right?' Alex uttered a rueful sound. 'So right, I

have doubts as to whether I shall be able to let you
go home.'

'Home?' She caught her breath. For a few moments
she had forgotten all about home, and Jane, and Roger.
In the last few minutes she had lost all memory of past,
present and future, and it was frightening to hear the
word on Alex's tongue. *Home!* She could go home now
that he had had what he wanted from her, she realised
bitterly. Her father was safe. She had paid his price. But
what a price it was, she dared not even contemplate.

'Yes, home,' Alex was saying now, nuzzling his face
against her neck. 'But not yet, hmm? We have still to
have some supper. And afterwards . . .'

'I don't want any supper.' Rachel swallowed
convulsively, turning her face away from his. 'Now
that—now that you've had your way, I might as well
make my farewells. What does one say in circumstances
like this? It was nice to have *known* you?'

'Stop it!' Alex turned her face back to his, his voice
taking on a cajoling tone as he smoothed her hectic
cheeks with his fingers. 'I know how you must feel, but
it isn't like that, believe me. I wanted you—I want you
still. And not for any other reason.'

'How can I believe that?'

'I'll have to try and convince you,' he replied softly,
turning on to his back and cradling her in his arms.
'But first we will have some supper. Then we will talk.'

Rachel twisted uncertainly against him. 'I don't
know——'

'I do,' he affirmed, releasing her to stretch his arms
above his head. 'Come—we will shower together.' His
lazy smile appeared. 'Then Karim will serve us.'

The bathroom adjoining the bedroom was as
impressive as the rest of the house. A circular step-in
bath, big enough for two, taps made of gold, and softly-
grained tiles underfoot that cooled, yet cushioned, her
feet. Rachel was too bemused with her surroundings to
feel embarrassed about their nudity, and catching a
glimpse of her reflection in a long mirror, she hardly
recognised the misty-eyed nymph who gazed back at
her. She looked so—so abandoned, she thought

incredulously, a wanton creature, all tangled hair and
luminous eyes and bruised, sensual lips.

The shower was scarcely big enough for two, and she
hung back uncertainly. But Alex drew her inside with
him, closing the fluted glass door behind them, and
turning on the shower to enfold them in a world of
falling water. Grasping a tablet of soap, he began to
lather her body from the shoulders down, lingering
longest at her breasts and at the intimate hollows below
her stomach. Rachel wanted to remain calm and
collected, but his probing fingers were unbearably
provoking, and she looked up at him helplessly, unable
to hide the emotion in her eyes.

'You're going to kill me,' he groaned, reaching for
her, the soap falling unheeded to the floor, and her
senses swam beguilingly as the magic engulfed her
again.

Some time later, after she had dried her hair with a
hand-drier Alex had provided, Rachel emerged from
the bathroom in search of her clothes. With a white
bathrobe, which was evidently too big for her, hanging
from her shoulders, she was unknowingly provocative,
and Alex turned from brushing his hair to gaze at her
emotively. He was already dressed, in moccasin-soft
suede pants that hugged his thighs, and a dark brown
knitted sweater, the lightness of his hair still artificially
darkened from the spray in the shower.

'Don't get dressed,' he said huskily, moving swiftly
towards her to slide his hands possessively inside the
loose neck of the bathrobe. 'Hmm, you smell delicious.
What is it?'

Rachel's lips parted. 'You, I think,' she confessed
teasingly. 'I mean,' she added, 'just your soap and
shampoo, of course.'

Alex's mouth quirked. 'What else?' he drawled,
exposing her full breasts to his possessive eyes. 'You
really are the most perfect creature, aren't you? I can't
keep my hands off you.'

'*Alexis!*'

He was gathering her to him, looking down at her
body as it was moulded against his, when the harsh use

of his name exploded with undisguised fury against their ears. Rachel, shocked out of the bemused state that Alex's lovemaking had induced, dragged the lapels of the gown desperately about her, and although Alex's jaw hardened at this unwarranted intrusion, he turned with undeniable alacrity to face his unannounced visitor.

'Grand-père,' he greeted the man politely, going forward to bow low before the intruder, and Rachel, unprepared and vulnerable, stared in amazement at the burnous-clad Arab who was facing her.

'Eh bien, Mariana avait raison!' the old man thundered furiously. 'Tu as une liaison avec une Anglaise! Tu es fou! Croyais-tu vraiment que tu pourrais commetre une telle abomination?'

'Will you speak English, Grand-père?' Alex requested smoothly, apparently unperturbed by his grandfather's wrath, for although Rachel couldn't understand all that was being said, she remembered enough of her schoolgirl French to comprehend that finding her here with Alex was not to his grandparent's liking. His grandparent! For a moment, belief seemed suspended. Was this elderly Arab really Alex's grandfather? she asked herself incredulously. Did that explain Karim's identity, the chauffeur, Hassan? And Alex's own references to white slavery, which she had paid so little attention to?

'Get rid of her!' the old man said now, very succinctly, but Rachel suspected he was only speaking her language so that she would be left in no doubt as to his feelings. Her own feelings were too chaotic to put into words, but her dearest wish was to put his request into operation. She had never felt so shamed or so humiliated in her life, and it didn't help when Alex's fingers, deceptively casual about her wrist, prevented her from doing as his grandfather desired.

'Rachel stays here,' declared Alex pleasantly, his thumb probing disturbingly down into the palm of her hand. 'But perhaps we should allow her to put on some clothes. Regrettably, you find us straight from the shower.'

Rachel thought the old man was going to explode. His gnarled cheeks took on a purplish hue, and his long-fingered hands plucked agitatedly at his robes. 'Mariana is here, Alexis,' he stated, with savage dignity. 'She is downstairs, now, waiting to speak to you. Must I tell her she is to wait while this—this—*garce*— clothes herself?'

'You may tell Mariana what you like,' replied Alex, his mouth hardening into a thin line, and Rachel, watching him, wondered who Mariana was and what she had done that he should have so little respect for her. Was she his sister? His girl-friend? She winced. *His wife*? 'She is, I am sure, in no doubt as to my feelings where she is concerned.'

His grandfather took a deep breath. 'We will wait downstairs,' he said with finality. 'For *you*. No one else.'

He withdrew, leaving the door open behind him, and with uncharacteristic violence, Alex crossed the room and slammed it shut. Then he turned to look at Rachel with eyes glinting steely-grey with anger.

'I'll get dressed,' she said unsteadily, turning quickly away, and with an ugly oath, he came back to her side.

'Don't be alarmed,' he said, with sudden gentleness. 'My grandfather's bark is infinitely worse than his bite. At least, so far as the family is concerned,' he amended wryly. 'It seems we must wait a little longer for our supper *à deux*.'

'Supper!' Rachel stifled a faintly hysterical sound. 'I don't think I want any supper right now. You—you speak to your grandfather and—and——'

'Mariana,' he supplied flatly, and she nodded.

'And Mariana,' she agreed. 'I shall go home, as I intended to do,' she glanced at her watch, '—hours ago!'

'I will take you home,' he corrected firmly, bending to pick up her strewn clothes for her. 'Later. After our visitors have left.'

'No——'

'Yes,' he insisted crisply. 'Now, do you want me to help you?'

'Play lady's maid, you mean?' she breathed huskily, shaking her head, but he nodded.

'Why not? I took them off,' he averred softly. 'I can put them on again.'

'No!'

She looked appalled and he uttered a soft laugh. 'You are right,' he conceded. 'I don't think my grandfather could stand for the inevitable delay. And there are certain situations I should not like him to interrupt.'

Rachel's face burned with colour. 'Go away, then.'

'Can't I watch?'

'No!'

'Very well.' Accepting his dismissal, he strolled towards the door. 'But don't be long. I may come back.'

In the event, he did come back before Rachel was as ready as she would have liked. She was dressed, it was true, and her hair had been coaxed into some semblance of order, although its wild beauty refused to be contained in any formal style. But she was still plying the brush when he entered the room, and her hand shook abominably when he came to stand behind her.

'Enough,' he said arrogantly, taking the brush from her grasp and putting it down on the chest where she had found it. 'It is beautiful hair. Don't try to change it.'

'I should have some make-up,' she exclaimed, touching her cheeks, the faint hollows beneath her eyes, and he smiled possessively.

'You do look a little—tired,' he conceded teasingly. 'But then so do I. A night's—sleep—will soon remedy that.'

Rachel bent her head. 'I should go,' she insisted, but Alex slid his hand down her arm, linking her fingers with his.

'Not yet,' he insisted. 'I want you to meet Mariana. She is not as frightening as my grandfather, and she is very eager to meet you.'

Rachel doubted that. There was something here that she didn't understand, and she was very much afraid she was being used in some way. But the fascination of

Alex's lovemaking was still upon her, making all thought of leaving abhorrent to her, and although she suspected she was being taken like a lamb to the slaughter, she let him lead her down a flight of stairs to the first floor landing.

Alex's grandfather and the young woman with him were waiting in the drawing room. At least, that was the designation Rachel put on the room into which Alex led her. The brief appraisal she was allowed revealed a luxurious room of generous proportions, whose moiré-silk walls were hung with Impressionist paintings. She saw turquoise silk sofas and chairs and several carved cabinets, but her attention was immediately drawn to the girl seated demurely to one side of the screened fireplace.

She heard his grandfather suck in his breath sharply when she entered the room at Alex's side, but Alex himself was unrepentant. 'Let me introduce you to my grandfather, Rachel,' he declared, drawing her insistently across the room. 'Sheik Ibrahim ibn Rachid: Miss Rachel Fleming.'

The old man standing on the hearth scarcely acknowledged her, but politeness would not allow him to ignore her completely. The faint inclination of his head was a confirmation of her presence, and with tightening lips, Alex moved to the other occupant of the room.

In the light from various shaded lamps, the young woman in the simple black suit was exquisite. Like Alex's, her skin was several shades darker than Rachel's own, but it had the smoothness and texture of a peach. Dark eyes looked out from between short black lashes, and hair the colour of ebony was drawn severely back into a chignon at her nape. The classic contours of her features were thus exposed, and with them, the faintly haughty air that characterised the old man's expression.

'Mariana,' said Alex politely, his mouth twisting with some emotion Rachel did not want to identify. Then: 'Rachel, this is Mademoiselle Mariana Rachid. My—cousin.'

*His cousin!*

Rachel forced a smile, but Mariana didn't even attempt to hide her feelings. The pebble-dark eyes merely flashed with undisguised fire, and she turned to look at Alex's grandfather as if appealing to him to rescue her from this unpalatable situation.

'So ...' Alex took the initiative, 'how are you, Mariana? You look well.'

*'Grandpère!'*

The young woman turned helplessly in the old man's direction, but before his grandfather could speak, Alex once again intervened. 'Why have you come here, Mariana?' he demanded, his voice low and controlled. 'We have nothing more to say to one another. Did I not make myself clear? What did you think to gain by involving our grandfather? I make my own decisions. You should know that by now.'

'Enough, Alexis.' His grandfather took an involuntary step forward. 'Mariana was right to come to me. Am I not the head of the family? She was distressed, confused; she understood, as you apparently do not, that I was the obvious person to be involved.'

Alex lifted his shoulders. 'What is done cannot be undone.'

'I disagree.' The old man hunched his shoulders. 'Alexis, Mariana has told me what happened. She has explained the misunderstanding——'

'There was no misunderstanding,' declared Alex harshly, but his grandfather wasn't listening to him.

'You were tired. Things are not always what they seem. You did not give her a chance to explain——'

'No explanation was necessary,' retorted Alex, with a shrug. 'I am not blind, or stupid. I know what I saw.'

'Alexis!'

His name came from Mariana's lips, an unmistakable plea for understanding, and Rachel, who had heard enough and didn't want to hear any more, shifted nervously towards the door. She was the intruder here, they knew it and she knew it, and what had begun as a reluctant adventure was fast becoming something much more serious, something she didn't want to be a part of.

'Stay!' Alex had noticed her attempted withdrawal,

and now he turned and came back to her side. 'Don't
go,' he added softly, touching an errant curl at her
temple, and Mariana uttered a disgusted sound at this
evidence of their intimacy.

'Alex——' Rachel began, only to have her words
overridden by his grandfather's anger:

*'Bon sang,'* he snapped violently, 'have you no respect
for the woman you are going to marry, Alexis? In the
name of Mohammed, have you no shame?'

There was a moment's pregnant silence after this
imprecation, and Rachel found herself gazing into
Alex's eyes with unconcealed accusation. She was to be
his wife! Mariana was his fiancée. That was what this
charade was all about. Mariana had evidently done
something to annoy him, and he had been using her to
punish the other girl.

'Is—is that true?' she got out presently, her throat so
dry she could hardly articulate the words, and seizing
his opportunity Sheik Ibrahim ibn Rachid stepped
arrogantly towards them.

'Of course it is true,' he snarled. 'Why else do you
think my grandson has brought you here? This
conversation does not concern you, yet Alexis wanted
you to hear it; or more accurately, he wanted Mariana
to see you. It is a fine revenge he has planned, and one
which hurts everyone but himself.'

Rachel quivered. 'Is this true?' she asked, dragging
her gaze from the old Arab's contemptuous features,
and Alex, who only moments before had been sharing
an intimacy with her, folded his arms. He looked
peculiarly Arab himself in that moment, she realised
inconsequently, her heart palpitating wildly in these
moments of stress. Was it true what his grandfather had
said? Was he seeking revenge? And if so, why had he
chosen her for his victim?

'He will not answer you, because he cannot,' declared
the old man, before Alex spoke. 'Why do you doubt
me? Sheik Ibrahim ibn Rachid does not deal in lies!'

'It is true, then.' Rachel moistened her lips with an
unconsciously provocative tongue. A terrible sense of
imminent disaster was gripping her, and she desperately

wanted to get away. 'I—did suspect——' She broke off.
'If you'll excuse me——'

'Not yet.' Alex broke his silence to lay a detaining hand
on her sleeve. 'Don't leave me—I have to talk to you.'

She shook off his fingers, turning unsteadily towards
the door. 'I think we've talked long enough,' she said,
noticing he had made no attempt to deny his
grandfather's words. 'Excuse me, but I want to go
home. Will you please ask Karim to give me my coat?'

The curved staircase took her down to the ground
floor and although she was aware that Alex had
followed her, she did not look back. Karim appeared as
usual, as if summoned by an unseen hand, but after
giving him his instructions, Alex made one final attempt
to reason with her.

'Won't you change your mind?' he exhorted, as
Karim was helping her on with her jacket, but Rachel
only shook her head. 'There is still the matter of the
fifty thousand pounds to be discussed,' he reminded her
harshly, using any means in his power to make her stay,
and her pale face hollowed at this indefensible attack.

'I'm sorry if you don't think you've had value for
money,' she said tremulously as Karim politely
withdrew. 'As I said earlier, I'll find some means to pay
you back. Even if it means using my body as you've
succeeded in using it!'

'Don't say that!'

His hand on her shoulder spun her round to face
him, and she saw the raw passion burning in his eyes.
For several tense seconds they just stared at one
another, and then, with a muffled groan, he jerked her
into his arms and his mouth fastened brutally over hers.

In spite of her anger and resentment, and humiliation,
Rachel could not deny the surge of emotion that
drowned out all other feelings. The angry caress
deepened and lengthened, her response causing Alex to
moan deep in his throat as her lissom form arched
against him, seeking a remembered intimacy.

'If you let anyone else touch you, I'll kill you!' he
muttered, against the curve of her ear, and his savage
words reminded her of why he had taken her innocence.

With a supreme effort she tore herself out of his arms, and although she knew she could not have got away unless he had intended her to do so, she flung open the front door and made her escape. The door closed heavily behind her, but she did not look back. It could have been Karim who attended to the task, or it could have been Alex's answer to her defiance.

## CHAPTER NINE

On Tuesday morning, Sophie was full of excitement over what had happened the night before. 'No wonder poor old Roger's got the push!' she exclaimed. 'You wouldn't catch me putting up with a TR7 if I could have a Lamborghini!'

'Sophie, the kind of car a man drives means nothing, absolutely nothing,' retorted Rachel heavily. 'And in any case, I wish you wouldn't talk about Alex Roche. He—he means nothing to me.'

Sophie regarded her intently. 'Doesn't he? That wasn't my impression.'

'What do you mean?'

'Well . . .' Sophie made a little moue with her lips, 'you didn't really like me talking to him, did you? I could positively feel the vibes emanating from the back of the car. If I didn't know you better, I'd have said you were jealous, Rachel.' She paused. 'But I could be wrong.'

'You are.' Rachel determinedly inserted another piece of paper into her typewriter. 'Even so, I'd be grateful if you didn't discuss this around the office.'

'Okay.' Sophie sauntered towards the door. 'I suppose you're afraid it will reach Roger's ears, aren't you? Are you and he likely to get back together again?'

'Who knows?' Rachel could think of nothing less likely, but she was not about to tell Sophie that. 'Now, I must get on—really. Mr Black is waiting to sign these letters before he goes to court.'

As soon as Sophie left the office, however, Rachel put her elbows on the desk and slumped forward, her chin resting in her palms. The letters were not urgent, but even if they had been, she doubted she could have kept to a schedule this morning. She felt terrible—sick and headachy, and tired, due no doubt to the fact that she had hardly slept a wink the night before. She felt shattered, mentally and physically, and it didn't help to remember that Roger had never made her feel this way. Even when they split up, she had not experienced such a sense of devastation; only a kind of emptiness that what had been planned was no longer to take place. Roger had been a habit, she reflected realistically; a regular part of her life, to which she had become accustomed.

Alex was not like that. There was nothing habitual about him. On the contrary, he was totally unpredictable; and ruthless, when it came to getting what he wanted. He had used her, as he had no doubt used Mariana, but whereas his cousin had had some reason to trust him, she had not. Was that why she had tried to avoid him, right from the beginning? Because she had known, even then, that he could destroy her in a way Roger never could?

She sighed. Jane had known something was wrong as soon as she arrived home the night before, but for once, she had been unable to confide in the other girl. What had happened had still been so brutally fresh in her mind, and the idea of confessing to anyone what a fool she had been was anathema to her. Instead, she had made up some story about going out for supper with one of the other girls, and left Jane to speculate why such an innocent occasion should have left her looking so distraught.

She didn't know what the other girl had thought about the cut on her hand. Her explanation that she had broken a cup in the office had not been convincing, and Jane must have known that Rachel would not have mentioned it if her friend had not noticed the elastic strips. Which was totally out of keeping with their usual openness with one another.

This morning there had been more of the same, and

Rachel knew she hadn't imagined the faintly strained atmosphere between them at the breakfast table. Her sleepless night had told in dark circles around her eyes and a certain lethargy in her walk, and it had been an effort to speak normally when she felt so utterly depressed.

How could she have done it? she asked herself for the umpteenth time. She, who had never even indulged in heavy petting with anyone other than Roger, and then she had always been in control of her emotions. How could she have allowed Alex to undress her, to undress himself, to take her to his bed with all the abandon of an experienced woman? It hardly seemed possible—but it was; she knew she was different, if only because of the unfamiliar aches in muscles never used before.

Her pulses quickened in spite of herself, and almost absently she allowed her arms to brush against her breasts. The nipples were sore, tender after the passionate assault Alex had made upon them, but even that slight abrasion was enough to evoke memories she would rather forget. Memories of Alex nuzzling her neck with his lips, tracing the outline of her ear with his tongue, imprisoning her beneath him, as he sought that final consummation . . .

'Dreaming, Rachel? I thought you were too sensible for that.'

Peter Rennison's teasing voice made her start, and she looked up in some embarrassment to find the young solicitor standing by her desk. 'I'm sorry,' she murmured, colouring, as she quickly rolled the paper down into her typewriter. 'I—er—I've got a bit of a headache. Perhaps I'm getting a cold.'

Peter Rennison regarded her consideringly. 'You don't look as if you're getting a cold to me,' he remarked. 'But you do look as if you've been burning the candle at both ends.'

Rachel bent her head. 'Did you want something Mr Rennison? Mr Black's leaving for court in—fifteen minutes.'

'Well, I did want to have a word with him, but it's not urgent.' The man grimaced. 'It can wait.' He paused, and then added: 'What's this I hear about you and Sophie getting into an expensive sports car yesterday evening? Has young Tennant got herself a wealthy admirer? Or—heaven forfend!—have you actually given old Roger the elbow?'

She sighed. 'News travels fast, doesn't it? Just because a—family friend gave Sophie and me a lift home, the grapevine is working overtime.'

'A family friend, eh?' Peter Rennison pulled a wry face. 'About thirty, and driving a Lamborghini Countach! What kind of family friend is that?'

Rachel looked up at him frustratedly. 'Who told you?'

'Who do you think?'

She shook her head. 'She said she wouldn't——' She broke off impatiently. 'Oh, what does it matter? You'll all know soon enough. Roger and I have split up.'

'Over the guy in the Lamborghini?'

'No!' Rachel realised belatedly how damning her words had been. 'I—what exactly did Sophie say?'

Peter endeavoured to be serious. 'Well, she did tell me in confidence,' he explained, and then, responding to Rachel's aggravated glare, he added: 'She said more or less what you've said . . .'

'Except?'

He sighed. 'Except that she seems to think you've fallen for this other chap.'

'Oh!'

'I didn't believe it,' he assured her fervently. 'And I can tell, you've taken this hard.' He paused. 'So how about joining me for a meal after work this evening? I promise I won't mention Roger or the other fellow. We can just have a nice cosy dinner for two.'

Rachel shook her head. 'Is that why you came here? To ask me for a date?' she demanded frustratedly. 'Did you know Mr Black was due in court this morning?'

He made a resigned gesture. 'Maybe.'

'Oh, Peter!' She expelled her breath wearily. 'I thought we'd had all this out months ago.'

'I thought you might welcome a shoulder to cry on,' he replied defensively. 'I don't expect you to fall into my arms. But—well, I care about you, and I'd like to help.'

Rachel sighed. This kind of complication was something she could do well without, but trying to be charitable, she made her refusal. 'I can't go out with you, Peter,' she said carefully. 'It was kind of you to think of me, but really, I'll be okay. Just give me a little time.'

'All right.' He was disappointed, but this time he took his dismissal in good part. Perhaps he had the idea that sooner or later she might be glad to change her mind, Rachel reflected ruefully. He must suspect, as much as she had, that men who drove expensive sports cars did not usually spare much time for common-or-garden office girls.

There was still the problem of her father to face, however, and with this thought in mind, she picked up the phone and asked for an outside line. Her father's office was near the Surrey Docks, but getting no reply from there, she rang his apartment.

His housekeeper, Mrs Webster, answered her call. 'I'm afraid your father's not here, Miss Fleming,' she responded to Rachel's inquiry. 'He's away—on business. I'm not sure when he'll be back.'

'Away?' Rachel was astounded. 'Away where?'

'I'm not sure, miss. I think he mentioned—the Gulf, would that be right?'

'The gulf?' Rachel blinked, and then a numbing thought struck her. 'Do you mean—the Persian Gulf?'

'Your guess is as good as mine, Miss Fleming. I just know he packed up and left yesterday morning. He said he didn't know when he'd be back!'

She gasped. 'I see.'

'Didn't he tell you, miss?' Mrs Webster sounded curious now, as if this might be a juicy piece of gossip to deliver to her married daughter, and Rachel quickly ironed over the cracks.

'Well, he did say he was going—on a business trip,' she lied, despising herself as she did so. 'I—just didn't expect him to go yesterday, that's all.'

'I see, miss.'

'I must have misunderstood what he said,' Rachel added, wanting to finish this call as quickly as possible. 'Er—thank you, Mrs Webster. I'll speak to him later.'

With her hand still resting on the replaced receiver, she stared blankly into space. Her father had gone away, she told herself silently. He had actually gone away without telling her. And to the Persian Gulf of all places! But why? *Why?*

It had to have something to do with Alex Roche, she decided flatly. There was no other alternative. But for what earthly reason could he have sent her father to the Middle East, without even mentioning it to her? She hunched her shoulders. Of course, he had wanted to talk to her last night, she acknowledged unwillingly. And about her father, or so he had said. But what she found hardest to bear was the knowledge that her father could disappear without even telling her that his debts had been settled, when he must know that some payment would be exacted.

The phone ringing again under her fingers gave her a nasty start, but she lifted the receiver swiftly, half hoping her thoughts had generated a response. But it was a call for Mr Black, and she put it through absently, forgetting in her confusion that her boss had left for Bow Street.

It was fortunate that Mr Black did spend most of the day out of the office. Rachel found it almost impossible to concentrate, and several times she picked up the phone to ring Alex Roche's house and put it down again. She had found his number in the directory; but although anger and bewilderment urged her to demand an explanation, pain and humiliation kept her silent. How could she ring him? she asked herself bitterly. How could she speak to him again after what had happened? No matter how agonising the decision might be, she had determined never to see him again, and if he had any decency, he would respect her feelings.

At lunchtime, she left the building deliberately, taking a bus to Oxford Street and spending the remainder of the time wandering through the large department stores that gave the street its reputation.

She bought little, only a couple of pairs of tights and a well-advertised skin conditioner, and arrived back at Fetter Lane soon after half past one.

'You had a visitor, miss,' Mr Hodges told her as she passed his cubbyhole on the ground floor, and Rachel's nerves tightened. 'It was that gentleman what came once before,' he added, leaning over his counter. 'Said his name was Roche, is that right? Tall bloke, with fair hair.'

She pressed the carrier containing her purchases to her. 'I—what did he want, Mr Hodges? Did he say?'

'He said to give you this,' declared the old caretaker, pulling open a drawer and extracting a white card. 'There's a note on the back. Something about his chauffeur coming round to pick you up from work.'

Rachel's face burned. The card was a simple business card, with Alex's name and address on it. On the rear, as Mr Hodges had paraphrased, were the words: 'I will see you this evening. My driver will call for you at five o'clock.'

'Thank you.' She thrust the card into her pocket and hurried up the stairs. She had been wise to leave the building at lunchtime. Alex Roche had no discretion where she was concerned. And no respect, she added painfully, tossing the hated card into the litter bin.

During the afternoon, she wondered uneasily what she should do. It was obvious that Alex was sending Hassim to apprehend her, as he had done once before, and the idea that he should think he could manipulate her without thought for her feelings filled her with indignation and mortification. She was not his toy, she thought angrily. Whatever the situation might be in his own country—and she suspected now that that country must be Bahdan—he must be made to see he could not treat her like some bought—*concubine*!

With some reluctance she phoned Peter Rennison's office about four o'clock. 'You know—you know what you said about—well, about having a meal after work,' she ventured, hating the pretence. 'I—are you still interested?'

'Are you kidding?' Peter sounded delighted. 'Do you mean to tell me you're accepting?'

Rachel sighed. 'For a meal only,' she insisted. 'No strings.'

'No strings,' he agreed eagerly. 'What time do you usually leave? Five o'clock?'

'Make it half past,'she said quickly, deciding that Hassim would get tired of waiting long before that time. 'You pass my office on your way out. I'll be waiting.'

'Fine.'

Peter approved the arrangement, and Rachel replaced the receiver. Almost immediately, she had misgivings, not least the knowledge that she was taking advantage of a married man. But it was just an innocent engagement, she consoled herself firmly. It wasn't as if she was trying to take Peter away from his wife. On the contrary, he would be safer with her than with some other, less conscientious, female. She wanted his company, nothing else. With Hassim, his protection didn't come into it.

At five o'clock she rang Jane and explained that she was having meal with one of the staff from the office.

'Male or female?' asked Jane flatly, still in the same mood as the morning, and Rachel sighed.

'Male,' she admitted unwillingly. 'But it's not what you think. We're just—friends, that's all. No emotional attachments.'

'Okay.' Jane accepted her explanation. 'I'll see you later, then. What time will you be home?'

'Oh, soon after eight, I should think,' responded Rachel swiftly, and rang off before her friend could ask who her date was.

She was applying a pale mauve eyeshadow to her lids when her office door opened. It was only about a quarter past five, and she looked up in surprise. 'You're early——' she was beginning, when her voice faltered unsteadily. 'You!' she breathed. 'What are you doing here? I thought you said—Hassim would—would pick me up.'

'It's just as well I decided to come myself, then, isn't it?' Alex averred sardonically, advancing into the room on suede-booted feet. In a dark blue mohair jacket and close-fitting corded pants, he looked lean and powerful, and unmistakably aggressive, his dark intense features mirroring his impatience. 'Why are you still in the office?' he asked, as she closed the box containing her eyeshadow and replaced it in her handbag. 'No, don't tell me. You're waiting for Hassim to go away. You really are transparent, Rachel. Now, get your jacket and let's go.'

'No.' Rachel pushed back her chair and got to her feet, unable to remain at such a disadvantage. 'I can't go with you. I—I've got a date.'

'Like hell you have!' Alex gazed at her angrily. 'Who is it? Not Harrington again? I thought I'd got rid of him!'

Rachel didn't stop to answer this outrageous statement. 'No,' she declared stiffly, 'It's not Roger. It's someone else—someone from the office. Now, will you please go. He'll be here any minute.'

'So that was what you meant when——' Alex broke off, and sucked in his breath. 'We're wasting time. Let's go. I have no intention of leaving here without you.'

Rachel gasped. 'How dare you!'

'What do you mean—how dare I?'

'After last night——'

'Yes? After last night?'

She caught her breath. 'You have no shame, do you?'

'Oh, not that again!' Alex rolled his eyes heavenward. 'Look, I don't want to argue with you. Where's your coat? Or did you come to work like that?' He eyed her plain white blouse and pleated skirt without expression. 'Rachel, don't keep me waiting.'

'You don't listen very well, do you?' She bent to stuff her handkerchief into her bag, too, avoiding his disturbing eyes. 'I'm not going with you. I'm having dinner with someone else. Go—go and spend your time with your fiancée. I'm quite sure your grandfather doesn't know you're here.'

'*Mon Dieu*, you would try the patience of a saint!' he snarled, sweeping her handbag to the floor with a savage gesture. 'Did I not make myself clear? You're coming with me.' He paused. 'Or would you rather take the chance that I might call in your father's markers?'

Rachel looked at him then, her eyes wide and tormented, and as if unable to meet that accusing gaze, he bent to gather the scattered contents of her bag together again.

*'Don't!'*

She bent, too, pushing his hands aside. But instead of obeying her, they fastened round her wrists, drawing her to her feet to face him, and she turned her face aside from his urgent pleas.

'Rachel!' he muttered. 'I didn't mean it. But, God help me, you make me say these things! Now, will you please stop wasting time!'

She steeled her features. 'You're—making me go with you then?'

*'Bon sang,* I'm *asking* you to come with me!' he snapped.

'As you *asked* my father to go to the Middle East, I suppose,' she countered. 'Without letting him speak to me first!'

Alex's face lost all expression. 'That was his decision.'

'I don't believe you.'

'That's your prerogative. It is the truth, nevertheless.'

'But *why* have you sent him away? *Where* have you sent him?'

'That is something we can discuss tonight.'

'And if I refuse?'

'Don't refuse.'

Rachel quivered. 'What about Mariana? Will she be joining us?'

Alex closed his eyes for a moment now. 'No,' he said flatly, opening them again. 'No, Mariana will not be joining us.'

'How can you be sure? Your grandfather said——'

'My grandfather is not my keeper,' he retorted harshly.

'But Mariana is your fiancée.'

His features stiffened. 'She was.'

'Was?'

'Yes, *was.*' He expelled his breath wearily. 'Now, will you come with me?'

Rachel bent her head. 'Why? Why can't we talk about my father here?'

'Why do you think?' He took a deep breath. 'I wish to make love to you, of course. In spite of your behaviour, I find I still want you. Does that answer your question?'

Rachel fumbled for her handbag. 'You—*want*—me?'

'Yes.' Alex was growing restless. 'Have I left you in any doubt? *Nom de Dieu*, what more do you want me to say?'

*That you love me, perhaps,* thought Rachel crazily, and then squashed the idea. She didn't love him, and she doubted Alex had ever loved anyone, even Mariana, although evidently she had once enjoyed his favour. But she had done something to upset him. Not all the nuances of that interchange last evening had gone over Rachel's head. Somehow, Mariana had blotted her copybook, and she, Rachel, was being used as a means of revenge. *But why her?*

The door opening behind them prevented her from making any response, however. Peter Rennison walked into the office with an air of confidence, only to halt in some confusion at the sight of the other man.

'Are you ready, Rachel?' he asked awkwardly, clearly aware of the tenseness of the atmosphere, and Rachel side-stepped Alex to make a rueful apology.

'Almost,' she said, securing the clip of her bag, but Alex's hand on her shoulder quelled her intention to escape him.

'No, she's not,' he said, almost pleasantly, only the sudden heightening of his accent revealing his innermost feelings. 'I'm afraid Rachel won't be joining you after all. She has a—previous engagement.'

'Is this true, Rachel?' Peter asked, as her face turned scarlet with embarrassment, and although she wanted to deny Alex's words, the grip of his fingers was both possessive and threatening.

'Oh—yes, I'm sorry, Peter,' she got out uncomfortably. 'I—I had forgotten——' She broke off. 'I don't know what to say.'

'You're all right, aren't you?' Peter eyed the other man with some misgivings. 'There's no—problem?'

'No problem,' echoed Alex smoothly, but Peter was still not convinced.

'Just now,' he said slowly, 'just now you said you were almost ready. Then you seemed to change your mind. You do want to go with—with this chap, don't you?'

'Well, I——'

'Perhaps you'd better leave well alone,' remarked Alex glacially. His eyes narrowed. 'Believe me, you would regret the alternative.'

His casual words were delivered quite politely, but Rachel sensed the vein of steel running through them. Alex would be a formidable adversary, even without his bodyguard, and she had no doubt that Hassim was hanging about somewhere close at hand. She couldn't let Peter get involved on her behalf. It just wasn't fair.

'Really, Peter,' she exclaimed, putting a note of lightness into her voice, 'I'm fine, honestly. And I really am sorry about tonight. Some other time, perhaps.'

Peter hesitated. 'Well—if you're sure.' Although he was a tall man himself, he did not possess Alex's lithe muscular build. Office work had taken its toll, and discretion was quickly getting the better part of valour. 'Okay, I'll see you tomorrow, then. Goodnight.'

'Goodnight.'

Rachel remained where she was until Peter had left the room, but then she turned on Alex like a veritable virago. 'How could you!' she choked. 'How could you humiliate me like that! Oh, why don't you go away and leave me alone? I hate you! *I hate you!*'

Alex's face darkened, his jaw hardening perceptibly. 'Well, regrettably, that is something you are going to have to learn to live with—at least, for the next couple of weeks,' he remarked harshly. 'I have to return to Bahdan, and you are coming with me. Just to prove to my grandfather that I mean what I say!'

# CHAPTER TEN

RACHEL had never travelled on a private plane before. She had seen them, of course, on film and on television, in the kind of glossy soap operas that were so popular at the moment. But she had never expected to ride in one. Her experience of aircraft had been limited to charter flights at holiday time, whose standard of service was nothing like that to which she was presently becoming accustomed, but although she could not fault it, she did not feel at ease.

The aeroplane was a Boeing, one of several owned by his grandfather, or so Alex had informed her, in the indifferent tones he had adopted since their confrontation at the office. Its interior was designed to resemble a comfortable lounge, with armchairs and occasional tables, and there was a desk, and hi-fi equipment, and a comprehensive communications system, capable of contacting any part of the world. The staff on board were all from Bahdan—with the exception of the pilot, who was French—and Rachel suspected she should have resisted more strongly before stepping so recklessly into the unknown.

But what could she have done? she asked herself yet again, staring blindly out of the window. Alex had given her no choice; he had given her an ultimatum; and had she chosen to ignore it, her father could have found himself in prison.

Nevertheless, Jane still thought she was mad to agree to such a trip. 'How do you know what he really wants?' she had demanded, when Rachel told her what she was going to do. 'Your father may not even be in Bahdan. And do you know for certain that he's paid that man off?'

'He showed me the slip,' replied Rachel dully, flopping down on to the couch. 'He brought it to the office this afternoon. Just to make sure I couldn't—

refuse. I don't know what Mr Black's going to say when he finds out I want my holiday moving forward by so many weeks.'

Jane sighed. 'But I don't understand. Why you? Isn't this going to jeopardise any chance of you and Roger getting back together again?'

Rachel coloured, bending her head. 'I don't think that's likely, in any case, Jane,' she mumbled, and the other girl frowned.

'You haven't—fallen for this Frenchman, have you?' she exclaimed suspiciously. 'Oh, Rachel, be careful! You don't know anything about him.'

'No.' Rachel was loath to discuss Alex with her friend, but as she looked up and found Jane's anxious eyes upon her, her courage deserted her. 'I don't know,' she said now, moistening her dry lips. 'I do find him—attractive. But I despise him for what he's forcing me to do.'

'For—asking you to pretend to be his fiancée?' Jane ventured slowly, and Rachel closed her eyes.

'It's not quite like that,' she admitted huskily. 'Oh, you might as well know, I was with him last night, not working late, as I told you. We—we went to his house. For—for supper.'

Jane shook her head. 'I suspected as much. Why didn't you tell me? What were you afraid I'd say?'

'I don't know.' Rachel opened her eyes again. 'I—I guess—oh, we had a row, and I suppose I felt too—upset—to discuss it with you.'

'Over this trip to Bahdan?'

'Oh, no, not that. I didn't know about that until today,' exclaimed Rachel revealingly, and then sighed. 'Something happened. I met his grandfather. And—and his ex-fiancée. They upset me. I suppose that was what it was.'

Jane looked sceptical, but for the life of her, Rachel could not confess what had really happened. How could she tell her friend she had gone to bed with a man she said she despised? How could she admit to acting like a fool, when all he wanted was to revenge himself on Mariana Rachid?

'So—who is his grandfather?' Jane asked. 'And how did he upset you?'

'He's an Arab, actually,' said Rachel, avoiding Jane's startled eyes. 'Sheik Abrahim ibn Rachid, or some such name.' She paused. 'He was angry because Alex had apparently broken up with his fiancée.'

'Who was there too?'

'Yes. Mariana. Apparently she's Alex's cousin.'

'I see.' Jane perched on the arm of a chair. 'Curiouser and curiouser.'

Rachel lifted her shoulders. ·'You don't approve.'

'Did you expect me to?'

'No.' Rachel was honest. 'So now you know.'

'Do I?' Jane regarded her friend wryly. 'Exactly what are you going to Bahdan as? His fiancée—or his——?'

She broke off, but Rachel knew exactly what she had been going to say, and her cheeks burned anew. 'I'm going because I have no choice,' she averred firmly. 'What else can I do?'

'Well, I hate to say this, but if you really are going for your father's sake, I'd think very carefully before doing anything rash. I mean—when has he ever been around when you needed him? If it wasn't for him, you might still be engaged to Roger.'

Rachel shook her head. 'I have to go.'

'Whatever this man Roche may expect of you?'

'What do you mean?'

'You *know* what I mean, Rachel. Alex Roche isn't just taking you along for the ride, is he?'

Rachel tilted her head back to look up at the concealed lighting that circled the cabin of the aircraft. That had been almost a week ago now, and remembering Jane's words she was uncomfortably reminded of her own fears in that connection. It was all very well telling herself that she despised the man seated in the chair opposite, but said in cold blood, her words lacked conviction. Just because he had allowed her to evade him for the past five days, while she organised her replacement at the office and made the necessary arrangements at home, it did not mean he could be relied upon to leave her alone. He still found her physically desirable—the occasional predatory gleam in his eyes told her that—and she was very much afraid of his power over her, and of how vulnerable she would be if he chose to exercise it.

With a mouthwatering lunch disposed of, Alex left his seat to come and join her, squatting on his haunches beside her until one of the stewards hastily produced a cushioned footstool for him to use. 'You didn't enjoy the food?' he queried, after giving the obsequious servant an impatient nod of thanks, and Rachel pressed her hands together in her lap as his muscled knee brushed hers.

'I wasn't hungry,' she said, surprised that he had noticed how little she had eaten. She omitted to mention the fact that her appetite had suffered since the anticipation of this trip, and Alex frowned consideringly.

'It wasn't to your taste?' he persisted. 'French food can be overly rich, I know. Are you sure there's nothing you would like instead? Marcel would be happy to prepare a simpler meal.'

'It wasn't anything to do with the food,' said Rachel, turning her face away. 'How long does this flight take? Is—is your grandfather's home far from the airport?'

Alex hesitated, and then, getting to his feet, he kicked the footstool aside. 'The flight should take approximately six hours,' he replied shortly. 'As to where my grandfather lives, you will learn that soon enough.'

Rachel took a deep breath, still not looking at him, and as if losing patience, he came down on the arm of her chair. 'What's the matter?' he demanded harshly. 'Is this journey so abhorrent to you?' He put his hand beneath her chin, turning her resistently to face him. 'What can I say to reassure you? You are acting as if I forced you on to the plane!'

'And didn't you?'

Her eyes challenged his, and reluctantly his features softened. 'Only indirectly,' he told her flatly. 'You could have refused to come.'

'And have you send my father to prison?' she

countered, her blue eyes sparkling with indignant fire. 'Come on, Alex, let's not be unrealistic. You made the situation—painfully clear.'

He sighed. 'You really believe I would have gone ahead with it?'

'Yes, I really believe you would have gone ahead with it,' she echoed. 'Or perhaps you cut off hands in your country, if someone gets irretrievably into debt.'

'In my country.' Alex inclined his head.

'Yes—Bahdan, or whatever you call it. Doesn't your religion call for the punishment to fit the crime, or something?'

Alex's mouth compressed. 'As I recall it, Christians are required to turn the other cheek, aren't they?' he remarked drily. 'Or am I wrong?'

Rachel gazed up at him. 'You're—a Christian?'

'What did you expect?'

She flushed. 'I don't know—a Muslim, I suppose. Isn't that what your grandfather is?'

'The old man may be many things,' declared Alex, with a shrug. 'I am not.'

'You're—his flesh and blood, aren't you?' she exclaimed, realising, as she did so, how ludicrous it seemed to describe someone with hair of that colour as an Arab, and Alex stiffened.

'I do have my grandfather's blood in my veins,' he agreed, his hand falling away from her quivering cheek. 'But my father is French, and I am considered to be of dual nationality.'

Rachel blinked. 'Your father is French?'

'That's right.'

'And your mother?'

'My grandfather's daughter, as you would expect.' Alex rose abruptly to his feet. 'I did not realise it would make such a difference.'

Rachel blinked. 'What do you mean?'

'I should have thought that was obvious.' His nostrils flared, ever so slightly. 'Did you really think you could hide your aversion from me?'

'I don't know what you're talking about.' She was confused.

'I think you do.' Alex pushed his balled fists into the
pockets of his leather jacket. 'You can no longer bear me
to touch you, can you? I should have guessed, after the
way you behaved at your office. Forgive me if I've been
obtuse. I misunderstood the reasons for your hostility.'

'That's not true!' Rachel got to her feet now, swaying
slightly as the aircraft banked to adjust its course. 'I
don't care who your father is—or your grandfather!'

'No?' His eyes narrowed. 'Yet you can't deny you've
changed towards me.'

'Changed towards you?' She gazed at him. 'You
know why.'

'Do I?'

'Yes, damn you, you do!' she exclaimed, her voice
rising and attracting the attention of the remaining
cabin steward. 'You lied to me. You—let me think you
were—attracted to me, but you weren't!' She cast the
steward a frustrated glance, but he didn't take the hint.
'You simply wanted someone to—to appease your ego!'

'That's your summation of the situation, is it?'
Clearly Alex had no compunction about speaking in the
servant's presence. 'And what if I don't agree with you?
What if I told you you were wrong?'

'I wouldn't believe you.'

Rachel turned her back on him, realising as she did
so, she was falling into his trap yet again. By forcing her
to defend herself, he had made her say things she would
rather not have said, and she expelled her breath
unsteadily when his hands descended on her shoulders.

'Then that's too bad,' he drawled, his teeth grazing
the side of her neck. 'Because I still want you—
whatever the reason.'

'*Alex——*'

She was intensely conscious of their audience, and as
if pandering to her reticence, he lifted his head to issue a
curt dismissal. 'You shouldn't let Mohammid's presence
trouble you,' he added, his hands sliding possessively
over the full swell of her breasts, outlined beneath the
thin fabric of her shirt. 'He's quite discreet, I assure
you. And he wouldn't do anything to arouse my
grandfather's ill-will.'

Rachel tore herself away from him, hurriedly refastening the buttons he had loosened. 'You mean— you wouldn't care if he was still watching us?' she choked, and Alex uttered an impatient imprecation.

'Have I offended your tender sensibilities?' he asked tautly. 'But then I am half Arab, am I not? And why should I object if the man gets some pleasure from it?'

'I don't believe you.' Rachel stared at him with horrified eyes. 'You don't mean that. You're just— trying to shock me.'

'Am I?' Alex's hot glance raked her quivering figure. 'And what if I wasn't? What if I am as—barbaric—as my maternal forebears? What then?'

Rachel sought the armchair behind her. 'I'd really rather not talk about it,' she said, desperate to regain some control over her emotions, and with a muffled imprecation he left her, disappearing through the door into the pilot's cabin.

The journey was long and nerveracking. Deprived of Alex's company, Rachel found she quickly regretted his departure, her troubled thoughts too active to allow her to rest. Nevertheless, she did doze towards the end of the afternoon, waking with a start when the steward set a tray of tea before her.

'You wish milk—or lemon?' he queried, kneeling beside her to attend to her needs, and Rachel shook her head.

'No. I mean—I'll do it,' she said, struggling up in her seat, and with a gesture of acquiescence the man bowed and withdrew.

'We have approximately thirty minutes before landing,' Alex remarked expressionlessly, and looking up, Rachel saw he was standing by the forward bulkhead. She wondered how long he had been there, watching her as she slept, and for the first time she hoped she didn't snore in her sleep.

'I—where do we land?' she asked, helping herself to a morsel of some spicy concoction and finding it very much to her liking. She had decided, before she fell asleep, that there was no point in refusing to speak to him, and her tone was politely enquiring as she met his studied gaze.

'We land at Bahdan,' he said, after a moment. 'The country is too small to support two airports. Or two cities either.'

Rachel licked a crumb from her lips. 'The city is called Bahdan, too?'

'As you say.'

Sipping her tea, she endeavoured to remain calm, but now that they were nearing their destination, her nerves could not be denied. 'And—and will I see my father tonight?' she asked, swallowing convulsively.

'Your father is not in Bahdan,' essayed Alex flatly, and Rachel, who had clung to this hope throughout the flight, stared at him disbelievingly.

'But—you said——'

'Yes? What did I say? Did I tell you your father was in Bahdan?'

'But I assumed——'

'The Middle East covers a vast area, Rachel.'

'But—his housekeeper said he had gone to the—the Gulf!'

'What gulf?' Alex was annoyingly obtuse. 'The Gulf of Aden; the Gulf of Oman; the Persian Gulf?'

Rachel sighed. 'Stop baiting me. Where is he?'

Alex hesitated, then he shrugged. 'I would guess he is somewhere in the United Arab Emirates.'

'But why?'

'You were not prepared to listen to me before,' he reminded her, and she bent her head.

'You've got what you want, haven't you?' she exclaimed bitterly. 'At least have the decency to explain what my father's doing.'

Alex moved away from the bulkhead to stand looking out of the window. 'I hope he is signing some contracts to aid that ailing company of his,' he replied, without expression. 'As I now own a part of Fleming Engineering, I expect to collect on my investment.'

Rachel gazed at the uncompromising width of his shoulders. 'You mean—you advanced him that money on the strength of a partnership?' she exclaimed, her cup clattering noisily into its saucer. 'Then—then what am I doing here?'

'You?' He turned to survey her with humiliating intentness. 'I thought I had made your position perfectly clear: You are here because I want you here. End of story.'

As the plane made its approach to the airport at Bahdan, Rachel hardly noticed the vast expanses of desert surrounding the city on three sides. She didn't see the skyline, set about with the tall modern business blocks that had sprung up since the oil boom. She was scarcely aware of the aircraft banking as it came in to land, or the smooth descent that followed it. Even when the wheels hit the tarmac, she made no reaction, and Alex, unfastening his safety-belt, came to stand over her with some impatience.

'We've landed,' he said unnecessarily, waving the attentive steward away. 'You are in my country now. Or rather, my grandfather's.'

'I want to go home.' Rachel looked up at him with eyes that sparked fire even though the flames were doused by her tears. 'You've brought me here under false pretences. Please take me back.'

'Eventually,' said Alex, reaching forward and unsnapping her safety belt. 'But not yet. Not until I have convinced my grandfather I mean what I say.'

She pressed her lips together mutinously. 'And if I won't do it?'

He sighed. 'Don't make me force you. I could, quite easily. Not least because in this country—*my* country—there are no laws but mine.'

The plane had taxied to a standstill, and already the doors were being opened and a draught of air surged into the cabin. It was desert air, hot and dry, and impregnated with tiny grains of sand, that invaded Rachel's nose and mouth. It was her first experience of the wind that blew at intervals in this area, and she caught her breath in protest when it swept her hair across her face.

Three men had accompanied the draught of air into the cabin. Two were dressed in Western clothes, but the third wore a loose-fitting *djellabah*, and it was he who bowed low over Alex's hand. They all spoke in their own language, which was neither English nor French, and Rachel decided, in some amazement, that they were a kind of official welcoming party, sent to handle such mundane matters as Customs inspection and Immigration. Several covert looks were cast in her direction, and she shifted a little uncomfortably beneath their gaze. Was Alex right? she wondered uneasily. Was his word law in this God-forsaken place? For the first time she peered through the window with something akin to unwilling curiosity.

It was early evening, and darkness was fast enveloping the surrounds of the airport. All she could see was a stretch of tarmac, and the usual floodlit airport buildings, with several other aircraft parked in separate bays.

'Come along.'

Alex's hand at her elbow was suddenly compelling her up and out of her seat, and although her eyes challenged his, she did not resist. The alternative of remaining here with the welcoming committee was less than tolerable, and accepting the jacket of her corded pants suit from one of the ubiquitous stewards, she allowed Alex to propel her through the door and down the flight of steps outside.

The wind was unpleasant, whipping up grit from the tarmac into her eyes and forcing her to cling to Alex's hand like a lifeline. If this was an example of the climate of Bahdan, no wonder his mother had married a Frenchman, Rachel thought tensely, cannoning into Alex when he unexpectedly came to a standstill.

She saw at once why he had done so. A sleek cream limousine was parked at the foot of the steps, and a uniformed chauffeur had emerged to open the rear door for them. Rachel scrambled inside on to squashy leather upholstery, and gulped for breath gratefully in the air-conditioned luxury of the car. Alex got in beside her, and the door was securely closed, cocooning them in a private world bound by the glass partition that separated them from the driver.

'The sirocco,' remarked Alex drily, as she endeavoured to bring some order to the tangled beauty of her hair. 'One of the less attractive features of Bahdan.'

'The wind?' Rachel was too bemused to remember that only minutes before she had wanted to stay on the plane.

'The wind,' he agreed smoothly, and with indolent ease he settled himself back in his seat.

The limousine glided swiftly across the tarmac, through iron gates opened by another bowing official. Then they were out on the road that led away from the airport, its lights disappearing rapidly behind them.

Away to their right, Rachel could see more lights, and she guessed that was the city of Bahdan. But, to her surprise, they did not turn towards them, and the dusty road on which they were travelling swerved decidedly westward, away from the coastal plain. Within minutes, all signs of civilisation had disappeared, and her world was encompassed by the confines of the car.

Beyond the car's headlights, there was little to see. They seemed to be alone in a vacuum of scrubby trees and drifting sand, the uncanny howling of the wind across these open spaces causing her to glance at Alex with something like raw panic. In the shadowy darkness of the car his expression was unreadable, but becoming aware of her appraisal, he turned his head towards her, tilting it slightly as he surveyed her evident unease.

'We're almost there,' he remarked. 'I'm sorry it could not have been under more appealing circumstances, but don't worry. Tomorrow things will seem infinitely different.'

'Different—but not better,' muttered Rachel, pressing her unsteady lips together. 'How long am I expected to stay here? When will we be going home?'

'I was born here,' observed Alex carelessly. 'You could say this is my home.' He paused, and then, when her nerves were stretched to screaming pitch, he added: 'As to when we'll be going back to England—well, shall we say—in a week?'

'A week?' She drew an uneven breath. A week was not so long, she told herself with some relief. What could happen in a week, after all? So long as she kept her head . . .

The car was slowing at last, and ahead of them she

could see the glimmer of lights spreading in a wide arc.
As they drew nearer, the flickering lights resolved
themselves into lamps guarding a wrought iron
gateway, set in a sweeping curve of sand-coloured
stone. Faintly, she could smell mimosa, and as they
drove between the rapidly-opened gates, she saw a
windswept bouquet of the blossom espaliered against
the wall. It was just one of the aspects of a garden more
formal than any she had expected to find in the desert,
but her attention was already being drawn to the house
that lay within its fragrant seclusion.

The car came to a halt before an arched colonnade,
and beyond the sculptured columns shuttered windows
folded as far as the dim illumination would allow. It
was impossible to judge the building's size, but Rachel
could see a sloping roof with hanging eaves, and palm
trees bending in the wind beside the stone basin of a
fountain. At present, the fountain was not working, but
even if it had been, she could not have heard it. The
wind was deafening as it gusted along the cloistered
arches, finding its way into every cranny and whistling
through the eaves.

There was a moment when she wondered if anyone,
other than the lodge-keeper, had heard their approach,
but then a narrow door was opened, and several
servants dressed in the loose-fitting robes Rachel was
coming to recognise came hurrying out to greet them.
Like a group of holy men, she thought imaginatively as,
burnouses pulled up to protect their heads, they
hastened to the car, and Alex got out swiftly and turned
to offer her his hand.

'Inside,' he ordered, propelling her unceremoniously
across the paved courtyard and in under the columned
terrace. Without time to wonder how she looked or
what the other members of the household might be
thinking, Rachel found herself thrust into a richly
decorated entrance hall, the subdued lighting of which
was still distinctly dazzling to her unwary eyes. It was
hot, too, breathtakingly so after the controlled heating
in the car, and the air was thick with the scent of
sandalwood, like incense all around her.

*'Alexis!'*

Rachel scarcely had time to observe the beauty of her surroundings before a musical female voice arrested them. As she attempted to brush the grains of sand from her clothes, a girlish figure appeared beneath an arched doorway, and after only a momentary hesitation, approached Alex with evident delight.

*'Chéri!'* the woman exclaimed, bestowing a warm kiss upon his cheek, and Alex's arms closed surely about her.

*'Eh bien, la fille prodigue est revenue!'* he declared lazily, enfolding her closely, and meeting Alex's eyes across the other woman's head, Rachel felt an unwelcome surge of emotion stirring in the pit of her stomach. She wasn't jealous, she told herself fiercely, *she wasn't*. But she was, and damn him, he knew it.

After a few moments Alex drew back again, and the woman turned to give Rachel her first real glimpse of her features. She saw, to her astonishment, that the woman was older than she had at first assumed, and although she was wearing European dress, her features were unmistakably darker.

'So this is the young woman your grandfather is so angry over,' she remarked, lacquered nails lingering against the cream silk of Alex's shirt, and her accent only added to the attraction of her voice. Her dark eyes surveyed Rachel in unnerving appraisal, and then she laughed. 'Introduce me, *chéri*, or she will begin to think you have a harem here at Hajat.'

Alex's lips twisted with sudden mockery, but his features sobered as he made the introduction. 'This is Rachel Fleming, Maman,' he announced, with casual emphasis, and Rachel knew an overwhelming sense of relief. 'My mother,' he added unnecessarily. 'Madame Roche.'

'How do you do, Miss Fleming.'

Alex's mother came forward now, holding out her hand in greeting, and Rachel took it automatically. 'How do you do, *madame*,' she countered, uncomfortably aware of her dishevelment when compared to this elegant little woman. With small hands and feet, and a diminuative frame attractively encased in a pale grey gown that brushed her ankles, Madame Roche was the epitome of Paris *chic*, and judging by the ebony chignon coiled expertly at her nape, Alex certainly didn't get his hair colour from her.

'I am sure it has been a tiring journey,' the older woman was saying now, turning back to her son. 'Miss Fleming must be forming a less than attractive opinion of our country. Believe me,' this as she turned back to Rachel once again, 'tonight is not typical of nights in Bahdan. And it is so hot in here because we must keep the wind out.'

'I understand, *madame*.'

A brief smile came and went on Rachel's nervous face, but Alex chose not to support her. 'Rachel did not want to come to Bahdan in the first place, Maman,' he remarked with embarrassing candour. 'She wanted to stay in London.' His eyes challenged hers. 'But I wanted her here, with me.'

'Really?' His mother intercepted the look that passed between them, and lifted her shoulders in a typically continental gesture. 'Oh, well, we must try and change her mind, mustn't we? And first, I think, she would like to see where she is going to sleep.'

## CHAPTER ELEVEN

ONCE she was left to herself, Rachel's first impulse was to tear off her clothes and throw wide the shutters sealing the windows. The air in the apartment was oppressive, and the heat, combined with the fact that she had eaten next to nothing that day, was making her feel quite dizzy.

But common sense prevailed, and instead, she sank down on to the huge cushioned divan, which she supposed was where she was supposed to sleep. At present a thick satin overlay, woven in shades of green and gold and blue, hid the springy mattress, but her limbs responded to its softness as her fingers went to unbutton her shirt.

The room into which the serving girl had shown her was high-ceilinged and spacious. It was imposing, too, with its veined marble pillars, and exotically coloured tapestries, although its absence of any of the furniture Rachel was accustomed to seeing in a bedroom was rather unusual. Apart from the bed, there was little else of note in the room, except an inlaid cedarwood chest and several ornately carved screens. Even her luggage seemed to have disappeared, and she looked about her frustratedly, wondering what she was expected to do. If only it wasn't so hot, she fretted, longing for the luxury of air-conditioning.

The opening of one of the heavily carved doors through which she had entered the apartment brought her head round with a start. For a moment she thought it might be Alex, and her fingers moved automatically to fasten her shirt again. But it was the maidservant who had shown her to the room who slipped inside at her bidding, and Rachel looked at her anxiously, wondering if she was about to be summoned.

The girl bowed, and although Rachel was unused to such behaviour, she found herself acknowledging the salutation before loosening her shirt again. 'It's very hot,' she said, fanning herself to show what she meant, and the girl frowned briefly before nodding her understanding.

'Très chaud,' she agreed, speaking in French, and Rachel expelled her breath gratefully. At least if the girl understood French, they might be able to converse in that language—though her schoolgirl abilities were not extensive.

With some trepidation, Rachel asked the girl's name, and was relieved when she answered: 'Jasira, mademoiselle. Je viens vous aider. Pendant que vous prendrez un bain, je m'occuperai de vos vêtements.'

Rachel sighed. 'You will attend to my clothes?' she echoed faintly, speaking the girl's language with rather less confidence, and Jasira nodded and gestured towards one of the tall screens.

'While you bathe, *mademoiselle*,' she agreed, speaking more slowly. 'Come: it is this way. I will show you.'

Rachel followed her behind the screen and caught her breath in surprise. Through an arched doorway, she discovered a dressing room, and beyond that a huge bathroom, with an enormous step-in tub. In truth, it was more like a small pool than any bath she had ever seen, and while she watched, entranced, Jasira turned on half a dozen golden taps. Water spurting from six faucets soon filled the porcelain basin, and Jasira added the contents of a cut-glass flagon to fill the air with its intoxicating fragrance.

Then she came back to the other girl, helping her off with her shirt, and indicating that she should take off the rest of her clothes. 'Your luggage is in the dressing room, *mademoiselle*,' she explained, embarrassing Rachel by her casual familiarity. The English girl was not used to olive-skinned hands plucking at her clothes, or to the admiring gaze of night-dark eyes, appraising her full-breasted figure.

'I can manage.'

Rachel moved determinedly away and the Arab girl lifted her shoulders dismissingly. 'If there is anything more you need, just call,' she declared, disappearing into the dressing room again, and Rachel was left with the uneasy awareness that she could return at any time. There were no locks here, not even a protective door to close out would-be intruders. If she wanted to step into the cool perfumed water, she had to accept this situation, and after hesitating only a moment, she complied.

It was delightful. The water was rather less than body heat, and its purifying softness was a balm to skin made sensitive by the wind. Rachel found that when she sat down in the water, it reached almost to shoulder height, and uncaring that her hair was getting soaked, she splashed about with real pleasure. It was like having her own private swimming pool, albeit a small one, and she moved her legs languorously, enjoying the new sensation.

She found a tablet of scented soap, left for her use,

and used it to cleanse her body. It, too, was luxuriously
soft, and the bubbles it created floated all around her.
When Jasira came back, Rachel was surrounded by a
sea of bubbles, her cheeks pink and unguarded, her hair
a skein of dark silk in the water. Jasira's presence was
disturbing, however, and Rachel looked up at her half
impatiently, glad of the concealing cover of the water.

'Yes?'

'I have come to help you dress, *mademoiselle*,' Jasira
responded smilingly. 'But first I will bring some fresh
water.'

'Fresh water?'

Rachel was confused, and she watched in some
bewilderment as the Arab girl filled several pitchers
from what Rachel had assumed was a drinking tap set
in the marble tiles. Then she came back, carrying one of
the pitchers, and Rachel was obliged to get to her feet
so that Jasira could empty its contents over her.

The water was much cooler than that in which she
had taken her bath, but its douche was invigorating.
However, by the time Jasira had emptied all the jugs,
she was glad to step out on to the soft rug spread for
her use, and she welcomed the enveloping folds of the
towel the girl draped about her.

'I can dry myself,' she said rather quickly, before
Jasira could offer her assistance, and she did so rapidly
while the Arab girl emptied the tub and replaced the
pitchers.

Then it was time to go into the dressing room, and
she saw to her astonishment that Jasira had unpacked
both her cases. The presence of an ironing board
revealed that the girl had also pressed those items that
had required it, and now she drew back the doors of a
cedarwood scented closet to expose the garments
hanging inside.

'You will wear the black gown, *mademoiselle*,' she
suggested, indicating one of the two evening dresses
Rachel had brought with her, and the English girl
frowned.

'Do you think I should?' she asked, but in this Jasira
could not advise her.

'The black gown is very pretty,' was all she would say, and it was left to Rachel to wonder whether Alex's family dressed formally for dinner.

By the time she was ready, Rachel was a mass of nerves. Perhaps if the night had been a pleasant one and she had been able to escape from the unfamiliar surroundings of her apartments, she would have felt less tense. But instead she had been confined for more than two hours with only Jasira for company, and her whole body felt sensitised to a finely-honed awareness.

The Arab girl had done her best to provide companionship, but she was only a servant and unused to being addressed in such a familiar way. She had brought some tea—a weak concoction flavoured with herbs the English girl couldn't identify—but Rachel had scarcely touched it. She was thirsty, but she longed for a drink of lemonade or a glass of Coke, and the sweet-smelling tea seemed a poor substitute.

It was almost nine o'clock when Jasira escorted her back along the corridors she had trod earlier. The palace—for it was too grand a piece of architecture to call a house—was a rabbit-warren of halls and corridors, and Rachel reflected, rather drily, that it would be virtually impossible for her to escape from here. Like Theseus in the labyrinth, she felt very much inclined to unwind a ball of string along the corridors, just to ensure she could find her way back again.

The corridors themselves were very grand affairs, and a little disturbing. Long marble halls, lit by electric bulbs in elegant bronze sconces, with exotically patterned carpets to cushion the feet, they were guarded by a series of uniformed retainers; and although no one attempted to detain them, Rachel was very much aware of their attention. Everywhere there were windows, shuttered like the bars of a prison, and the muted sound of the wind outside, as it tore itself to pieces.

After what seemed like an age, they reached a part of the palace where no guards stood on duty at the doors. Jasira led the way through an arching portal, and from there through an outer chamber into a large well-lit salon.

The first person Rachel saw was Alex. Or perhaps it was that her eyes sought him before anyone else, she reflected half impatiently, annoyed to feel any sense of pleasure in his presence. At her entrance, he rose with indolent grace from the couch on which he had been lounging, and Jasira bowed in deference before taking her departure.

The room had three other occupants: Alex's mother was there, she saw with some relief. She had liked the older woman. And, disturbingly, Mariana; and a man, whose resemblance to Alex could be in no doubt, who like his son rose to greet the newcomer. There was no sign of Alex's grandfather, but Rachel was not reassured. That gentleman would be joining them, she was convinced, and for the present there was Mariana's hostility to deal with.

Alex came towards her, more elegant than she had ever seen him, in a dark blue velvet dinner suit. The fall of snow-white lace at his throat only accentuated the attractive darkness of his skin, and the soft fabric of the suit moulded his muscled body like a second skin. He looked sleek and well fed, like a pet leopard, she thought fancifully, or perhaps a pet cobra was more to the point.

'So,' he said, reaching her, his remarks audible to her ears alone, 'at last you wear something for me.' His fingers brushed the curve of her jawline. 'An attractive choice, albeit a disappointing one.'

'What do you mean?' Rachel had thought the simple lines of the black dress most suitable. It had been bought to attend a rag-trade dinner with Roger, and its cowl neckline and bat-wing sleeves were all-concealing, an appropriate choice in a country where women were protected from inquisitive eyes.

'I had hoped to see more of you,' he remarked, resisting her efforts to escape him, and delivering a deliberately sensuous kiss at the corner of her mouth. 'Don't fight me, or my parents may begin to suspect our relationship.'

'I don't care about our relationship!' she hissed, endeavouring to tug her fingers out of his grasp, but

Alex's warning: 'You want to go home, don't you?' brought a wave of startled colour into her cheeks.

Fortunately, their exchange had not been observed by the others in the room, although meeting Mariana's cold gaze a few moments later, Rachel suspected she had seen the kiss Alex had bestowed. However, Alex's father unknowingly defused the situation, taking her hand politely, and offering her his greeting.

'My wife tells me this is your first visit to this part of the world,' he remarked, his lean good looks very like his son's. Like Alex, too, he was wearing a dinner suit, though he was shorter and there was a revealing bulge behind the single button of his jacket.

'Yes.' Rachel was still trying to gather her composure, but she managed to make some polite comment.

'Miss Fleming is from London, Hugo,' put in Alex's mother, glancing thoughtfully at Mariana. 'Alex met her—quite by accident, I believe. After his return from America.'

'That's correct, Maman,' her son said agreeably, and Rachel felt him move to stand behind her. 'We have got to know one another—very well, in an incredibly short time.'

Rachel refused to acknowledge this deliberate challenge, and turned instead to Mariana. 'How do you do, Miss Rachid?' she smiled, attempting to be sociable. 'It's—nice to see you again. Do you live in Bahdan?'

'Mariana's mother is my younger sister,' Madame Roche answered for her. 'She lives here, with my father. Mariana does not.'

'I live in London,' the girl said now, her lips twisting scornfully. 'I work for the oil company. With Alexis.'

'I see.'

Rachel's eyes flickered over the man who had now moved to stand beside her, and he lifted his shoulders in a gesture of dismissal. 'A lot of people work for the oil company,' he remarked carelessly, and Rachel's lips tightened at the implied reassurance.

'Including Malcolm Cross,' interposed Mariana, with

sudden vehemence, and Rachel saw Alex's reaction with a curious feeling of unease.

'Including Malcolm Cross,' he conceded, after a moment, but Rachel had the feeling he was not as indifferent as he would like her to think.

As if not liking the direction the conversation had taken, Madame Roche gestured for Rachel to come and sit beside her on the couch. With something like relief Rachel obeyed, but her eyes still probed the arrogant mastery of Alex's features, only darting away in embarrassment when he met that intent appraisal.

'Tell me all about yourself,' invited Madame Roche firmly. 'What do you do? Where do you live? Are your parents still alive?'

Rachel hesistated. 'I'm a secretary, *madame*,' she said at last. 'I work for a firm of solicitors. And yes—my parents are still alive.'

'You live with your parents?' suggested Alex's mother in some surprise, and her son strolled across the room to join them.

'Rachel is an independent girl, Maman,' he inserted smoothly, before she could explain. 'Naturally, she does not live with her parents. She shares a flat with a friend. A *female* friend,' he added, as if that could be in any doubt.

Rachel flushed. 'My parents are divorced, *madame*,' she declared stiffly. 'My mother remarried, and now lives in Australia, but my father——'

'—lives in London,' Alex finished for her smoothly. 'He runs a small engineering company. You remember?' He exchanged a knowing glance with his father. 'I told you.'

'Of course.' Hugo Roche inclined his head. 'The firm was in some difficulties, I believe,' but before Rachel could take up the cudgels in her father's defence, they were joined by two other people.

The first Rachel identified only too well. Alex's grandfather was just as forbidding this evening as on that other memorable occasion when they had met, his flowing robes and rope-bound *kaffiyeh* setting him apart from the other members of the party. His choice

of garb might be traditional, but Rachel had the feeling
he wore it deliberately, alienating himself and his ideals
with an intentional display of arrogance.

The woman with him was less Eastern in appearance.
Like Alex's mother, she was wearing a high-necked
evening gown, and Rachel reflected how, even in their
European clothes, they deferred to traditional ideals.
Even Mariana's gown was demure, although the splits
in its skirt gave it an added sophistication.

'My sister, Sofia,' murmured Alex's mother, and she
and Rachel rose automatically. Sheik Rachid had that
effect on people, and the English girl knew a
momentary chill as his arrogant gaze met hers.

His younger daughter, Mariana's mother, surveyed
the gathering intently, her dark gaze lingering longest
on the English girl, too. So much resentment, and all
directed at me, thought Rachel uneasily, and was
almost relieved when Alex came to her side.

'Let me introduce you to my aunt,' he said, his hands
at her waist propelling her insistently forward, and
conscious of everyone's eyes upon them, she had to
obey.

'Miss Fleming.' Sophia was scarcely polite, her
haughty stare causing Rachel no small degree of
embarrassment. 'I would like to talk to you later. I
should like to learn about the girl who has caused my
nephew to ignore his family commitments.'

'Perhaps you should speak with Mariana, then,'
drawled Alex, his ironic smile for her alone, and with a
polite bow, he drew Rachel away.

'They all hate me, don't they?' she murmured, almost
inaudibly, looking up at him with troubled eyes. 'You
should tell them the truth, Alex. Then they might realise
I didn't engineer this.'

'What is the truth?' Alex's brows arched in quizzical
interrogation. 'Truth is like beauty—in the eye of the
beholder.'

The evening meal was announced by a bowing
manservant, and Rachel was obliged to accompany
Alex into the dining salon. Like the room they had just
left, this apartment, too, was beautifully appointed,

with long side tables loaded with plates and cutlery in burnished silver. The floor was spread with a huge oval carpet, and dinner was served on a low table around which piles of cushions had been arranged.

'My grandfather enjoys adhering to the traditions of his ancestors,' Alex told her softly, as she showed her surprise. 'Sit down. It's quite comfortable really. And rather romantic, don't you think?'

Rachel could see little of romance in taking dinner in company with people with whom she shared no point of contact. If she had been Alex's fiancée—girl-friend—she might have felt differently, but knowing she was there under false pretences made the whole affair that much more distasteful. They didn't want her here, and she certainly didn't want to be here, she told herself. Though her determined aversion for Alex took a distinct reversal when he took his place beside Mariana.

His grandfather had arranged things, of course. He himself took his place at the head of the table, with Alex on his right, and Hugo Roche on his left. The four women were ranged lower down the table, with his elder daughter seated beside her husband, and Sofia occupying the place next to Mariana. That meant Rachel was seated beside Madame Roche with Mariana's mother immediately opposite, and she looked a little anxiously in Alex's direction, as the distance between them seemed to stretch to insuperable proportions.

She was relieved to find the food was at least European in appearance. Cold *hors d'oeuvre* were followed by a spicy consommé, and the lamb that formed the main course was served with rice and vegetables. The dessert was more of the sticky confectionery she had tasted at Alex's house, and the coffee was thick and black and delicious. No wine was served with the meal, only a fruity concoction, which Rachel nevertheless found quite heady, and by the time the meal was over she was glad of its potent qualities.

In spite of her determination not to show any interest, her eyes were continually drawn to the opposite end of the table. Even though she told herself she had no reason to care what Alex might be saying to Mariana, or his grandfather, she couldn't ignore the swelling core of indignation inside her. He had brought her here, against her will, and now he had abandoned her in favour of the girl he was supposed to have jilted. Exactly what game was he playing? she wondered resentfully, unable to avoid Sofia's evident satisfaction at these developments. She was not jealous, Rachel told herself fiercely, only angry, and her eyes flashed fire as she attacked the sweetmeats the manservant had provided.

When the meal was over, more coffee was served, and conversation expanded. Hugo Roche leant past his wife to ask Rachel about the firm for which she worked, and after learning of its identity, he remarked that Colin Harrop, a barrister known to Rachel, had represented his company in a court action concerning oil pollution. 'One of my tankers was holed off the Scillies,' he explained, with some regret. 'A section of the coastline was affected by an oil slick, and one of the conservancy committees brought an action against us.'

'The birds all died,' his wife put in sadly. 'Poor Hugo! It was not his fault, but he was held responsible.'

'It was my vessel,' commented her husband drily. 'But happily, those things do not happen too often. Wild life is important, not only for our children, but for our children's children. Eh, Alexis?'

Alex smiled, and Rachel, watching him, knew a sudden pang. Was he aware of his effect on her? she wondered crossly. And then: of course he was. He must be. How else could he depend upon her participation in this outrageous masquerade, unless he secretly suspected she was helpless to defy him?

'As I have no children that I know of, how can I reply?' he was saying now, in answer to his father's challenge. 'I care about the destruction of our environment—of course I do. But man is reproducing himself so fast he is rapidly outstripping his best intentions.'

'But you want children, Alexis, don't you?' Mariana inserted now, her sloe-black eyes fixed on his face, and Rachel waited apprehensively for his reply.

'Eventually,' he agreed at last, his gaze flickering mockingly in Rachel's direction, and she bent her head in sudden weakness at the flagrant provocation.

'Perhaps Alexis will have no children,' Mariana's mother put in insidiously, and meeting the malevolent stare that accompanied her words, Rachel felt oppressed. If Alex did not have children with Mariana, he might not have children at all, was what she was implying, and the threat was quite believable in this medieval atmosphere.

At last the party broke up, and Rachel found Madame Roche by her side. 'Come,' she said, 'I will escort you back to your apartments,' and although Rachel saw Alex looking frowningly in her direction, she went gladly with his mother.

'You must not let Sofia upset you,' the older woman remarked as they traversed the endless corridors. 'She is afraid her daughter will not become mistress of Hajat. Since Mariana was born, she has been waiting for the merging of our two families. Her husband died, you see, and poor Sofia has always been envious of me.'

The words were said quite calmly, and without conceit, and Rachel looked at her unhappily: 'Madame,' she murmured awkwardly, 'I don't think you understand about—about Alex and me——'

'Please . . .' The older woman's hand on Rachel's sleeve silenced her. 'You do not have to explain your relationship with my son to me. I married outside the family, too, remember? And like Alex, I met the same opposition. But my son's character is every bit as strong as my husband's, and whatever he decides, we will support him.'

'But——'

'No more.' Madame Roche patted her sleeve. 'Ah, here we are at your door. Goodnight—Rachel. We will meet again tomorrow.'

Jasira was waiting, and Rachel's nerves tightened. She could not face the Arab girl's ministrations this evening, however well meant, and lifting up her hands, palms outwards, she gestured her away.

'I can undress myself, thank you,' she assured her,

speaking in French as before. 'I'll—I'll see you in the morning. Goodnight.'

'Goodnight, *mademoiselle*.'

Jasira was disappointed, but she left obediently enough, and Rachel lifted her arms to unzip the back of her dress. The soft black material slid unheeded to the floor, and with it went her slip and panties, and the fragile tights, which nevertheless had been too warm this evening.

Then she went into the bathroom, rinsing her face at the porcelain basin and examining her reflection as she cleaned her teeth. She looked tight-lipped and frustrated, she decided bitterly, and trudged back into the bedroom with a feeling of discontentment.

Before leaving, Jasira had folded back the coverlet from the bed, and now Rachel slipped between fine silk sheets, that rustled against her skin. Reaching out her hand, she turned out the final lamp, then slumped on the pillows, alone in the darkness.

Only then did she realise that the wind had subsided. There was still the taste of dryness in the air, but amazingly, the heat had subsided, too, and the air in the room was pervaded by the scents of the garden which must lie beyond the shuttered windows. Rachel was tempted to get out of bed and open the shutters, but her isolation kept her safe within the contours of the bed. She would see the garden tomorrow, she thought, with some resentment. And tomorrow, and tomorrow, until Alex decided she could go home.

She didn't want to think of Alex then, but his image was inescapable. She didn't want to think of him exchanging pleasantries with Mariana at the dinner table, she didn't want to think of Mariana's mother, spreading her veil of malice; and she didn't want to remember her own treacherous feelings as she watched him with the girl his grandfather had decreed would be his wife.

She must have been tireder than she thought, because her eyelids grew heavy and she drowsed a while, only to wake with a start at the realisation that someone else was getting into the bed. Panic flared as a lean warm body moved determinedly across the mattress to reach her, but as her lips parted to utter a horrified cry, firm fingers closed over her mouth.

'Who did you expect?' Alex's lazy voice intoned in her ear, his lips playing tantalisingly with her lobe. 'Now don't scream, or you'll bring the guards in to eject me—and that could be rather embarrassing for both of us.'

Rachel tore his hand away, her fingers reaching urgently for the bedside lamp. When its golden illumination flooded over the bed, she gazed at Alex angrily, her earlier feelings eclipsed by his unashamed audacity.

'The guards?' she echoed, momentarily diverted, and he nodded.

'This is the female section of the palace,' he conferred outrageously. 'I had the devil's own job getting in here. God knows how I'm going to get out again.'

'You're crazy!'

'Very probably.'

Alex was unconcerned, but Rachel came quickly to her senses.

'And what do you think you're doing?' she demanded, hugging the silk sheet to her body. It had been so warm, she had not bothered to wear a nightgown, and she was irresistibly aware of his naked body outlined beneath the cover.

'What do you think I'm doing?' he enquired drily, linking his hands behind his head. 'Did you really think I'd let you escape me so easily?' His eyes darkened. 'I've been waiting all evening for this.'

'Oh, really!' Rachel was too distraught to be discreet. 'I suppose when you were entertaining Mariana, you were thinking of taking me to bed! Or did *she* reject you, and I'm a convenient substitute!'

Alex's hands moved swiftly from behind his head to imprison her shoulders, and ignoring her attempt to keep him at bay, he bore her back against the pillows, crushing her body with his. 'You'll never know, will you?' he snarled, with savage vehemence. 'And don't look now, but your eyes have turned green. What's the matter? Did I really succeed in making you jealous?'

'Jealous!' spat Rachel, twisting her head from side to side. 'You have to be joking! I was glad you left me alone. I hoped you'd got the message.'

'Oh, I got the message all right, and it wasn't like you say,' retorted Alex, imprisoning her hands above her head and looking down with infuriating superiority into her flushed face. 'If I hadn't been sure of my welcome, I shouldn't have come here.' His lips parted sensually. 'And you're wasting time. I have to be gone before morning.'

His lips descended on her quivering mouth, and their sensuous mastery sent her senses spinning. With consummate skill he explored her mouth, arousing her and drugging her all at the same time, so that although she started by beating her fists at his back, she ended by curling her nails into his smooth skin.

'Better, much better,' he murmured, his mouth seeking the tender curve of her nape. 'And so considerate of you to put the light on.' He kicked the sheet aside with careless abandon. 'Your body is so beautiful, I can never seen enough of it . . .'

'Alex——'

Her plea for sanity was ignored, and in any case, she was no longer capable of denying him anything. With his muscled flanks entwined with her legs, and the unmistakable heat of his desire thrusting against her stomach, she didn't want to resist him, and she shifted beneath him to facilitate his demands.

'You drive me crazy,' he breathed, pressing his face between her breasts, and she gripped the hair at the back of his neck to bring his mouth back to hers.

Their lovemaking was even more thrilling than before. Rachel had learned from that previous encounter, and her instinctive responses seemed to drive Alex to even greater depths of feeling. He was demanding, insatiable, his hungry body taking and giving so much pleasure that by the time they fell into an exhausted slumber just before dawn, she was quite content to sleep in his arms. She didn't want to think of the morning, and what it might bring. For the present, she was satisfied with the knowledge that for the past few hours, Alex had thought of no one but her . . .

# CHAPTER TWELVE

THE feeling of contentment lasted no longer than it took for Rachel to awaken the next morning. Opening her eyes to the brilliant light filtering in between the shutters, she was immediately aware that she was alone in the huge bed. The only evidence of Alex's occupation was in the tangle of the covers and the unmistakable scent of his body lingering on the sheets.

She had no idea what time it was, but she still felt utterly lethargic, and realising that something must have wakened her, she looked about her a trifle apprehensively. Jasira's appearance from behind the screens was both a reassurance and a disappointment, but she shrugged away the traitorous hope that perhaps Alex might have changed his mind, and watched the girl from between her lids as she carefully opened the shutters.

The onslaught of so much brightness caused Rachel to turn her face away, however, and observing that her charge was awake, Jasira came to the bed.

'Good morning, *mademoiselle*,' she greeted her smilingly. 'Did you sleep well?'

Rachel managed to conceal her real feelings behind the sheltering shade of her arm. 'Um—reasonably, thank you,' she responded, blinking in the light. 'What time is it?'

'It is almost noon, *mademoiselle*,' replied Jasira, with dismaying simplicity. 'Monsieur Alexis left instructions that you were not to be disturbed, but Madame Nadine suggested that you might wish to be awakened now.'

'Heavens, yes.' Rachel struggled up in the bed, and as she did so her senses were assailed by the entrancing

vista that was visible now through the opened jalousies.
Beyond the environs of her apartments, an arched
cloister gave access to a paved patio that circled the
green waters of an ornamental pool. There were palms
and other blossoming shrubs, and box-hedged gardens
bright with the vivid colours of the flowers. A narrow
stone bell-tower was set at one corner of the gardens,
and from its latticed turrets the soft cooing of doves
could be heard.

Her gasp of delight attracted Jasira's attention and
she turned with the tray she had set on the bedside
cabinet earlier in her arms. 'La Cour des Lis,' she
announced smilingly. 'Do you like it?'

'The Court of the Lilies,' murmured Rachel to
herself, and then in French: 'It's beautiful.'

'But first, breakfast,' declared Jasira, setting the tray
across her legs, and Rachel tucked the sheet beneath her
arms to prevent an embarrassing exposure.

The tray was set with warm *croissants* and curls of
butter, tiny jars of fruit preserves, and a squat jug of
coffee. It was late in the day to be having breakfast,
Rachel reflected, but deciding the hollow feeling inside
her was probably physical in origin, she tackled the
food with determination.

Two *croissants* and three cups of coffee later, she felt
a little better. The events of the night before had
assumed the unreal qualities of a dream, and although
she knew it was a temporary reprieve, she had
succeeded in pushing what had happened to the back of
her mind. However, Alex would not be so dismissed,
and although she despised herself for doing so, she
couldn't prevent herself from asking where he was.

'He has gone riding, *mademoiselle*,' Jasira explained,
with unwitting candour. 'He, and his grandfather, and
the lady Mariana; they left more than two hours ago to
visit the home of Sheik Rachid's brother.'

Rachel thrust the tray aside and wrapping the sheet
about her, she got out of bed. 'More than two hours
ago, you say?' she remarked tautly. 'When will they be
back? Do you know?'

'Not before this afternoon,' replied the Arab girl,

leading the way into the bathroom, and now Rachel
saw what Jasira had been doing earlier. The sunken
bath was filled with bubbles, and with an appealing
gesture, she indicated that Rachel should step into it. 'It
is too hot to ride in the heat of the day,' she explained,
as Rachel hesitated. 'Come, *mademoiselle*. You will feel
better after bathing. And Monsieur Alexis was most
concerned that you should enjoy a rest.'

I'll bet he was, thought Rachel grimly, shedding the
sheet and stepping down into the tub in one fluid motion.
He had no compunction about taking Mariana with him
on his ride, in spite of what he had said in London. And
Rachel had the feeling, he was enjoying the manoeuvring,
as his grandfather schemed to achieve his own ends.

Dismissing Jasira, she spent some time in the bath,
and then dressed slowly in a sleeveless cotton tunic,
whose dropped waistline was reminiscent of her
mother's generation. However, the short pleated skirt
was flattering to long shapely legs, and leaving them
bare, she slipped high-heeled sandals on to her feet.

She was standing on the patio, brushing her hair in
the brilliant sunlight, when she heard a sound behind
her, and turning, she found Mariana's mother just
coming through the arched doorway. Sofia Rachid was
dressed again in black, albeit today's dress was a slight
concession to European fashions. The neckline was not
quite so high as the gown she had worn the night
before, and the hemline reached only to her calves, and
not her ankles. However, she was just as intimidating,
and watching her approach, Rachel felt the unfamiliar
chill her presence evoked.

'*Madame*,' she said politely, wondering if the woman
had knocked and she had not heard her, but Sofia's
expression was not encouraging.

'So, you are still here, *mademoiselle*,' was her
overture, and Rachel wondered half impatiently how
she had expected her to leave last night.

'Yes, still here, *madame*,' she said now, putting her
hands holding the brush behind her back. 'It's a
beautiful morning, isn't it? Much different from last
night. Does the sirocco often blow?'

'Here we call it the simoom, *mademoiselle*. Sirocco is the name for many winds. And generally it blows at this time of the year.' She paused. 'It has been known to drive people to distraction.'

'I can believe it.' Rachel tried to keep the conversation going. She didn't know why Mariana's mother had come here, and she didn't want to know. 'It's not an experience one could forget.'

'You think not?' Sofia regarded her intently. 'Nor perhaps an experience one would wish to repeat.'

'No.' Rachel forced a slight smile. 'Er—is it time for lunch? I'm afraid I overslept and I'm still a little confused.'

'Not only about the time, *mademoiselle*,' inserted Sofia coldly. 'Whatever my nephew may have led you to believe, he is going to marry my daughter. And your presence here can only be an embarrassment: to my father, to my daughter, and to me.'

Rachel sighed. She had guessed this was coming, and she hoped Mariana's mother would think it was the sun which was responsible for the sudden colour in her cheeks. 'I'm sure you're right,' she murmured unhappily, unwilling to get into an argument. 'And now, if you'll excuse me, I do have to finish getting ready——'

'Not yet.' Sofia stepped squarely into her path, and looking into the older woman's features, Rachel knew a sudden sense of unease. There was about Mariana's mother an air of grim determination, that boded ill for anybody attempting to thwart her plans, and however blameless Rachel's motives might be, Sofia was unlikely to listen to any explanation.

'I don't think you understand,' Rachel attempted now, choosing her words with care. 'Alex—Alex and I are not planning on getting—married. We—we're just—friends, that's all.' Her face burned. 'You have no need to get upset, *madame*, I assure you.'

Whether or not Sofia believed her, Rachel couldn't tell, and besides, with her face shining like a beacon, she was hardly the picture of innocence. She looked guilty, and she felt guilty, and why not? she asked herself bitterly. She *was* guilty—or at least Alex was.

'I don't think you understand, *mademoiselle*,' averred
the older woman harshly, and Rachel thought how
strange it was that the bright day should suddenly seem
so overcast. 'Oh, I know why Alexis is using you—
Mariana told me. There was some mix-up over her and
a young Englishman who works for the company.
Alexis thought they were having an affair, and like the
hotheaded young devil he is, he chose to humiliate her
in the most public way possible. And with an *English*
girl!'

Rachel felt a sudden jolt. 'A mix-up?' she echoed
faintly, as her stomach churned sickeningly, and Sofia
nodded impatiently, pressing her palms together.

'Mariana is a beautiful young woman, and the man,
Malcolm Cross, took advantage of her while Alexis was
in New York. It was all quite innocent, of course, but
Alexis refused to listen to reason. Instead he involved
himself with you, taking you to his house in London,
bringing you here; degrading the family by introducing
you to his parents!'

Rachel wished there was somewhere to sit down.
What Sofia was saying was all, *horribly*, believable.
Only yesterday she had glimpsed Alex's reaction when
Mariana had used the other man's name, and
unwillingly she was recalling the very first time they
met. Alex said he had just come back from New
York, she remembered, and since that night he had
pursued her with a diligence she herself had found
difficult to understand. He had not cared about
Roger, because Roger was just another Englishman,
like the man with whom he thought Mariana was
having an affair. What greater irony than to destroy
their relationship just as the man from the oil
company had destroyed his.

'I see you do not dismiss my explanation,
*mademoiselle*,' the now hateful voice continued. 'Whatever Alexis may have told you, it is of no matter. His
grandfather will not permit him to marry outside the
family. With an unpredictable sheikdom to control,
Alexis would never dare marry an outsider.'

Rachel blinked, swaying a little in the bright sunlight.

'A sheikdom to control?' she echoed blankly. 'I—don't understand——'

'My father is the uncrowned ruler of Bahdan, *mademoiselle*. And Alexis is his heir. Did he not tell you?'

The two men walked into the palace together, both tall and impressive, the one in modern riding gear, the other in the traditional robes of his ancestors. Mariana went ahead of them, hurrying to find her mother, and the consolation she so badly needed. It had been a humiliating day for the young Arab girl, and she was determined to pack her bags that evening and leave the palace for good.

Alex would have left his grandfather when they entered the building, but Sheik Rachid put a staying hand on his arm, his gnarled features twisting into an expression of reluctant entreaty.

'A moment, my son,' he muttered harshly. 'Let us not part in this way. I do not wish you to leave the palace.' He sighed. 'On the contrary, my greatest wish is that you should make your home here, not in Paris or London.'

'On your terms?' suggested Alex bleakly, running a weary hand inside the opened neck of his shirt. His skin felt damp and gritty, and he was looking forward to a bath. And then ... Rachel, he thought, with some satisfaction. It was amazing how quickly he had come to depend on her, to *need* her, and his senses stirred at the memory of how he had last seen her.

'That is something we have to talk about,' his grandfather stated now, not without some regret. 'Perhaps I have been too pedantic, too inclined to adhere to old edicts, when all I really wanted was your happiness——'

'*Grandpère*——'

'At least have the goodness to hear me out,' exclaimed the old man tensely. 'You cannot expect to bring this girl here and gain immediate approval. Mariana—Mariana may have been wrong for you. Maybe I have been blind in that respect. But how do

you know this English girl will make you any happier?
*Bon sang*, Alexis, by your own admission, you have
barely known her for three weeks!'

Alex's dark face grew sardonic. 'Is this your idea of
tolerance, *Grandpère*? Of—talking this out?'

'Alexis——'

'We will talk it out, *Grandpère*, I promise,' his
grandson declared equably. 'But not now. Now, I am
tired. Now, I need a bath.' He paused. 'And Rachel
must be wondering why I have deserted her for so long.'

Sheik Rachid's nostrils flared. 'This man—her
father—what of him?'

'He's weak,' Alexis shrugged. 'But he will learn.'

'At your expense!'

Alex hesitated. 'Fleming Engineering can succeed,
given the right opportunities. So far as his debts with
the man, Devlin, are concerned, I think it will be some
time before he tangles with him again.'

'And when he does?'

'I will handle it.' Alex grimaced. 'Convincing Fleming
of my sincerity is not the problem. Convincing Rachel
is something else.'

His grandfather stared at him. 'What do you mean?
The girl is besotted with you.'

'Is she?' Alex's muscles tensed. 'Well, we will see.'

He was about to turn away towards his own
apartments when his mother came gliding into the hall.
In apricot silk lounging pyjamas, Nadine Roche looked
absurdly boyish, and Alex had opened his mouth to
make some comment when her expression silenced him.

'What is it?' he demanded, a sixth sense warning him
that something was wrong, and even his grandfather
hesitated, troubled by the look on his daughter's face.

'You've been so long, Alexis,' she exclaimed,
grasping his hands and gazing up into his dark face.
'Oh dear, I don't know how to tell you this, but Rachel
has gone. She has left the palace!'

With Mrs Bently's help, Rachel spring-cleaned the flat,
using all her pent-up energies in a splurge of washing
and dusting and polishing. Because she had arranged to

bring her holidays forward, she couldn't go back to the office, and she was glad of the unaccustomed activity to exhaust her pent-up emotions. She seemed full of energy, but it was of the nervous variety, and certainly not a result of her current way of life. She ate little and slept badly, and Jane was most concerned about her.

'Call him,' she said one morning, as Rachel was arming herself with a paintbrush and emulsion paint ready to whitewash the bathroom. 'I'm sure by now he'll have forgiven you. And there's still time to make the arrangements.'

For once she had Rachel's whole attention, and the younger girl gazed at her blankly. 'Call who?' she asked, for a moment too confused to comprehend her, and Jane sighed impatiently as she took the paint pot from her and set it down.

'Roger,' she said flatly. 'Call him. Whatever your differences, they're over now. At least give it one last try.'

Rachel caught her breath, a sob rising in her throat at the realisation that Jane actually thought this was about Roger Harrington. 'I—no,' she said at last, unwilling to get into explanations that she couldn't handle right now. 'It's all right, Jane, really. Once I get back to work, things will be fine.'

'You don't really believe that, do you?' Jane made an impatient gesture. 'For heaven's sake, Rachel, take a look at yourself! You look terrible! I'm sure if Roger could see you——'

'Which he won't.'

Jane frowned. 'I suppose I could call him——'

'*No!*' Rachel was horrified now. 'No, you mustn't. I—I don't want to see Roger—please! Believe me.'

Jane regarded her doubtfully. 'Why not?' She paused, and then went on: 'Rachel, this isn't about Alex Roche, is it? I mean, I know when you came back from Bahdan you said it was all over, but it seems to me you haven't really relaxed since then.'

'Oh, Jane . . .'

'Well, it's true. I thought at first everything was going to be all right, but it isn't. You're not eating, and by the looks of you, you're not sleeping. If it's not Roger, it has to be Alex. For pity's sake, Rachel, what did he do?'

Rachel sighed. 'Nothing. He did nothing—I told you. He took me out there to prove to his grandfather that—that he couldn't be forced to marry someone he didn't want.'

'And he proved that in twenty-four hours?' Jane was sceptical. 'What I don't understand is why, if you flew out there in a private plane, you didn't come home the same way.'

'I told you,' Rachel bent her head, 'there wasn't a plane available. And besides, I was coming back alone, not with—not with a member of the *Royal* family!'

She was sardonic, but Jane was still not convinced. 'So why don't you want to see Roger?' she persisted. 'You still love him, don't you?'

'Jane, what is this?' Rachel's voice had risen dangerously. 'Since when have you been a founder member of the Roger Harrington fan club?' She took a deep breath. 'All right, I'll tell you. I don't love Roger. I don't know if I ever did. There, does that satisfy you? I don't want to marry him.'

Jane regarded her with troubled eyes. 'And you think that consoles me?'

'It should.'

'Well, it doesn't.' Jane expelled her breath heavily. 'What do you think I am, Rachel? Some unfeeling person who goes around with her eyes shut? If you're not pining for Roger Harrison, then I really am concerned about you. Because if it's not Roger who's causing all this upset, then it must be Alex Roche!'

'Oh, *Jane!*'

Rachel could sustain her composure no longer, and sinking down into the nearest chair, she buried her face in her hands. It was such a relief to let her feelings go, and although it was past the time Jane should have left for school, she squatted down beside her and put her arm about her.

'I should have known,' she muttered impatiently. 'A man like Alex Roche: you never should have got involved with him.'

'Do you think I don't know that?' mumbled Rachel, groping for a tissue and blowing her nose hard. 'Oh, that's a laugh, isn't it? He didn't leave me any choice.'

Two days later, Rachel was just stepping out of the bath when the doorbell rang. It was early afternoon, and after scouring the kitchen, she had taken the opportunity to have a bath before preparing the evening meal.

Deciding it must be Mrs Bently who had forgotten something, she wrapped her damp hair in the towel and pulling on a fleecy bathrobe padded barefoot to the door.

The woman who stood waiting outside was the last person she had expected to see, and Rachel's heart took an uncontrollable little plunge before righting itself again. 'Madame Roche!' she exclaimed, running her tongue over her upper lip. 'What a—surprise!'

'Can I come in, Rachel?' Alex's mother looked pointedly beyond her, and Rachel looked back uncertainly over her shoulder.

'Oh—yes. Yes, of course,' she murmured, stepping obediently out of the way, and the other woman stepped purposefully past her and into the living room of the flat.

In a trim-fitting navy blue suit and perilously high heels, Nadine Roche looked totally out of place in the commonplace environs of the flat, and Rachel was made overwhelmingly aware of her own dishevelment when compared to this elegant little woman. But deciding her appearance could mean nothing to Alex's mother, she gestured to the couch and invited her to sit down.

'Can I get you something? Some tea, perhaps?' she asked, not quite knowing what to say, but Nadine subsided on to the couch and shook her head.

'Not just now, my dear,' she answered, patting the seat beside her. 'Won't you join me? This won't take long.'

Rachel hesitated, but then, realising she could hardly ask the other woman to wait while she put some clothes on, she complied with her request. 'Thank you,' she said awkwardly, wondering why Nadine was here. Had Alex sent her? It didn't seem likely. And in any case, what was there to say?

Nadine looked at her now, and Rachel felt her colour rising. What was Alex's mother thinking? she wondered. That she looked pale and unhealthy, and older than her years? She certainly felt that way at this moment, and her knees trembled a little as she tucked the folds of the bathrobe around them.

'You must be wondering why I've come to see you,' the older woman remarked now, and Rachel guessed her expression was quite transparent. 'But you left my father's house so precipitately, you must have guessed we would be concerned about you.'

Rachel took a steadying breath. 'Your sister knew where I had gone.'

'Sofia? Yes, she knew. But don't you think you owed Alex an explanation, before you made such a—a hasty departure? I mean, you were his guest, not Sofia's. He was most—disturbed—when he came home and found you were gone.'

Rachel flushed. 'I'm sorry.'

'Are you?' Nadine regarded her intently. 'Or are you not just the tiniest bit smug, that you succeeded in hurting him so badly?'

She gasped. *'Hurting him!'*

'Yes, hurting him.' Nadine spoke crisply now. 'Stealing away like a thief in the night! How did you think he would feel?'

Rachel schooled her expression. 'I imagine he was— annoyed,' she declared tautly. 'But I'm afraid I don't care how he felt. My—association—with Alex is over. I just want to get on with my life, and I wish he would do the same.'

'What do you mean?'

Rachel sighed. 'Alex sent you here, didn't he?'

'No, he did not!' Nadine's response was too spontaneous to be assumed. 'I've no doubt my son would be furious if he knew where I was. But something has to be said, and if he is not prepared to say it, then I must.'

Rachel shook her head. 'Look' she said carefully, 'I'm sorry if you think I—spurned your hospitality. That was not my intention. It wasn't like that. You should ask Alex to tell you the truth about us. It's not what you think, believe me!'

'No?' Nadine lifted her silk-clad shoulders. 'You will tell me next that my son is not in love with you. Well, believe me, *Miss Fleming*, I know him as well as, if not better, than you do.'

The colour drained out of Rachel's face with disturbing thoroughness, and her lips were grey and parched as she listened to this last statement. 'You—don't understand,' she persisted, wetting her quivering mouth. 'Alex was only trying to get back at—at Mariana. Our relationship was just—just a game he played. A cruel game, but a game nonetheless.'

Nadine gazed at her steadily. 'You really believe that?'

'It's the truth.' Rachel bent her head. 'I know that doesn't excuse the way I behaved to you and the other members of your family, but Alex didn't really give me any choice.'

'He broke up your engagement, I know.' Nadine surprised her by this knowledge. 'But he did say that your—fiancé and you were having problems anyway.'

Rachel nodded. 'That's true.'

'So maybe he did you a favour, *non*?'

She nodded again. 'You could say that.'

'So why did you run away?'

'You know why.' Rachel stared at her. 'I've just told you.'

'No,' Nadine shook her head, 'all you have said is that your relationship with my son began with a game.'

'Began and ended,' said Rachel bitterly. 'Oh, please, *madame*, can we talk about something else?'

'Very well,' Nadine nodded, but Rachel's relief was shortlived. 'Let us talk about Alex's relationship with Mariana—and the events that precluded their eventual break-up.'

'Madame——'

'What did Alex tell you?' Nadine was not to be diverted.

'Alex told me nothing——'

'*Eh bien*, I will—how do you say?—fill you in, eh? Then perhaps you can judge for yourself which of us is telling the truth.'

'It's nothing to do with me, *madame*——'

'I disagree. And Alex, I suspect, would regard the information I am about to give you as a betrayal of weakness on his part.' She paused. 'Mariana has been having an affair with an English boy who works at the London offices of the oil company.'

'I know,' Rachel interrupted her, and then, comprehending the older woman's surprise, she added: 'Your sister told me. But it was all a mistake.'

'Ah!' Nadine stared at her now with something akin to understanding. 'Sofia spoke to you before you left. She did not tell us that.'

Rachel sighed. 'Does it matter?'

'It does if you still think there is some doubt about Mariana's guilt. Oh, yes, she was having an affair, Rachel, be assured of that. Alex came back from New York and found them together. Need I say more? They were drunk, or so he says. Whatever, he took a bottle of gin out of the apartment and poured it down the drain.'

Rachel blinked. 'Gin?'

'Yes.' Alex's mother sighed again. 'Mariana's mother does not know this, of course. She would be most distressed if she learned that her daughter had been drinking. It is one of the things she feels most strongly about. A—link with the old days, you might say.'

Rachel swallowed. 'That—still doesn't alter——'

'Doesn't it?' Nadine didn't let her finish. 'Look, my dear, if Sofia said anything to you—if she hinted——'

'*Hinted!*' Rachel got unsteadily to her feet. 'Oh, why don't you be honest, *madame*? Alex may have been piqued because I walked out on him, but it's Mariana he's going to marry. His grandfather will see to that!'

'He won't.' Alex's mother rose now also. 'Rachel, Alex is not going to marry Mariana. Whatever you may have thought, whatever lies Sofia may have cooked up, Alex will never make Mariana his wife.

He has told my father so.'

'Oh, well——' Rachel sniffed, not looking at her. 'He got what he wanted, then.'

'No, he did not get what he wanted,' explained Nadine fiercely. Haven't you been listening to me? My son wants you—surely you must know that? I thought he had made it abundantly clear.'

'When?' Rachel swung round to face her. 'When he talked with Mariana all through dinner the night I was at the palace? When he took her riding the next day— *all day!*'

Nadine's lips twitched. 'You were—jealous?'

Rachel quivered. 'Does it matter?'

'Of course it matters. Listen, Rachel, I love my son, and I know that his feelings are tearing him apart. He wants you. He wants to see you!'

'Then why hasn't he come here?' demanded Rachel tremulously, grasping the back of a chair for support. 'He was never backward in interfering in my affairs before.'

Nadine sighed. 'That may be why.'

'What do you mean?'

'Oh, Rachel . . .' She moistened her lips. 'From the little he's confided in me and his father, I'd say he feels he's done everything he can. I realise I don't know everything that's passed between you, but I do know he's not the man he used to be.' She shook her head. 'I'm afraid for him, Rachel. I believe he's living on the edge of a complete breakdown . . .'

Rachel drove the Mini to Eaton Mews. It was some time since it had had an airing, but the little motor responded happily to the demands she put upon it. However, it took her some time to find a place to park, and the sight of the silver-grey Lamborghini parked outside Number 3 made her fingers all thumbs.

Ringing the doorbell some time later, she wondered what she would do if Alex refused to see her. There was a distinct possibility, in spite of what his mother had said, and it was conceivable that she might have made a mistake. Alex might be fretting for Mariana, not her, and as Rachel waited for the door to be opened, she knew an urgent desire to run.

But then the heavy door swung inward, and the manservant, Karim, was gazing down at her, an enigmatic expression guarding his inner feelings. 'Good afternoon, *mademoiselle*,' he greeted her politely. 'Won't you come in?'

Nothing surprised Karim, thought Rachel wryly, climbing the steps and following him inside. Unless he was prepared for her visit, she reflected uneasily, wondering whether Madame Roche had completed her afternoon's calls by coming here.

'I—were you expecting me, Karim?' she asked now, allowing him to take her coat with some reluctance, but the manservant shook his head.

'I am merely happy to see you again, *mademoiselle*,' he assured her smoothly. 'If you will wait here, I will inform my master of your arrival.'

'No, wait——' Rachel put out a detaining hand and then withdrew it again. 'I mean—don't announce me, Karim. Just—tell me where he is.'

Karim looked doubtful. 'I believe my master is in the library, *mademoiselle*,' he conceded slowly. 'But I am sure——'

'Later, Karim,' said Rachel swiftly, dropping her handbag and making for the stairs. 'Honestly, I'll tell Alex—I mean, your Mr Roche—that I insisted, hmm?'

Karim was hesitant, but there was about him an air of unfeigned relief which Rachel could only regard as hopeful. Perhaps, like Madame Roche, Karim was worried about Alex, too. Rachel shook her head. The man had feelings, after all.

However, by the time she reached the top of the stairs, her momentary confidence had fled. Was she being utterly presumptuous in coming here? she wondered. Could she honestly depend on his mother's assessment of the situation? And what if she was wrong, disastrously wrong . . .

Running her sweating palms down the seams of her narrow-legged velvet pants, she raised her hand to tap on the panels of the library door. But something, some

inner caution, urged her not to warn him of her
presence, and instead she turned the handle and allowed
the leather-studded door to swing inwards.

Alex was seated at his desk, and hearing the tentative
rattle of her fingernails against the handle, he gave a
heavy sigh. *'Va-t'en*, Karim,' he exclaimed warily,
then followed these words with others in the language
Rachel had heard spoken in Bahdan. She did not
understand the words, only the meaning, which
indicated unmistakably that he did not wish to be
disturbed. He did not even look up. He simply
continued to study the documents laid on the desk in
front of him, and only when, by her silence, he realised
something was wrong did he lift his head.

*'Rachel!'*

His hoarse use of her name was a small indication of
the strength of his feelings, but looking at him, Rachel
had little doubt that his mother had not been
exaggerating when she said he was on the verge of a
breakdown. The lean contours of his face had been
honed to a brittle thinness, and it hardly seemed
possible that in a little over two weeks he should have
lost so much weight. The grey eyes were dark and
hollowed in their sockets, and even the brilliant lustre
of his hair seemed dulled.

'Hello, Alex,' she said, closing the door behind her, and
she saw the nervous tension in his hands as he pressed
down on to the desk to lever himself out of his seat.

'Rachel,' he said again, more normally now, 'did
Karim announce you? I'm afraid I didn't hear him.'

The formality of his tone was almost her undoing,
but ignoring the persistent anxiety that perhaps she was
presumptive, even now, Rachel advanced towards him.
'I persuaded Karim to let me come up alone,' she said
huskily. 'How—how are you, Alex?'

'Me?' He made a dismissive movement of his
shoulders, and she knew an inner pang at the awareness
that he was still wary of her. 'Oh, I'm fine.' He glanced
down at the desk. 'Working hard, as you can see.'

Rachel sighed. 'I see.' She paused. 'I'm interrupting
you, then.'

'Yes, you are.' He expelled a short breath. 'Perhaps you'd better tell me why you've come here. Surely your father hasn't got into any more difficulties?'

'No.' Rachel touched the lacings of the jerkin she was wearing over a full-sleeved blouse. 'As a matter of fact, he seems to be making an effort to prove himself at the moment. I don't know what you said to him, but he's a changed man.'

'I'm pleased to hear it.' Alex's mouth compressed. 'So—if it wasn't Fleming who brought you here, what was it?'

Rachel caught her breath. 'Don't you know?'

He uttered a brief mirthless laugh. 'I don't know anything any more,' he retorted. 'Perhaps you've come to apologise for walking out on me—well, forget it. It's too late now to have second thoughts.'

His words were crippling, not least because Rachel was having the greatest difficulty in believing that she could be responsible for his disintegration. His mother must have been wrong, she told herself. Alex didn't love her, he despised her; and far from wanting a reconciliation, he evidently resented her intrusion.

'I'm sorry,' she said, backing towards the door. 'I shouldn't have come here. I thought—oh, it doesn't matter what I thought—I'd better go.' And turning to the door, she fumbled for the handle.

'Oh, *God*!' She heard his muffled oath and his footsteps across the carpet, which was still the same one, she saw inconsequently. Then his hands on her upper arms stilled her frantic efforts to escape him, and she allowed herself to be drawn back to rest against his body. 'Rachel, Rachel,' he groaned, resting his face in the hollow of her shoulder, and she knew, with sudden exhilaration, that his mother had not been mistaken after all.

'I love you,' she said simply, lifting her face to rub her cheek against his, and he turned her, ever so slowly, seeking her mouth with his.

He was hungry for her, and for a long time there was silence in the quiet room as he drank his fill of her compelling sweetness. His mouth possessed her,

his hands sliding possessively across her body,
reminding her insistently of how much she had missed
his touch.

'Why did you leave me?' he muttered at last, pulling
her down into one of the soft armchairs with him,
burying his face in the silky darkness of her hair. 'Was
it because of my mother? My grandfather? Was it my
whole alien background that frightened you so much?'

'No. No.' Rachel burrowed against him, parting the
buttons of his shirt so that she could press her lips
against the exposed bones of his throat. And then,
realising he could only be told the truth, she breathed:
'I—I thought you were going to marry Mariana, after
all. In spite of what you had said, you seemed—very
close.'

'Oh, *God*!' Alex groaned. 'If you only knew! The day
you chose to walk out on me, Mariana and I had had
one hell of a row, in my grandfather's presence,
incidentally. I told her—and him—that there was no
chance of my marrying anyone I didn't love. And I
never loved Mariana. I don't think I've ever loved
anyone—until now.'

'Oh, Alex!'

'It's true.' He tilted her face up to his. 'I've been crazy
about you since that night you played the Good
Samaritan. Oh, I admit I didn't always want to believe
it, but God help me, it's the truth!'

Rachel shook her head. 'But what about Mariana?
You did want to hurt her, didn't you?'

He sighed. 'Mariana was having an affair with
another man while I was in New York,' he said flatly.
'That night—the night we met—I had just left her
apartment. Yes, I wanted to hurt her. I wanted my
revenge. Only later it seemed I'd only hurt you—and
myself.'

She touched her mouth to his, drawing back when his
tongue probed her lips. 'So I was to be the victim.'

Alex looked rueful. 'I guess so.'

'And Roger.'

'If Harrington had had any faith in you——' Alex
broke off. 'Did you love him?'

'Roger was a habit,' said Rachel truthfully. 'He didn't—we didn't——'

'—Make love. I know.' He gave her a wry look. 'So you forgive me?'

'Do I have any choice?' Her lips probed his ear. 'Did I ever have any choice?'

'I have to tell you, my actions were deliberate,' he muttered, after a moment. 'To begin with, I thought it was just a game I could play, but it didn't work out that way. Once I fell in love with you, I knew I had to have you—any way I could, fair means or foul.'

Rachel stroked his neck. 'Was that why you gave my father that money?'

'I used him, I suppose,' agreed Alex honestly. 'But it was a small price to pay if I could somehow bind us together. But the more I fell in love with you, the more you seemed to fight me, and when you finally left me in Bahdan, I just—went to pieces.'

Rachel wound her arms around his neck. 'You've lost weight. You're so thin!'

He grimaced. 'I haven't noticed.'

'You look——'

'Awful?'

'No, haggard.' Rachel's smile came and went. 'I've not been sleeping very well either.'

His fingers cupped her nape. 'Don't depend on sleeping with me,' he breathed. 'I can think of much better things to do.' He tugged free the laces of her jerkin. 'Like right now, for instance . . .'

Some time later, Rachel opened her eyes to find him watching her, his eyes warm and compelling in that disturbing dark face. 'I want to marry you,' he said, without preamble, moving closer to her in the wide bed. His hand slid beneath the tangled weight of her hair. 'This month; this week; today, if that were possible,' and Rachel thought how little it really mattered when or how they got married so long as they did. 'I want you to be my wife before we fly back to Bahdan.'

She blinked a little anxiously now. 'To Bahdan?' she echoed, her expression revealing. 'But won't your

grandfather object? I mean, your aunt Sofia said——'
She bit her tongue, and then continued awkwardly: 'I
mean, do you think it's a good idea?'

But Alex had heard the 'Sofia,' and his free hand
turned her face to his. 'Tell me,' he said insistently,
'what did Sofia say? And when? I'd like to know.'

'Oh, Alex . . .' Rachel sighed, 'does it matter?'

'I think so. My mother suggested something of the
kind several days ago, but I wouldn't listen to her. I'll
listen to you.'

Her palms moved possessively over his shoulders, as
he imprisoned her legs with his. 'It was nothing,
honestly,' she murmured, not very convincingly. 'She
just—well, she implied that your grandfather would
never let you marry anyone who—who wasn't a
member of your family.'

Alex muttered an oath. 'I should have known,' he
muttered huskily. 'I should have suspected——' He
broke off. 'But after that night we spent together, I
couldn't believe that anything anyone said could
convince you that I didn't want you.'

Rachel looked up at him through her lashes, her
fingers curling in the hair at his nape. 'Yet you went off
with Mariana. What was I supposed to think?'

'I had to talk to her and my grandfather—hey!' His
eyes grew teasing. 'You were jealous!'

'Mmm.' Rachel pulled his head down so that she could
touch his mouth with hers. 'I have feelings, too, remember.'

Alex smiled then, the wonderful lazy smile that she
adored. 'Well, it may please you to hear that my aunt
Sofia has decided she has had enough of the desert for
the time being. She left Hajat over a week ago, she and
Mariana both. I heard they are planning to buy a
property in Italy.'

Rachel absorbed this with some relief, and then, as he
nuzzled her shoulder, she ventured: 'Will we have to live
in Bahdan—after we're married?'

'Would you mind?' His eyes were intent, and after a
moment she shook her head.

'So long as I'm with you, I don't care where we live,'
she murmured, coiling her arms round his neck.

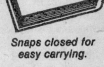